# ONE TASTE OF LOVE

A ONE TASTE NOVEL

AMANDA SIEGRIST

*Happy reading!*

*Amanda S.*

ISBN-13: 978-1542736824
ISBN-10: 154273682X

## ALSO BY AMANDA SIEGRIST

*A happy ending is all I need.*

**One Taste Novel**

One Taste of You

One Taste of Crazy

One Taste of Sin

One Taste of Redemption

**Lucky Town Novel**

Escaping Memories

Dangerous Memories

Stolen Memories

Deadly Memories

**Consequences Novel**

Dark Consequences

**McCord Family Novel**

Protecting You

Trust in Love

Deserving You

Always Kind of Love

**Holiday Romance Novel**

Merry Me

Mistletoe Magic

Christmas Wish

Snowed in Love

Snowflakes and Shots

**Perfect For You Novel**

The Wrong Brother

The Right Time

**Standalone Novel**

The Danger with Love

**Mona & Mason**

The Paranormal Chronicles

**Conquering Fear Novel**

CO-WRITTEN WITH JANE BLYTHE

Drowning in You

Out of the Darkness

*He won't let anyone hurt her.*
*Not her meddling father...or the killer.*

# 1

A gentle hand landed on his shoulder, making his torture the past few months escalate to the point of pain. He tried not to cringe from the pain or groan from the longing. He didn't need to turn to know who it was. Her touch always made him ache for more. Not that she'd ever give him more. Just little touches here and there that made him want to cry, and he wasn't a man who cried. Turning around seemed inevitable, but he didn't want to.

"Ben, would you like something to drink?"

He finally swiveled his head and glanced at her hand. She jumped back immediately in her calm, collected manner she always displayed. She never got riled up. Not once. He was waiting for the moment, any moment, when Rina would display any sort of anger or frustration. Even in anger, she spoke softly, calmly, and stood with poise. Sometimes, he just wanted to provoke her. Provoke her to the point of breaking that anger out. Like, now. Because he was breaking inside.

"I'll have whatever Zeke's having." He pulled a smile from nowhere, sighing inside as she nodded once and walked out of the living room. He could never bring himself to provoke her, no matter how many times he wanted to.

"Oh, man. Come on!" Zeke threw an irritated hand at the TV. "Did you just see that move? He should've caught that."

Ben turned his attention back to the TV where they were watching football. He grinned, for Zeke's benefit, and laughed. "Yeah, he's been missing catches all season. What the hell do you expect?"

Zeke slapped his knee as he laughed. "Dude, they didn't even throw the ball. They ran it. I was just seeing if you were paying attention. Clearly, you weren't." A huge smirk emerged. "You were glued to Rina, like you always are. When are you finally going to ask her out? Don't you think it's time?"

"Please, Zeke, talk a little louder. I'm not sure if Rina heard you," Ben said through clenched teeth.

"Oh, someone's grouchy. I don't need two babies in the house. One is plenty. Plus, she's cuter than you."

Ben smiled, despite himself, as Zeke lifted his little baby girl closer to his chest, kissing her forehead.

"I can't believe she's sleeping so peacefully with you yelling at the TV like that."

"Zabrina can sleep through a lot. Except at night. She loves to keep Mommy and Daddy up. I've been taking a lot of the night feedings lately. Zoe goes back to work soon, and I want her to get plenty of rest before she does." Zeke kissed his daughter's head again.

"Zoe's one lucky lady. You spoil them too much."

"Nah, I don't spoil them enough. You'll see when you finally ask Rina out. Love does something to you."

Ben jerked. "I don't love Rina. I'm not going to ask her out. Just drop it already."

Zeke raised a brow, his smirk widening even further. "I've known you a long time. I see the look in your eyes. You can lie to me, but you really shouldn't lie to yourself. I can help—"

"Just stop." Ben held his hand up, cutting Zeke off. "Please, just stop. Not a conversation I want to have when that very person is in the house and going to walk back into the room at any moment."

"Fair enough. I'll bug you later."

"Oh, joy," Ben mumbled under his breath, suddenly sitting straighter when Rina walked into the living room holding two bottles of beer.

She handed one to Zeke first, even though she had to walk past Ben. Then she approached him and slowly held out the bottle.

"Sorry it took so long. Zoe's trying to make a grocery list and she needed my help. How's the game?"

Her sweet voice rocked him to the core. He could listen to her speak all day, just saying nonsense. He loved her voice. A shiver rippled through him.

Love.

No, he just loved her voice, not actual love.

Heart pounding, he grabbed the bottle and tried not to display the trembling he felt through his entire body.

"Great. Wanna watch some?" He scooted over toward Zeke to make room for her. The invite spilled out before he could stop himself.

She eyed the spot he cleared and then swiftly lifted her eyes to his as she bit her lip. "Zoe still needs my help. Just shout out if you two need anything else."

"Thanks again," Ben said, lifting his bottle slightly and turned back to the TV. He refused to watch her walk out like she did every single time he saw her.

Always walking away from him.

"Well, that's a start."

Ben glared at Zeke. "A start? I asked her to watch the game with us and she said no. Imagine if I asked her out on a date."

"So you do want to ask?" Zeke grinned. He nudged Ben in the shoulder when he refused to remove his glare. "It's football. Zoe's not big into it either. It doesn't mean she doesn't love me. And it doesn't mean Rina would say no if you asked her out. Baby steps. You can do this."

"Shut up."

He raised the bottle to his lips, wanting to down the contents in one long swig. Drowning his sorrows with beer sounded like a great idea. Before one wonderful taste could hit his lips, his phone went off at the exact same time Zeke's rang. They shared a look.

Ten minutes later, they were in Zeke's car heading to a crime scene. Ben didn't want to talk anymore, especially about Rina. Resting his head against the window with his eyes closed, he hoped Zeke got the message. When Zeke called about watching the game, he had wanted to say no. Then his empty house stared back, laughing at him. Of course, if he had known Rina would show up, he would've never said yes. Probably why Zeke never mentioned it.

"Really, man. Can't a guy get some rest here." Ben lifted his head from the window with a frown to Zeke, who just threw a napkin at his face.

"You didn't eat your cookie. Can I have yours? It's only two o'clock in the afternoon. You looked tired when you came over. Didn't you get any sleep last night?"

Did he get any sleep? Sure he did. After he had multiple dreams about Rina that left him aching with pain. Sleep was hard to come by. Talking about it with Zeke would get him nowhere but more teasing. He wasn't sure how much more of that he could take. Not that he didn't deserve it. He had been brutal with the teasing when Zeke first started dating Zoe.

He handed his cookie that he had absolutely no desire to eat to Zeke, who smiled wide with excitement.

"I can't believe you don't want yours. Zoe's been going a little crazy. She's been buzzing around the house, baking cookies, cleaning, just all this...energy. I think it's nerves. She's nervous about going back to work."

"Why? Is it because she's going back to work, or leaving Zabrina?"

"I think a bit of both. She's not sure she wants to be a secretary anymore. She's contemplating going back to school, or maybe even staying home with Zabrina for a few years. She hates to think about her going to daycare. I'm not too keen on the idea either."

"Can you swing Zoe not working?" Ben asked, surprised. They had a great job working at the St. Cloud Police Department, but they were by no means getting rich off their job.

"I can swing anything for Zoe. If that's what she wants, I'll try to get some overtime. It's not like we don't get it already."

"True." Ben leaned his head against the window again. He worked more overtime than Zeke did. Unlike Zeke, he had nothing waiting at home for him.

"You seem out of it. For a while now. What's going on, Ben?" Zeke asked, shoving a quick bite of the cookie into his mouth.

"Nothing."

"Still lying."

He sat up, then shrugged. "It's been crazy around the office. It feels like our caseload gets larger every day."

"You sound like you need a vacation. Those two weeks I had off when Brina was born were the best." Zeke shoved another bite of the cookie into his mouth, half-chewing, half-speaking as he added, "Or maybe you just need to get laid. Didn't you have a date with what's-her-name?"

Ben rolled his eyes at Zeke and watched him shove the remaining part of the cookie into his mouth and snap his fingers as his mind whirled around for the answer.

"Trina...Trisha...no, Tabitha, that's her name."

"It was Bethany," Ben said dryly.

"Well, shit, I was way off." Zeke laughed. "You guys had a date last week. How did it go? You never did tell me."

"It's not going into a second date."

"I think having some sex might help this," Zeke said, waving his hand up and down.

"You just pointed to all of me."

"Yeah, man, you're a mess. Trust me. A nice, steamy round of sex helps me."

Ben shuddered. "TMI, don't wanna hear that shit."

"Why don't you just ask out Rina? It's way past due, like, a year past due."

Ben closed his eyes to shut out those damaging words. "Let's drop the subject, Zeke."

"Come on, man. One little date. Zoe and I will even double date with you, if you want."

"I don't like Rina like that. I've told you guys this since the beginning." Could he lie any longer to his best friend? Because that statement was a bald-faced lie. He liked her so much it hurt to breathe sometimes.

"You're a horrible liar, Ben. She likes you. Just ask her out."

"Drop it." Ben glanced out the window to see if they had made it to their destination yet. Was Zeke driving slowly on purpose to torture him about Rina? Next time he'd drive himself.

"Didn't you see the way she looked at you back at the house? She'll say yes. Then you two—"

"She'll say yes? No, she won't," Ben yelled, whipping his head toward him.

Zeke smirked. "Yep, too much bottled-up tension. She would never say no."

"You don't get it." He shook his head, releasing a tired sigh.

"Get what?"

A muscle ticked in his jaw as the words slowly left his mouth. "I did ask her out. A few months ago. She said no. Why don't you and Zoe just knock it off already. I'm sick and tired of hearing about Rina and how I should ask her out. Quit the teasing. Quit the nagging. Just quit it."

He could still hear her soft voice telling him no. He had stood there like an idiot from the beginning, asking dumb questions about her coffee. She had been sitting outside a café with a white mug, sipping coffee and reading a book, looking like a beautiful angel. Every time he saw her, his nerves ventured forth like a speeding bullet. That's why he never had the courage to ask her out. She just seemed too unattainable. And he had been right. He should've never asked.

Zeke's mouth dropped open. "No, no, that's not right. She's got the hots for you. I know this—"

"You don't know shit. I'm telling you I asked her out and she said she can't."

"Back to interrupting me. That hasn't happened in a long time. Don't do that. She said she can't. Why the hell not? What does that mean?"

He shrugged. "Hell if I know. If you say one more word

about this, I'm going to hurt you. And don't you dare say a word about this to Zoe. Just drop the subject and forget we ever had this conversation."

Ben could tell Zeke wanted to say more but wisely kept his mouth shut. Because he seriously would've contemplated punching him in the face. He tortured himself enough. He didn't need his best friend adding to it.

Before long, Zeke pulled up to the crime scene. Ben hopped out of the car without one word and trudged up the walkway to the front door without glancing at or waiting for Zeke.

He walked inside the house, an officer pointing him to a bedroom that held the dead body of a woman. He couldn't stop the grimace that crossed over his face as he took in the sight. Not reacting had become second nature. But this. The horror in front of him couldn't stop the disgust from emerging. Halting near the doorway, he almost considered walking out—something he had never done before at a crime scene.

A woman in her twenties lay on the bed, arms and legs spread wide, naked for the world to see, and a dark-red scarf tied around her neck. The sight of her body displayed in such a manner made his stomach churn with unease. The deep bruises covering her arms, legs, and unfortunately near her lower regions gave him a clue he didn't like knowing. She had been raped.

"What do we have so far, Susan?" Zeke asked, coming up quietly next to Ben.

He heard the disgust in Zeke's voice easily. No doubt, he was thinking the same thing as him. Just one of the things that made them great partners—thinking alike.

Susan looked up from where she was bent over the bed collecting evidence from the sheets. "Not a lot. Dr. Everly stepped outside to take a call, but he did estimate time of death last night around midnight or so. As you can see, most likely by strangulation. Obvious signs of sexual assault as well. Her name's Beth Darlington, age twenty-six, single, and works at a salon, Style Me."

"How'd you figure all that out so quickly? We just got the call," Zeke asked, giving the room a cursory glance.

Ben followed the same path Zeke's eyes took, noting nothing out of place. No sign of a struggle. It seemed better to look at the room than at her tortured body, except he couldn't seem to help himself. Bile rose in his throat as he gave her another glance.

"Her best friend came to check on her. She found the body. She spoke to the responding officer, who then relayed everything to me. Diane, the best friend, also called her brother, Timothy. She was distraught, almost hysterical. He took her home. Before he left, I think he mentioned to Officer Johnson that he was going to Beth's house to tell her parents. He wanted to be the one to do it. Diane and Beth were close...really close. I guess Timothy is also really close to her parents."

"Everyone deals with death differently. Saves us the trouble, but that seems very odd. Was he dating Beth?" Ben barely recognized his own voice, or that he finally found the energy to say something. For whatever reason, this scene was hitting him harder than he had ever experienced before.

"I don't know. Based on the information from Officer Johnson, no," Susan said, sealing her evidence bag after she placed a light-brown strand of hair in it.

"Well, I guess we'll find out when we talk to him. Sounds like we need to talk to him first." Zeke glanced at Ben, who nodded in agreement.

"Any signs of how the perp got in?" Ben asked.

"Not yet. I started in here. A brief walk around the house showed no signs of anything disturbed. Either she let the person in, or they jimmied a lock open somehow. Don't worry, I've got it covered," Susan said with confidence and a small wink.

A small frown suddenly formed on her face, her eyebrows dipping into confusion. She slowly lifted Beth's arm and rolled her to her side. The movement made Beth's hair that had been fanned out lovingly on the bed brush over her face, covering her features.

Ben's heart stopped beating as sweat trickled down the middle of his back. The bile rose again in his throat as he took a step back.

Air. He needed air. Lots of it.

The sight of the woman made him want to drop to his knees and scream in agony. Clenching his fists, he focused on controlling his breathing. Drawing in a decent breath just wouldn't come.

"What did you find, Susan?" Zeke asked, oblivious to Ben's tortured expression.

"A piece of paper. I thought this was one hell of a scene just by the brutality of her body. Now I'm just creeped out," Susan said with a shudder as she slipped the paper into an evidence bag and sealed it tightly.

Zeke held his hand out. With a slight shake of her hand, she passed the evidence bag to him.

"Red for the heat, I love so deep," Zeke said quietly, reading the note. "What the hell does that mean?"

"I don't even want to know," Susan muttered as she rolled Beth a little more.

Zeke finally looked at him and puckered his brows. "You okay, Ben? Did you hear what I said?"

Ben tore his gaze from the battered woman to Zeke's concerned eyes. He had no idea how he managed to do that. Her body. Her hair covering her face. Those bruises. He needed some damn air.

"I heard you."

Zeke stepped closer to him and whispered, "I'm sorry about what happened in the car."

Ben pointed to the dead woman on the bed. Her body still on her side, her sleek auburn hair lightly covering her face. "Look, Zeke. Who does she look like? The hair, the body type, just look."

Zeke turned to the bed. Susan busily worked at collecting her evidence, taking pictures of the scene, unaware of their current tension.

Zeke shrugged. "I'm not—"

"Rina. She looks like Rina. I think I'm going to be sick now," Ben muttered as he walked out of the room.

## 2

Z eke shut the front door, the loud click gaining a stern voice to prick his ears.

"If you so much as wake that little girl up with your loud ways, you're gonna get it."

Smiling wide, he held his arms open as he walked over to her. "Oh, what am I going to get?"

"Not what you're thinking, that's for sure. I just put her down." She pressed her head against his chest and wrapped her arms tightly around him. "I don't want to go back to work."

He kissed the top of her head. "We talked about this. You don't have to."

She lifted her head and grabbed a quick kiss. "You work too much as it is. If I quit, you'd have to work even more. It just isn't feasible."

"For you, I'll do anything. Just say the word. If you want to take time off, then do it, sweetheart. I want you happy and I want our little Brina happy." Savoring another sweet kiss, he walked her backwards toward the wall. "Now, how about a little some-some while our angel is sleeping."

She laughed against his lips. "I have to fold the laundry, look over some bills, and everything else on my list that I didn't get done while she was awake. Or bedtime would be good, too."

"I've been denied a long time. You're finally free to engage in sex anytime you freely want. I want to start engaging in that. I feel very deprived," he said, nibbling on her neck.

She opened her neck to give him better access. "You shouldn't. You got plenty last night, and if my memory serves correctly, this morning. I have no idea how we managed that either. I'm dead on my feet, Zeke. Bedtime seems like it should move to the top of the list."

He peppered small kisses up her neck until he reached her lips, shifting his body closer as she moaned delightfully in his mouth. "I will always manage to find time to love you. Make no mistake on that."

"And while I want to right now, I need to get stuff done before she wakes up," she whispered regretfully, pushing him away.

"This feels wrong," he teased, following her into the kitchen. "Can you keep a secret?"

She turned around, holding the refrigerator door handle, raising a brow in disbelief. "Since when can't I keep a secret?"

"Hmm, let's see, darling, you have a weakness divulging things to Dee and Rina." He snatched a kiss to lighten the truth of his words and grabbed a plate from the cupboard.

"If you want me to keep it to myself, I can. Honestly, that hurts you think I can't." She gave him a sly smile, telling him she was kidding, but her voice held a hint of pain.

"I love you."

"I love you, too. Dish already." She opened the lid to the

container and scooped some of the chicken dinner onto his plate.

"Ben's been in a funk lately. I kinda needled him about it. Did you know he asked out Rina a few months ago?"

Zoe dropped the spoon as her jaw dropped.

"Yeah, that was my reaction, too. He's crushed. I could hear it in his voice."

He crossed his arms as he blew out a breath. Talk about the worst friend on the planet. He had teased Ben up and down almost every day to ask her out. Not once had Ben given the impression he had. Just laughed at it or ignored him. They had been friends for a long time. He should've seen through it.

"Crushed? What did she say? There's no way she said no."

"She shut him down. She never gave you any indication he asked her out?"

"Hell, no. I would've told you that. He has to be giving you a line so you stop teasing him. I bet that's what this is."

He shook his head, wishing it were true. The devastation on Ben's face hadn't been faked. "I'm telling you, he asked her out and she said no."

Zeke dropped his arms and took a step toward Zoe when she started to wipe her hands on a towel. "What are you doing?"

"Calling Rina," she said, her voice trailing as she walked away.

"I said to keep it between us, Zoe."

"Fat chance on that. She's one of my best friends and he's one of yours. I refuse to believe she would tell him no. She likes him." She turned around with her hands on her hips as she stood in the threshold of the hallway. "I'm calling her. I think I heard Zabrina. You hollered, your turn."

Zeke watched her walk away, his daughter's beautiful cries perforating the air. Well, that didn't go how he'd expected.

----

BEN PULLED a beer out of the fridge, twisted the cap, and took a long swallow. The cool liquid did nothing to soothe his nerves. After downing half the bottle, he stared at it, his eyes blurring until he only saw Rina's face. Not in the way he wanted to either.

That damn crime scene.

The body laid out on the bed, almost as if she were posed. The bruises lining up and down her body, showing the brutality she'd experienced. The red scarf wrapped around her neck, almost in a loving way. And her face. No matter how many times he tried to see the victim's face, he only saw Rina.

The entire drive home he had the insane urge to drive to her house and make sure she was okay. Insane, he knew. She wasn't the victim or involved in the case in any way, but the worry had formed the minute she swapped faces with the victim. His stomach coiled every time the image appeared. Which, since it happened, was every few minutes. He couldn't erase it.

Why would the case be easy either? Nope. Nothing had been easy. He should've known by the pristine look throughout the house. No sign of a struggle or how the perp got in.

Beth's parents weren't helpful, to say the least. Neither could form coherent thoughts. Blind numbness had taken over. Losing their daughter in such a horrible way tore the spirit right out of them.

Timothy, the one person to prick their senses as a good suspect by what Susan told them, was still at the house when they arrived. He had been trying his best to console Beth's parents. It hadn't worked well for him.

He had answered their questions without an issue and was very straightforward. Nothing about him had seemed to rub him or Zeke the wrong way. He was a pretty boy, dressed in khaki pants and a blue polo shirt with his blonde hair combed back, not a strand out of place. He had worn glasses that fit his face perfectly and gave him an air of intellect. He looked like he was pulled from a GQ magazine, ready to win the ladies over with a thousand-watt smile.

Ben leaned against the counter as the conversation with Timothy rolled around his mind. Looking back, revisiting every angle always helped. He would do it until they found their killer.

"How well did you know Beth?" Zeke had asked. "I'm assuming pretty well, since you wanted to tell her parents what happened."

"She's been best friends with my sister since they were eight. She's part of our family. Her parents lost their son about two years ago in a car accident. The cop who showed up to relay the news wasn't very delicate about it. So forgive me if I wanted it to go better this time. As you can see, they didn't take it well regardless." Timothy had looked at the couple sitting on the couch, hugging each other tightly as the tears spilled down with despair. "But I think it went better than some jerk of a cop relaying the news."

"We aren't jerks when we do it," Ben had said as nicely as possible.

"Maybe you're not."

"Is she seeing anyone? Have you ever dated her?" Zeke had asked

"She broke up with her boyfriend, Steven, a few weeks ago. I don't know the reason why. I haven't seen her as often as I did when we were kids. I've never dated her. She's my sister's best friend."

"When's the last time you saw her?" Ben had asked.

"About two weeks ago. I saw her downtown at a coffee shop. She was shopping with Diane. She seemed happy. That's when I found out she wasn't dating Steven anymore. She didn't seem heartbroken or anything." Timothy had smoothed a hand through his hair, messing up the perfect strands. Yet, it had still fallen down looking almost perfect.

"Did Beth have a problem with anyone? Is there someone you think would hurt her?" Zeke had asked.

"Beth was a sweetheart. She wouldn't hurt a fly or a spider," Timothy had said with a sad laugh. "I killed a few spiders for her."

"Here's my card. If you think of anything else. Give us a call," Ben had said, handing Timothy his card. "Where were you last night?"

Timothy had taken the card and answered the question without appearing insulted. "I was at home. And yes, by myself. I live alone. Beth was like family. I just can't get over the fact she's gone."

Ben took a swig of beer. He knew he wouldn't get a phone call from Timothy. Beth was a sweetheart. The entire night did nothing to bring them closer to an answer. Not even her boyfriend had been helpful. He had been distraught, almost to the point as her parents when they interviewed him. He said the breakup had been amicable. They had split just three weeks ago, the relationship dying because they were better friends than lovers. Steven couldn't think of a single person who had a problem with Beth.

Her co-workers had relayed the same information. She

rarely had problems with people. A few disgruntled customers, but women, not men. Almost immediately, they discredited a woman to have committed the crime. Preliminary results indicated she was raped. Despite defensive wounds marring her body, someone held her down with brute strength. The person didn't have to tie her up to violate then kill her with the scarf. The person did it by simply holding her down with their body weight. Someone heavier than her, stronger than her. Someone like a man.

Susan had informed them a window from the bedroom closest to the living room had been unlocked. She dusted for fingerprints but came up empty. Every other window, including the doors, was locked when Diane came to her house and found her. She had a spare key. They were like sisters; even Beth had a key to her house. The first thing Ben told Diane was to change her locks. They had no idea if the killer searched the house and found the key. Better to be safe than sorry. Like an insensitive jerk, he'd actually said that to her. The fear that lit up her eyes made him regret saying it so matter-of-factly. He had no excuse. And if he did, it'd be the sight of Beth's body. The way she reminded him of Rina.

Taking another swallow, he clutched the bottle tightly. He wanted to get that image out of his mind. Thinking about the case wasn't helping. His fingers itched to grab his keys from the hook on the wall and drive to Rina's. She'd probably politely smile and say she was fine, then dismiss him with ease. Like always.

The only solution to the problem would be to solve the case immediately. It wasn't looking good. Neither voiced it, but a bad sensation had swirled around them as they worked. This case wouldn't be simple. This killer had watched, waited, planned, and carefully attacked Beth.

Damn this case.

He chugged the remainder of his beer and grabbed the fridge door handle. It tasted good, settling his stomach a little. He couldn't drown his sorrows earlier, but he could now.

Was that what he should do?

Food didn't sound appealing and he didn't think he could eat one bite if he tried. He nearly got sick in the victim's house.

But beer...that sounded good. It just might take the edge off. Maybe even put him into a stupor so he could sleep tonight. Because the way his day was going, he wouldn't get a wink of sleep. Instead of having sweet dreams of Rina, he'd have terrifying nightmares of her body bruised and strangled. Not going to happen.

He yanked on the handle and grabbed another beer. Only five more left. Would that be enough to make him forget? Probably not.

Clenching the cap, he twisted it sharply as another image of Rina floated by.

That's all he ever thought about. Since the day he met her.

Over the course of the year, with Zeke marrying Zoe, she slipped further and further into his mind. If there was a party, she was there. If he went out for a drink with Zeke, Zoe showed up with Rina and Dee in tow. If he decided to hang out at Zeke's, Rina suddenly showed up. He couldn't escape her. He also couldn't turn away from her beauty, her sweetness, her perfection.

He knew she was too good for him. Too beautiful. Too high-class for a guy like him. He had nothing to offer her. He was nothing but a cop, who worked too much and didn't get enough pay. Yet, Zeke managed just fine. He found a beautiful, amazing woman, juggling his new life with ease.

So why couldn't he have the same thing? That's why he had decided to ask her out. He thought he saw the same desire mirrored in her eyes. The small, tentative glances she would give him, displaying a yearning as strong as his own. Boy, had he been wrong.

She turned him down flat in her sweet, soft way she always spoke with. It broke his heart worse than if she would've sneered in disgust. He almost would've preferred that reaction instead of her gentle words. "I'm so sorry, Ben. I can't. Thank you for asking, though."

He couldn't believe when she turned him down, or that he read her so wrong. Too embarrassed, the pain still fresh in his heart, he had kept her rejection to himself. Now he wished he still had. It bugged him knowing Zeke knew.

A loud ringing echoed throughout the house. He jerked, the beer almost slipping through his fingers as his heart pounded from the interruption. Who the hell was ringing his doorbell at ten o'clock at night? If Zeke stood on his porch, Ben almost had the temptation to punch him in the face. Maybe he would. Maybe that would take some of his pain away. Not that any of this was Zeke's fault, but he just needed someone to take it away. That's what friends were for, right? Or was he here to talk about Rina again?

He stalked to the door, ready to lay into him. He wanted to drop the conversation about Rina in the car. What made Zeke think he wanted to start it back up again? Maybe punching him wasn't solely about taking the pain away. He just wanted to unleash his anger for all the teasing he'd endured the past three months. No more. He'd had it.

Whipping open the door with a biting retort on his lips

for Zeke, he staggered back. All of his anger swept away instantly.

"Rina, what are you doing here?"

She stood rigid, her hands clenched tightly by her sides. Not a normal look for her. Then she spoke in her sweet, delicate voice he loved hearing every time he saw her. "I hate you, Ben. I could slap you right now." She raised her hand to do just that.

He caught her wrist with a strong, yet gentle grip before she connected with his face. Her soft words cut him deeply, as if she'd yelled fiercely.

*I hate you, Ben.*

What in the world had he done to garner such words? He'd left her at Zeke's with a beautiful smile on her face. As usual. Even when he had asked her out, she smiled so beautifully at him.

He had hoped to anger her, and now, apparently he had.

"I think I deserve an explanation of why you want to slap me and then maybe I'll let you." He said it just as softly as she had expressed her biting words.

"Let me go, Ben." She glanced at her wrist.

"You come over to my house, you knock on my door, and then you try to slap me. Tell me why, Rina."

Her soulful eyes lifted again toward his. "It's embarrassing when my friend asks me why I told a man no after he asked me out. I just figured that would be something between the two of us, not everyone else."

A deep tremble escaped from her. Did she really think he would hurt her? He softly rubbed his thumb over the rapid pulse beating on her wrist. She hated him. He hated Zeke at the moment. Damn him! He just had to tell Zoe. Now, not only did Rina not want to date him, she hated him.

She had asked him to let her go. He couldn't find the

strength. He couldn't find any words either. Her silky skin tortured him even more than he ached before. The only thing he wanted to do was remove the hatred she had for him by pulling her into his arms and kissing it away. Soothe them both in a torrid embrace. What would she do if he did that? Probably follow through on that slap. That's the last thing he wanted. He dropped her wrist as if she'd burned his hand and tried to banish all thoughts of kissing.

"Go ahead and slap me. I told Zeke not to tell Zoe. What's the big deal?" he said, trying not to sound bitter as a deeper pain formed in his heart.

"You should know better. They never keep secrets from each other. Ever." She grabbed her hand, rubbing her wrist lightly.

"Did I hurt you?"

She glanced down at her wrist again. "No." Glancing up at him, her eyes sprinkled with sadness. "I can't believe you told Zeke."

That sadness. Couldn't she see his?

He didn't hurt her. Thank goodness. Because that's the last thing he'd ever do. But damn, she was tearing him apart.

"Is this where I feel sorry? Maybe I just got sick and tired of Zeke telling me I had to ask you out. Why haven't I done it yet? She'll say yes, buddy. Right, she'll say yes. Boy was he wrong," Ben muttered, then took a sip of beer. The flavor, unlike before, went down with a rancid taste. He never spoke like this to her and he hated himself for it, but he couldn't stop the words from leaving.

"I'm sorry, Ben. I can't date you."

"Stop saying can't, Rina. Just why in the hell can't you?" he asked with his jaw clenched tightly. She wouldn't holler, then neither would he.

"You...you're not right for me. It's better this way. Please, don't get mad at me."

"This day just keeps getting better and better. Hey, while you're at it, speaking these lovely words to me, why don't you dig that knife just a little further into my heart. I don't think it made it all the way through yet. Why don't you slam the door in your own face, Rina. I'm done here."

He turned around, leaving her staring wide-eyed and shocked at his words. Yeah, well, she shocked him rushing over here, telling him she hated him. Telling him she can't date him. He wasn't right for her. Well, who in the hell was right for her then? That's what he wanted to know.

Walking to the sink in the kitchen, the liquid fell out in a smooth stream as he started to pour the beer down the sink. Why couldn't his life go smoothly? He had no taste for anything now. He felt like throwing up the last beer. His heart had been wounded when she turned him down three months ago. Now his heart felt like a mangled piece of meat torn up from a grinder.

She hated him. Hardly any of her other words penetrated through his thick skull because those other damaging words kept repeating themselves. *I hate you, Ben.* Yeah, he hated himself. Why did he speak to her that way?

Gripping the edge of the counter, his fingers pressed painfully into the steel sink. He had no idea how to deal with this sort of pain. He had dated quite a few women, his longest relationship two years. They both instinctively knew marriage wasn't in their future, so they broke it off. The feeling of losing his girlfriend of two years compared nothing to this feeling of losing Rina before he even had a chance to have her.

Desire rippled throughout his body as a small hand clasped his shoulder. Her tiny voice, sweet like fresh rain, tore at his heart. As usual. "I'm sorry, Ben. Please don't hate me."

He slowly turned around, her hand falling to her side. The counter dug into his back as he slumped against it. "I never said I hated you, Rina. You're the one who said those words to me."

She frowned as she took a step back.

Now she needed space from him. Did she truly believe he would hurt her? "I've never met anyone who could slice me into two without raising one part of her voice. Your soft words, the things you say in general, always manage to come out as if you're yelling, putting a person in their place. I would never hurt you, no matter what you said or did to me."

Her face fell into agony. "I don't do relationships well. I rarely date. It's best I don't. I didn't mean to say those words. Honestly, Ben, I'm sorry for ever saying that. Please believe me. I know you'd never hurt me."

What did she mean, *it's best I don't*?

The anguish written on her face made him want to wrap her up into his arms and kiss the daylights out of her. Her hands trembled by her sides. Why did it still look like she thought he'd hurt her?

"Let's just move on, Rina. Now that Zeke and Zoe know, they'll quit bugging me to ask you out. No hard feelings."

She hesitated before saying, "I'm sorry for knocking on your door so late. It won't happen again."

"No worries. I apologize for getting upset and speaking to you the way I did. I'll walk you out." He gestured for her to lead the way.

She had to leave. Now. Each minute that ticked by made him want to throw caution to the wind and pull her into his arms. She stood close to him as they walked to the door, the tantalizing scent of vanilla wafting to his nose. He wanted to get closer to find where the smell originated from. Her neck? Her hair? Her mouth? She smelled so sweet.

As they approached the door, she reached for the doorknob first. His heart dipped to the floor as she started to turn the knob. Watching her leave wasn't something he was fond of. What he wouldn't give to change this all to his favor. But that would never happen.

Her hand suddenly stiffened. She turned around with one hand still gripping the knob behind her back. "I'm so sorry, Ben. I said I can't date you. It doesn't mean I don't want to."

Her face bloomed a deep red. His eyes flared as he took a few steps toward her, leaving barely an inch between their bodies.

"Do you enjoy messing with my heart, Rina?"

Her eyes zoomed to his lips. "No."

"Then why would you say I'm not right for you, and in another breath, say you want to date me but can't. What am I missing here? When I ask a woman out, it should be a simple yes or no."

"Nothing in my life is simple. I always wanted a simple life."

"I always thought you had a simple life. What's wrong? You know I will always help you." He boxed her in further by putting his hands, one on each side of the door, near her head.

"You can't help me, Ben," she whispered with a desperation that scared him.

"I really hate the word *can't* every time it leaves your mouth. Because, damn it, I *can* help you. If you're in trouble, I need to know." His voice held no arguments, just a demand she tell him the truth.

"I should go. Can you move?"

Leaning closer, he finally saw it, something he missed every time he spoke to her. A flame of desire.

His mouth brushed her lips. "No, I can't."

He closed the distance, moving his lips tenderly across hers. She barely moved as he removed his hands from the door and cradled her cheeks. That movement made her shiver, bringing her even closer, almost molding into his body. Her mouth opened wider and his tongue dove in.

A sweet burst of chocolate attacked his senses. She tasted divine. She felt divine. Why would she lie to him? She felt perfect in his arms. Now he knew she couldn't resist him.

Slowly, she curled her arms around his neck, every inch of her body pressed against his as the kiss deepened into new territory. He couldn't get enough of her. The kissed turned harder, deeper. His aching heat begged to touch her more intimately, yet he knew this couldn't go much further. The only problem was his body didn't agree as he pushed into her.

She tore her mouth away, pushing lightly against his chest. "No, Ben, stop."

He backed away immediately. A small amount of fear mixed with desire poured from her eyes. "I'd never hurt you, Rina."

She pressed a tender hand to his chest as if she still needed some sort of connection with him. "It's just...too much, too soon."

He placed a hand over hers and lightly rubbed with his thumb. "Does that mean I have a chance? Will you go out with me?"

She bit her lip as she grimaced. "I can't."

He stepped away, letting her hand drop from his chest.

"This makes absolutely no sense. You fit perfectly in my arms. You belong in my arms. Can you honestly tell me you felt nothing? Was that nothing to you? Why do you keep saying you can't?"

"I'm sorry."

Before he could stop her, get a reason why she refused to give in, she pulled open the door and fled to her car. He watched as she drove away, taking his heart with her. He should've never kissed her. Now he knew what she tasted like. He'd never get that taste out of his system. She had ruined him for life.

---

RINA WIPED the tears with one hand as the other tried to keep the steering wheel steady.

Dumb! Her entire behavior tonight had been utterly ridiculous. How had she honestly expected to confront Ben like that and not fall into his charm? She could never resist him. His sweet, innocent charm.

She lied to him. Just as she kept lying to herself. It wasn't that she didn't want to date him. It was that she couldn't.

*Can't.*

The dreaded word she kept telling him over and over again.

If only he never asked her out that day at the café. Life would still be dull and pleasant instead of painful and difficult. The best solution would be to stay as far away from Ben as she could. No more showing up when she knew Ben would be there. She was doing nothing but torturing herself —and him.

The ultimate torture. Not seeing him again. She just couldn't help wanting to be near him. His handsome face.

His kind words. The gentleness he always displayed when it came to her. No matter what she said, or how she treated him, he always treated her with kindness and respect. She didn't deserve a man like him. She didn't deserve anything.

The tears refused to stop. Images of Ben refused to diminish. The way he had pinned her between the door and his body. His warm, hot body that she had wanted even closer. As close as two people could get.

She had done it on purpose. She knew that now. Walking out of that house without telling him the truth—part of the truth—had been impossible. His hand on her earlier had created havoc on her body. The burning tingles of desire that ramped up to an inferno anytime he touched her. She had wanted more. That's why she opened her dumb mouth and dug the knife further into his chest.

Even though it was a horrible thing to want. She loved touching him. She always tried to find a simple reason to touch his gorgeous body.

So many times she yearned to brush her fingers through his black hair that needed a haircut. A little longer, especially in the front, it made her ache even more to sweep his hair back.

Or to caress a tender hand across his cheek, a hint of stubble that she knew would feel rough but sweet. Just like him. She normally saw him after a long day of work. Rarely did she see him early in the morning. That meant his jaw always had the wonderful scruffy look. She loved that look on him.

She loved touching his shoulder, as silly as it seemed. The picture of running her hand from his shoulder, down his arms, and caressing back up his chest was enough to make her lay a gentle hand on him. Each and every time she touched his shoulders, she died with the temptation to do just that. Of course, she never did. She settled for the torture of touching his shoulder, envisioning the rest in her mind. Every time she touched him, she could feel a difference. He had to be working out. She could feel the definition in each muscle.

She craved to touch him everywhere. To feel the strength in him. To feel a little bit of love for once.

It should all be so simple. Just like he said. But it was the furthest thing from the truth.

It had been on the tip of her tongue to blurt out her problems. To lay it out at his feet, let someone else fight her battles. She figured if she ever dared to let Dee and Zoe know her issues, they'd fight for her as well. Yet, knowing all of that, she couldn't find the nerve to say one word. She just couldn't.

Her problems would stay as they were. Hers.

As she pulled into her driveway, her face still wet, she knew she would never do anything so reckless like that again. Staying away from Ben was her number-one priority from now on. No matter how difficult it would be.

She went through the motions of getting ready for bed, barely registering what she was doing. Curling under the soft, plush blankets, she pulled a pillow closer as she conjured a picture of Ben. She closed her eyes and replayed every moment he held her in his arms. The tears came back as a part of herself died inside.

All she wanted in life was Ben. And she could never have him.

## 3

"What's with the look?" Dee asked as she perched her butt on the edge of Rina's desk.

She glanced up from her computer, failing miserably at hiding her grimace at Dee's intrusion. She tried to play it off anyway. "What look?"

Dee raised her eyebrow with mock disgust. "Are you seriously trying to lie to me, Rina? Girl, don't start with me. What's going on? Do I need to call Zoe?"

Rina rolled her eyes. "I'm surprised she didn't call you already."

"What's going on, Rina? Since when do you roll your eyes?"

"It's nothing. I don't want to make it into something big when it's not."

"Ooookay. What are we not making into something big? You lost me."

Rina fiddled with the keyboard, refusing to look Dee in the eyes. "Ben asked me out a few months ago. Zeke and Zoe just found out last night, and Zoe kind of interrogated me why I said no."

Dee nearly fell off the desk. "And what did you tell her? Why would you say no to that man?"

Rina looked at her. "I thought you didn't like him. I've heard you call him a douche."

Dee shuffled a hand through her unruly hair and rolled her eyes. "That was, like, forever ago. Ben's a sweetheart. Zeke still has douchey tendencies, but still borderline sweetheart. I'd totally fall for Ben if he asked me out, which he never would because his eyes are always glued to you." Dee leaned closer. "Why would you tell him no? I always thought I saw the same kind of spark in your eyes."

"Let's just get back to work. Oh, and we need to finish planning Zoe's welcome back party," Rina said, grabbing some papers as if she needed to input the numbers into the system, even though she already had.

"Look, Zoe and I have always tried to steer clear of this part of your life and respect it. But Zoe's not here to stop me. Did something bad happen to you, Rina? Is that why you're afraid of men?"

Her eyes zoomed to Dee, suddenly shameful, afraid she would see the fear. "I'm not afraid of men. In fact, I have a date this weekend. He's a very nice man, very respectable. He's a lawyer. Anthony Tollhorn."

"He sounds like a douche," Dee said without faltering, raising her eyebrow again.

"You don't even know him to say that. That's not even nice."

"He's a lawyer. I don't need to know anything else. I'm going to tell you what's not nice: not giving Ben a chance. Quite frankly, I'm shocked that you wouldn't."

Rina sighed heavily as Dee walked away, then placed a light touch to her lips.

His sweet lips, the way they melted her senses with one

teasing touch. The way his tongue dove in and claimed her with ease. To have his delicious mouth on her lips again.

Forget it. Forget him. She had no choice in the matter. This was her life. She needed to forget all about Ben. Think about Anthony, the douche lawyer.

She lowered her head onto her desk in frustration and tried to hold in the tears that wanted to release.

---

BEN SHOVED THE DOOR OPEN, breathing in the fresh air. He took an extra-large gulp, trying to dispel the horrible image of Beth from his mind—again.

"You okay, partner?" Zeke asked, coming out behind him.

"Yeah, I hate autopsies. Do we really need to be there?" Ben asked, making his way to the car.

"Well, we wanted a break from the office."

"Yeah, what a break. Just to hear the same crap we already know. Died by asphyxiation due to being strangled with a scarf. Raped, repeatedly, hence the damn bruises marking her body. No semen present. No DNA for them to collect. Nothing. I didn't need to see her body again." Ben yanked the passenger door open and slumped into the seat.

Zeke slid into his seat and started the car as he gave Ben a quick glance. "I'm sorry I told Zoe about Rina."

"And I said drop it. I never had a chance with her."

"Well, that's not true. Zoe just thinks—"

"You know what, Zeke. I don't want to know what your wife thinks. I know my situation. Please, feel free to let your wife know that as well."

"Shit, I'm sorry. Rina gave you no clue at all what's going on with her?" Zeke put the car in gear.

"No. Do I think something's going on in her life? Yeah, but she wouldn't tell me. Remember that long month of torture you had when you thought you lost Zoe forever, that you'd never find her, make it up to her for treating her like a prostitute?"

Zeke's hands tightened on the steering wheel. "Yeah, hard to forget. It was the worst month of my life. You're reminding me of my idiocy, why?"

"Triple that for me. Three months of torture, Zeke. I even tried again last night with the answer still no. I'd appreciate it if we didn't talk about Rina. Let's focus on the case."

Thankfully, Zeke decided to follow his words as silence descended within the car. He might've seriously considered socking him in the face if he hadn't. His heart was already torn to shreds. He didn't need Zeke adding to the torment.

The rest of the day dragged with the tension still hanging in the air. Tension they normally didn't have between them. Ben figured it was because Zeke knew one little word about Rina and he would fly off the handle. Smart man. He would. Problem was, Zeke wanted to say a lot about her. Hence, the tension.

After interviewing more of Beth's friends and co-workers, with little results, Ben wanted to drop the case and walk away. Something he had never contemplated before. Thinking about Beth always brought Rina to his mind. He really didn't need that reminder, especially when at every avenue of the case things remained a mystery. None of her neighbors remembered hearing or seeing anything that night. A wily bastard. Slipped inside in the dead of night, slipping right back out without an issue.

He liked his job, the tedious work it involved, the solving of a puzzle. Why did this case have to hit him differently?

Only because of Rina. Every time he saw Beth's battered

body, he saw Rina instead. It made his stomach churn with trepidation. When would the killer hit again? Who would be his next victim? Because he knew this psycho wasn't finished. He prayed Rina resembling Beth was a coincidence. Nothing more. That, when the killer decided to strike again, he didn't have a type.

He couldn't have Rina. He would learn to live with that. But losing her to the brutality in which Beth endured, he'd never survive that. She deserved to live a long, happy life. Even if he wasn't the one to give her that.

Damn, he missed her. Forgetting the taste of her lips or the way her body molded perfectly to his hadn't come yet. He'd probably never forget.

He thought of Rina and her beautiful body all the way home, creating a raging hard-on. He had no way of releasing that without diving into the shower, letting the cold pelt him until he simmered down.

Barely eating again, he couldn't find the energy to care. Not even thinking about the possible lecture from Dickens for not taking care of himself gave him energy. A lecture from Dickens was a high possibility since he hadn't shown up to the gym in a few days. Dickens had the eyes of a hawk. He knew when his clients didn't show up to the gym with their regular routine. He also had a nasty habit of gaining information like a bartender; listening to their woes and trying to lift them back up with hard work.

Thirty minutes on the elliptical. A strenuous time lifting weights. Or even taking a lap or two in the pool. Ben always managed to leave feeling a little better.

He really should head over to the gym and get that happy feeling back, but he just couldn't find the energy.

He chuckled as he grabbed a beer from the fridge. The lunacy of it all. Dickens, lately, the gym demon from hell, managed to make him feel better than his own best friend, Zeke. He figured Zeke could thank himself for that. He's originally the one who finagled Ben to join the gym.

Ben ended the night by downing two beers, a small package of saltine crackers, just to pacify himself that he knew how to eat, and plopped into bed hoping for a restful night.

It never came.

His mind flashed horrible images of Rina, bruised and strangled. A scarf, the color unclear, wrapped tightly around her neck. He woke in a panic, drenched in a heavy sweat. He walked around the house just to calm himself down.

A scarf.

No discernible color. Nothing.

She would not be a victim. She had nothing to do with the case. Just because she resembled the victim a tiny bit didn't mean she would be next.

Then why couldn't he shake the nasty feeling?

The next day consisted of more digging into Beth's life, finding her routine, her habits, and interviewing anyone she knew. She liked to work out at the gym, same as his, Pump It Up Fitness. Although, he never recalled seeing her there. Ben braved going to the gym to talk to Dickens.

"Do you remember Beth Darlington?" Ben asked Dickens. "She was a member." Avoiding full eye contact would be futile. Dickens would lay into him at any moment.

"Yep. Sweet girl. Pretty decent routine. Came in every Monday, and if she missed that day, she always came in on Wednesdays. Where have you been, Ben?"

"Working. Lots of work," Ben said sheepishly.

Dickens crossed his arms, making his body appear bigger, which made Zeke, who was standing next to Ben, take a step back. "That sounds like an excuse, Ben. We talked about this. You need to make time. You can't fall off your schedule. When you fall off your schedule, you fall behind, you lose the motivation. You can't lose the motivation, Ben."

Ben cleared his throat, throwing him what he hoped was an eager smile. "You're absolutely right, Dickens. I'll be in this week. Back to Beth. Did you ever see her have any issues with anyone? Any problems that you know of in her life? You're a friendly guy. People open up to you. Did she tell you anything?"

"She talked about breaking up with Steven. Although, she didn't seem too concerned. She said they were great friends. She had a great schedule. Very focused. Not like you. I want to see you this week, Ben. No negotiations, my friend. Bring your buddy along. I think it's about time you joined, Zeke." Dickens smiled wide, turning his head toward the front desk. "Johnny, grab me some paperwork."

Zeke looked panicked, glancing at Ben for help, who smirked wide and planted his feet a little more firmly to the ground. Zeke glanced at his watch. "Oh, geez, Dickens, look at the time. We have to get to another interview. We...ah...set an appointment."

"It'll only take five minutes," Dickens said warmly, puffing up his chest a little.

"We could probably spare five minutes. Right, Zeke?" Ben said, enjoying his discomfort immensely. Served him right after the way he teased him relentlessly about Rina.

"No, I really don't think so."

Ben laughed but finally conceded that they needed to leave. Why did he let Zeke skate by again without Dickens getting his way? Zeke's discomfort gave him a small window into his anguish, lifting his spirits. When he centered his mind back on the case, his happiness came crashing back down.

Beth liked grabbing a cup of coffee from the diner near the salon every morning before work. Same time every day. No one in the diner could provide any useful information. She always grabbed her coffee, said good-bye with a friendly smile, and went on her way.

She had just booked a cruise with her friend Diane. She wanted to get away and pamper herself after breaking it off with Steven. While she knew they were better as friends, she still felt the heartache of losing him. She had been looking forward to the getaway.

Steven's alibi indicated he was home alone that night, which really gave him no alibi, but they didn't get the feeling he'd committed the crime. Timothy hadn't given them a funny feeling either.

Who did that leave as a suspect?

The day offered nothing to help find a good suspect. Or the next day.

Ben went home that night, his mood no better than yesterday. He went to bed with the same hope he had the night before. He just wanted some sleep and a peaceful night with no brutal nightmares of Rina.

Of course, the phone ringing in his ear dashed his hopes. He rolled over to his nightstand, barely needing to rub his eyes clear of sleep, considering he really hadn't been sleeping, and groaned. Only 1:15 in the morning.

"Hello," he mumbled, not even bothering to check who was calling.

"We got another dead body. Do you want to meet me, or should I pick you up?" Zeke asked, the tiredness evident in his voice.

"Shit. Please tell me it's not related to Beth's case." Ben sat up, throwing the covers off.

"I wish I could, buddy."

"Come get me. I'll be ready in five." Ben started to walk toward the closet, then almost stumbled as he froze. "Do we have an ID yet?"

"Susan just called me and said she would meet us there. The victim's husband found her." Ben heard a pause and a slight breath escape. "It's not Rina, if that's what your crazy head was thinking. I'm not even sure why you'd think that."

He found the strength to finish walking and yanked a shirt off the hanger. "What can I say, Zeke? I can't get her out of my mind."

"I hear ya. That's why when I tell you what I know, I hope you don't hate me for relaying the news."

"What the hell are you talking about?"

"I'll be there in ten."

"Zeke, tell me now."

Ben stared at the phone when silence answered him. How could Zeke hang up on him like that? He threw his phone on the bed, then started to change his shirt. Every time his fingers attempted to loop a button, he had to take a breath and try again.

Rina.

He was going to tell him something about Rina.

## 4

**B**en crawled into the passenger seat and slammed the door shut. "Do we know anything else?"

"I know as much as I told you on the phone." Zeke tried to sneak a glance at Ben.

"Whatever it is you feel you need to tell me, don't. Does it have to do with Rina?"

"Yes."

"Then I don't want to know."

"But I think—" Zeke threw up his hand. "And don't you dare cut me off. I think you should know."

"What you think and what I want are two separate things. I've lost my energy."

Definitely lost his energy. They always had a war, throwing pencils back and forth when they teased each other. He couldn't remember who started it. Perhaps he did. Roberta, the supply goddess, hated seeing their faces when they tried to get a new box of pencils. "Seriously, how do you two go through so many so fast?" Ben always grinned and replied, "I just love seeing your face." She would always blush and hand him a new box without a problem after that.

"If I had a pencil right now, I wouldn't even have the energy to throw it at you. What does that tell you?"

"That I have no idea how to make my best friend feel better. I'm sorry, man."

Ben shrugged. What else could he say? He was sorry as hell, too.

Ten minutes later, Zeke arrived at a white rambler house. He parked a few houses down, considering the street and driveway was already filled with other police personnel.

Officer Spencer stood on the porch, hands on his hips, wearing a morose expression. "Chance. Stoyer. I don't know how you guys do this shit day in and day out."

Ben stood by quietly. Zeke normally liked to take the lead on things. With his energy gone, he really didn't care. Half the time he would mockingly rip at Zeke for always going first or talking first. Not now.

"Compartmentalizing. What do you know?" Zeke asked.

"Victim's name is Ashley Patterson. Her husband's inside sitting in the living room. They've been fighting lately, and he's been staying at his brother's house. He had a little too much to drink tonight and came back home to talk to his wife. Sort of like drunk dialing, but he decided to do it drunk-in-your-face instead." Spencer gestured toward the door. "He's a mess. I saw her body. I'd be a mess, too, if I saw my wife like that."

"Thanks, Spencer." Zeke walked inside, ignoring the officer and the husband, who sat huddled on the couch, tears streaming down the husband's face.

Ben followed suit, coming behind Zeke as he stepped inside the bedroom. The same pristine scene like Beth's room hit his eyes. Bruised woman, auburn hair, a scarf around her neck. No signs of a struggle.

"Hey, guys," Susan said with little fanfare.

Zeke walked closer to the bed. "It's an orange scarf this time. Is he bringing his own, or are these the victims'?"

"I think he's bringing them. Beth didn't have many scarves in her house, except for an old knit scarf, probably for winter. Ashley here, just a quick glance inside her closet, dresses up a little fancier than Beth did. But this is a silk scarf. Very high-end. Ashley's clothes are nice, but not *that* nice. The color of the scarf he chooses seems to go with the lovely creepy notes he leaves."

Susan rounded the bed with an evidence bag and handed it to Ben, who stood the closest to her. "Check it out. I have no clue what this bastard's getting at."

Tiny goose bumps flushed his skin as he read the note. *Orange for the glow, that hangs so low.* He passed it to Zeke. Nobody probably wanted to hear the words spoken. "Could be the husband. They've been fighting and he found the body."

"Yeah, he looks good for it, except he's kind of an idiot. He's been a blubbering mess, and while he looks like a big guy, he doesn't seem smart enough to pull this type of crime off. This guy is methodical. The killer had to know she would be alone. She still has her wedding ring on. He knew she was married, yet broke in anyway and did this," Susan said, whipping a hand at Ashley.

Ben instinctively followed her hand, cringing when his eyes landed on the body.

Rina all over again. Same hair color, same body type. Why did they have to look like her? Like he wasn't already in enough pain.

"Is Dr. Everly here yet? I don't recall seeing his vehicle," Zeke asked.

"Not yet, but I'd say the same manner of death. She was strangled and raped. Bruises show enough indication of that. Cover her face, picture a different color of scarf, and you have a mirror image of our last crime scene. He has a type. Auburn hair, slim woman, younger, and I would've said single, but obviously Ashley is married."

"So what, we let every auburn-haired, slim woman in the St. Cloud area be aware?" Ben snapped.

Susan stepped back, her face twisting with confusion. "Did I say something to upset you, detective?"

Running a hand through his hair, a few strands slipped onto his forehead. "I'm sorry, Susan. I didn't mean to snap. Anything else you can tell us?"

"No. Why don't you two leave so I can do my job?" She turned back toward the bed, dismissing them.

Ben walked out first.

*Idiot.*

Taking out his despair on Susan. She didn't deserve that. She was one of the nicest in the crime lab, usually bumping stuff up for him and Zeke with a sweet smile whenever they asked.

He just couldn't erase those vicious images from his mind.

A rough hand grabbed his shoulder, shoving him around. Zeke pursed his lips as he shook his head. "That was uncalled for, man."

"I know. I said I was sorry."

"Maybe you need to take a few days off and get your head together. In all the time I've known you, I've never seen you act this way."

"We have two murders to solve."

"I'll handle it. You're no help to me when you act like a jackass, especially to Susan."

"I can't—"

"This is me interrupting you for once. It wasn't a suggestion. Don't make me go to the captain and tell him why I think you need time off. I know you're hurting about Rina. Figure that shit out and then come back. I don't know what else to say. We normally joke around, and we haven't done that in a while. Where's my best friend at?"

"I was wondering the same thing. I'm not taking time off. Go talk to the damn captain if it'll make you feel better."

---

"WHAT'S it like to be back?" Dee asked, filling up her coffee cup.

"It kind of sucks. I'm so glad I don't officially start until Monday. It's already Thursday. I don't have much time left. I feel like a noose is around my neck," Zoe said, placing a soft hand over the blanket where Zabrina peacefully slept in her car seat.

"Why are you coming back then? We'll miss you here, but it's not like these stuffy accountants can't find a new secretary. I mean, Mary, who's been filling in for you, she's been doing a nice job. Do what's best for you, Zoe," Rina said quietly as she looked at Zabrina.

"Did you just say stuffy? Since when does our Rina speak like that?" Dee pierced a hard glare at her, then just as suddenly softened her features.

"I don't see the big deal," Rina said with a shrug. See what happened when she tried to say what she really wanted. She got called out on it. It was so much better to stay quiet.

"I don't think Mr. Young would like it if I left. After last year, when Mills and Murphy were murdered, he said as much. I mean, he gave me a raise and has been making sure everything is always easy for me. I have it easy here." Zoe sighed, then shared a look with Rina.

She knew what Zoe just did: redirected Dee's attention. It certainly didn't mean Zoe wouldn't hound her later about what the problem was.

"Mr. Young is pretty great. I still can't get over the fact he slept with Murphy's wife. That was his partner and friend. I guess it could be because I'm his secretary that I still like him, but the new guy who replaced Mills and Murphy, Donaho, he's sort of douchey," Dee said.

"He's sort of hot, too," Zoe added.

Rina couldn't resist. She laughed along with them. Zoe hit the nail on the head. He'd never be hotter than Ben, though. No one would probably ever surpass him.

"I like hearing you laugh." Zoe smiled, then slowly frowned. "Are you really going out with some lawyer? Where did you meet this guy?"

So much for Zoe waiting to pounce on her later.

"I really don't like having to explain myself all the time. Does it matter where I met him? He's very nice. We changed our date. We're going out tonight instead of Saturday."

Fleeing sounded like a great plan. She couldn't handle this interrogation, especially from her two best friends. Sooner or later, they would know what a terrible liar she was. If they didn't already.

"You're becoming much more aggressive with your words, Rina. So unlike you. If you feel better lying to us, then so be it. But lying to yourself isn't going to help you any. Have a nice date tonight," Dee said, almost as softly as she would've spoken. It hit her squarely in the chest as if Dee had sucker-punched her. Was that what she did to people when she spoke softly?

"I need to get back to work. See you Sunday, Zoe. We're all going out for drinks still, right?" Dee asked, glancing between the two.

"Of course. I promise not to bring up Ben, Rina. We're just worried about you and what's going on. Because something is definitely going on. You always told me to talk it out with Zeke, so I'm not sure why you're not talking out your issues with anyone," Zoe said.

Rina could hear the worry and the concern in both of their voices. Seeing it in their eyes as well would just break her heart further. She couldn't look at them. They would see everything written in her eyes. The pain. The shame. The fear.

"Some issues aren't as easily solved as you two would like to think." Rina finally looked up, her face expressionless. At least, she hoped so. "I'll see you Sunday."

She walked out of the break room first, heading to her desk like a fuse on a stick of dynamite just lit up. She wanted to imagine a lovely date with Anthony tonight. She met him once at her father's house and didn't lie about him being nice. He seemed like a gentleman. Every time she conjured his face, which was difficult to do, she couldn't imagine going anywhere with the man. Not like when she thought of Ben.

Why did she torture them both? Why couldn't she be stronger and give Ben a chance? She wanted to so badly. But the fear, like always, held her back. She may sound strong to everyone, but she was a wimp. A lowly wimp. A disgrace.

She left work without saying good-bye to Dee, something she had never done before, and felt the rebel in her sneaking out more and more as time went on. She needed that rebel to stay out and fight. When she arrived home to see her father's car sitting in the driveway, she knew why the rebel always hid away in the deep recesses of her mind.

"You're late," her father said with annoyance, glancing at his watch. His scowl did nothing to help her nerves that were already wired. He walked around his car, clicking the automatic lock with a quick press of his thumb.

"Traffic was not good, Father. It's only 5:30. My date isn't arriving until seven. I'm not sure what the problem is." Rina unlocked her front door, not even waiting for her father to follow.

"Don't take that tone of voice with me, Rina. You need to look your best. Anthony comes from a good family. Our families have been friends forever. You two together would be perfect," her father said in the normal insolent tone he always used with her.

Rina dropped her keys into the bowl on her dining room table and took a deep silent breath before she turned around to face her father. "I'm looking forward to this date."

"Good. Do something beautiful with your hair. Put it up in a nice coiffed hairstyle. Wear something black. You always look elegant in black."

Her father glanced around the room, his nose lifting in disgust. "Honestly, Rina, don't you know how to keep a clean house. This is embarrassing. If you invite him in, he'll be disappointed at how filthy everything is."

Tears pricked the corner of her eyes. She pressed her lips together to keep the tears at bay, knowing her father didn't like tears whatsoever, and glanced around the dining room and kitchen that connected as one. Besides a coffee mug from earlier this morning that sat on the kitchen counter, nothing was out of place. Her house was spotless, especially when she knew her father would make an appearance.

The damn mug. She should've known better than to leave it on the counter.

"Let me pick up and then get ready."

"I'll take care of it. You'd think you'd know better by now. You'll never find a suitable man on your own."

A weak smile emerged. Anything to pacify her father and show that she agreed. Any other response would just start a whole new tirade. She could barely stand this one.

She walked out of the room before the tears fell like a waterfall. Her father was wrong. She could find a suitable man on her own. She had found one—Ben. She just couldn't have him.

Rina managed to get ready with a speed she knew would satisfy her father and fixed her hair with his approval as well. She wrapped her hair into a tight bun, leaving the right side into a deep wave that clipped to the back. Even she liked it.

She had several black dresses to choose from, but pulled two from the closet. One could be called conservative, leaving it up to the man's imagination of what was underneath. The other was a little too revealing for her tastes. Two tiny straps, a little more than a hint of cleavage, her back half-bare, and it reached midway between her hips and knees. She would feel utterly naked if she wore that one.

The rebel who appeared earlier at work spoke loudly. Without thinking, she tossed the conservative one to the floor and strapped on the provocative dress before she could change her mind. Her father was bound to blow a gasket. Oh well. That was nothing new.

She didn't want to impress Anthony. She wanted to scare him away.

Except when she opened the door for Anthony, she saw the appreciation in his eyes. He liked the dress, and the entire time they ate, he couldn't keep his eyes on her face. She continually shifted in her seat as his piercing stares centered on her chest, making her more and more uncomfortable as the night dragged on.

She had thought him a nice man, but the longer the date went on, the more she realized he was just like her father. Arrogant and rude to what he considered people below him. Like the waitstaff.

The date seemed never-ending. But a serious problem had surfaced. Her father liked him and expected a relationship to develop. Not just a relationship, but something very, very permanent. Her father expected her to marry this man. Anthony had insinuated as such. If she were honest with herself, her father had as well. Ignoring the obvious didn't make it go away.

"I had a lovely night, Rina. You are absolutely breathtaking. Your father raised a beautiful woman. And all on his own. You never know what sort of lady appears considering that," Anthony said, flickering a glance her way, his eyes roaming down her legs.

Shifting unobtrusively, she tried to pull down her dress a little. "Thank you, Anthony." She smiled politely, knowing any other retort would get her nowhere. Just like her father. It made her want to throw up.

"I would love to bring you to the country club on Sunday. My mother will be there."

She shifted in the seat again. "I would love to, but I already have plans."

She turned her head in time to see him clench his jaw, then just as quickly, a smile formed. "I would love to see you tomorrow. There's this play I've been wanting to see. Join me."

She smiled, then glanced away to look out the window. What could she say to get out of that one? He really hadn't phrased it as a question. More like a demand. She didn't want to date Anthony. Dealing with her father drove her insane at times. Having to deal with another man just like him would probably send her straight to the mental ward. Sometimes in life, a person couldn't escape the inevitable.

She started to turn her head back to him with a fake smile and false words when he pulled into her driveway. Her throat clogged, unable to respond with even one little lie. Someone stood on her porch.

"It's nine o'clock. It seems rather late for a visitor, Rina."

She pressed her lips together to hold in the laughter. The audacity of the man. He couldn't even hide his annoyance. Did he think she would just magically fall at his feet no matter how he acted? Laughter wouldn't help her situation, but she really wanted to laugh. The absurdity of the entire night. She would've never had a pitiful date if Ben had been by her side.

*You two together would be perfect.* Damn her father. Of course, Anthony assumed she'd take whatever abuse he delivered her way. He was just like her father. Most likely even had a long chat with him about her.

She almost rubbed her eyes to make sure she was seeing things clearly when she got a better look at her visitor. A huge weight suddenly lifted off her shoulders, for the very tiniest of a moment, until she realized how this would look.

"Do you know who that man is?" Anthony asked, grabbing her arm when she placed a hand on the door handle.

Glancing at him, she then looked at his hand. He hadn't

grabbed her roughly, but the feel of his hand sent disturbing tingles up her arm. "Please let me go."

He let her go immediately. "My apologies. Do I need to call the police? Do you know him?"

Just like that, he feigned concern. What a masterful actor. Rina adjusted her dress and opened her door. "Yes, I do."

She stepped out with as much elegance as she could muster and slowly approached Ben, who stood on her porch with his hands in his pockets. "Hi, Ben. What are you doing here?"

"Care to explain who he is yet, Rina?" Anthony asked without waiting for Ben to respond, barely giving Rina a chance to speak.

"Who are you?" Ben retorted, then glanced at Rina with disgust.

He probably hated her for her actions earlier this week. If he didn't, he certainly did now by the look on his face.

"Rina's boyfriend. I'd like to know who you are and why you're at her house so late at night," Anthony replied without missing a beat.

"Well, shit, Rina, how long have you been dating this guy?" Ben shoved a hand in Anthony's direction.

The anger imploded on his face made her lose her words. What could she say to that? It wasn't true. Not really. One date didn't constitute dating, did it? Or did the fact her father expected her to date him make it true?

"Do not speak to her that way. Who are you?" Anthony took a step closer to Ben.

"Nobody. Absolutely nobody." Ben walked down the stairs, then stopped in front of her and whispered, "You could've shared this news a few days ago. Instead, you let me kiss you."

He took a step away. Her panic rose to the surface. She couldn't be alone with Anthony anymore. She never wanted to go out with him in the first place. All she wanted was Ben.

Instinctively, her hand reached out and grabbed his jacket before he stepped too far away. "Don't leave, Ben. Please."

He looked at her. A crease formed between his brows as he frowned. He touched her hand temporarily to give her reassurance, then turned toward Anthony. How had he known she needed that? Everything suddenly felt better. Safer.

"Well, continue on your way, Ben," Anthony said, his voice enunciating his name with a bit of venom.

"I need to talk to Rina. I'll wait for you to say good night." Ben offered a friendly smile, shifting his body a little closer to her, brushing his arm against her bare shoulder. Shivering with delight from the contact, she wondered how Anthony would react if she suddenly wrapped her arms around Ben. How would Ben react, for that matter? But that's what she needed. His warm arms around her.

"You're making Rina nervous. Don't make me call the police. I'll have you arrested without an issue. I'm a lawyer. Anthony Tollhorn." He smirked.

Ben moved his jacket to put a hand on his hip, displaying his badge clipped to his belt with pride. "Not sure what officer would dare to try and put handcuffs on me when I haven't broken the law."

Anthony looked confused, yet with a hint of anger lingering in the depths of his eyes. "Is everything okay, Rina? If you have a problem, I can help you. You don't need him to help you with anything."

"He's a friend. My best friend is married to his partner. There's nothing wrong. I'll call you tomorrow." Rina offered him a sweet smile that would hopefully diffuse the situation brewing. Ben still stood very close to her. He tensed immediately at her softly spoken words.

To her surprise, Anthony walked over and grabbed her by the shoulders with a little more force than he had used in the car. He moved her away from Ben. "I don't like the looks of him. Police or not. I'm not leaving you alone until he leaves."

"He'd never hurt me. You don't have to worry."

His fingers began to increase in pressure. The sickening feeling from the car intensified to unbearable as she grimaced. His fingernails grazed her skin as Ben suddenly shoved him off. He took a stance in front of her, blocking her view of Anthony.

"You touch her like that again, Anthony," Ben said, enunciating his name with venom this time, "and I'll arrest you for assault."

"Do you have any idea who you're dealing with? I am Anthony Tollhorn. My father is David Tollhorn, best criminal lawyer in the state."

"What is it with assholes like you always mentioning dear old dad? My dad owns a hardware store, which I'm damn proud of, but if you wanna play the dad card, then I'm game. My partner, Detective Chance, his dad happens to be the best judge in the state. I'm like a son to him. You want to keep going back and forth here, or are you going to get the hell off Rina's property? In fact, Rina, do you want this joker coming back?"

Ben stepped to the side, one eye on Anthony and the other on her. He looked ready to fight to the death for her, yet the concern pierced his eyes. "Rina? Do you want him coming around anymore?"

His worry, his compassion made her want to cry. She

tore her eyes away and glanced at Anthony. Nothing but arrogance and disappointment. Disappointment like her father always displayed.

Screwed either way. Anthony would tell his father, who would tell her father, no matter what she said. Anthony's condescending voice helped her decide rather quickly.

"Like she'd pick you over me."

She grabbed Ben's hand, squeezing hard. "No, Ben, I don't want him coming around here. Anthony, I don't believe we will be having a second date. Please leave."

"You're making the worst decision of your life, Rina. I wonder what your father will have to say." Anthony gave her a look of disgust and left without another word.

Rina let go of Ben's hand and quickly unlocked her door as the tears pooled in the corner of her eyes. Sniffling once, she had to keep them back. Breaking down in front of Ben would make her look even more pathetic. She couldn't be any more embarrassed. What did Ben think of her now?

The door swung open with a little more force than she anticipated. Barely hiding her stumble, she walked away with the door wide open. Ben could decide whether he wanted to come in or not. She didn't want to see the disappointment in his eyes. The disgust that she actually chose willingly to go out with a man like that.

The keys jingled as they hit the bottom of the bowl. No other sound echoed around the house. Did he even close the front door before he left?

A tear slid down. Her feet immobile. What direction did she go? To her bedroom or to check the front door?

A soft hand clamped her arm. "Rina, look at me."

She closed her eyes, unable to move. He shouldn't sound so concerned. She didn't deserve any kindness from him.

"Don't ignore me." He walked in front of her instead of

pulling her toward him, his warm hand still holding her arm.

His soft touch soothed her just as his sweet voice did. A finger brushed her cheek, wiping away another tear, then his arms circled around her, pulling her as close as possible. "Please don't let that asshole make you cry. He doesn't know what the hell he's talking about. I can't imagine your father would like him anyway. He'll probably—"

"Stop." She lifted her head, finally opening her eyes. "My father likes Anthony. Do you want to know why I can't date you, Ben?"

"Yes, I do."

Wrapping her arms tightly around him as she rested her head against his chest, she whispered, "Because my father would never allow it."

Clutching him tighter, she refused to look him in the eye. What would she see? He still hadn't given her one look of disgust or contempt.

"He'd probably make you feel like you didn't matter. He would never approve of me dating a cop. That's not good enough in his eyes. Sometimes, I think I'm not even good enough in his eyes."

She probably wasn't. A mere secretary. The only time in her life she defied her father and he let her get away with it.

Another tear escaped as his arms still held her tightly. He probably had no idea how much she needed him just to hold her. To offer comfort when she didn't deserve any.

"If you still didn't back down on dating me, he'd probably offer you money to walk away. It's happened before. I dated a sweet guy when I was nineteen. I was head over heels for him. He worked at a coffee shop. He didn't need to work there anymore after my father got done with him. See where this is going, Ben?"

He pulled her away from his chest and wiped another tear away. "Yeah, your dad sounds like an asshole."

She laughed lightly at the truth in those words, yet she still loved him. He was her father. How could she not? "Ben...I...he's my father. I've never disobeyed him, unless you count me taking a job as a secretary. He's still not happy about that. He expects me to be something better. Something worthy. It's just me and him."

"You are worthy. There's nothing wrong with your job. What's he going to do when he finds out you sent Anthony packing? Has he ever hurt you?"

"Never. He won't be happy about Anthony, for sure. He'll probably find out more information about you and deal with it in his own way."

He cupped her face, lightly brushing her lips. Everything in the world felt better by that simple touch. "You do realize you can hurt somebody without physically touching them. I'm not scared of your father."

"You should be. He's a powerful man," she said with a shiver. He still held his warm hands on her face, wishing for another kiss to touch her lips.

"Do you really want nothing to do with me? You, Rina, not what your father would want. If the answer is yes, I will leave you alone. I'll never bother you again. But if you want me as much as I want you, then just say the word. Just be completely honest with me."

"Ben, you claimed a part of me a long time ago. The day you finally asked me out, my heart soared. It broke me just as much as you to say no. I want you, I do, but—"

He broke her words with a crushing kiss. He devoured her mouth, her tongue matching pace with him. His passion melted her senses, making her forget everything but him holding her.

"There are no buts, Rina. You need to stop letting your father dictate your life. I'm not scared of him. Let's see where this can go."

"He's my father." She stepped away, missing his touch the minute she did, but she needed space.

She walked to the fridge, pulling the door open as he responded, "You're a grown woman. You can do whatever the hell you want."

"Water?" she asked, holding a bottle for him to take.

"No. I just want you," he said simply.

Her hand wavered in the air as his words sent burning tingles of desire throughout her body. The bottle puffed out like it wanted to explode as she exerted pressure on it. The fridge door slowly closed behind her. "Why did you come over?"

He looked away, his expression a brooding one. "I just needed to."

"Is something wrong?" She couldn't stand the pain in his eyes. Her footsteps were slow, but very steady as she walked over to him where he leaned against the counter.

He didn't hesitate to pull her into his arms as soon as she got within reaching distance. "I had a rough day. Zeke and I have these cases right now...they're bad. I just needed to see you."

She smoothed a hand down his chest, enacting one of the many fantasies she played in her head. Defined ridges answered back. How easily could his shirt disappear? "I don't understand."

He grabbed her hand, clutching it. "I got home tonight and I just started going out of my mind. I needed to see you. I needed to make sure you were all right."

"You still have me confused. You look tired."

"I am tired. I don't even want to leave you tonight."

There was so much more hidden in those words. What was bothering him? Why wouldn't he just tell her?

"I'll be okay. You don't have to worry about me."

He pulled her hand to his lips, lightly kissing it. "What about Anthony? If I hadn't shown up..."

Tucking her head against his chest, the rapid beating of his heart echoing in her ear, she tried to conjure the right words. There were none. She had no idea what would've happened. Most likely, she would've accepted his date, even though she couldn't stand the thought of it.

Ben must've known that as he wrapped his arms around her tighter. He never insisted on an answer. They stood like that for a few minutes. Enjoying the silence, the comfort of each other's arms. Rina knew what she had to do. For once, something for herself. Perhaps it would soothe his nerves about Anthony, no matter what her decision might've been if he hadn't shown up.

She lifted her head and kissed him. Nothing urgent and strong, just light and brief. "Ask me out, Ben?"

"I never get the answer I want." His face, instead of beaming with happiness as she'd hoped, held a lot of worry.

"I ruined my chances. You're too good for me."

"I think that's the other way around. You're beautiful. You're amazing. And you're perfect for me." He smiled at her, yet she saw the worry line his face. "Will you do me the honor of letting me take you out on a date? Cup of coffee, maybe?"

Her heart that had shattered into pieces thinking she lost her chance lifted instantly. "I would love to. Why wait? Stay for a while. Watch a movie with me."

"I love watching movies. Can we act like teenagers and make out some?" he asked with a silly grin.

She giggled. "I never made out as a teenager. What does

it entail?"

He grabbed her hand and led her out of the kitchen. "Oh boy, I can't wait to show you. It involves a lot of kissing, touching, maybe even some exploring, like hunting for treasure."

Another giggle escaped. Happy for the first time ever. She knew her father would eventually ruin this beautiful thing with Ben. But for the moment, she would soak up every minute with him as if it were the last time. Which it just might be.

"I should go change. My movies are in the little cubby beneath the TV." Her fingers slipped from his as she backed up a step.

---

HIS EYES slowly took in her appearance. The gorgeous way her hair was swept to the side, giving her face the attention it deserved. The dress showed more of her than he had ever seen. A small rage started to boil inside that she had worn this dress for Anthony. He could only imagine how much that man ogled her throughout the night. The dress hugged her body like a silk glove, showing her cleavage in a way that had him wishing he could touch. Her legs ran on for miles as the dress stopped just short of mid-thigh. Too short. He didn't want anyone else to see her like this. Only him.

To his horror, he was doing exactly what he hated Anthony for probably doing. Ogling her! She knew it, too, as she stood waiting for him to say something. Words left his brain. He didn't know what to say. This was the first time he took a good long look at what she actually had on. The only thing occupying his mind outside had been how not to punch Anthony in the face and shove him off her property.

"Ben?" she whispered delicately.

"What?"

"I'm going to go change. I'm just making sure you're okay. You looked a little bit lost there," she said with a small laugh.

"I'm definitely not lost." He took a step toward the living room, needing to escape from the temptation standing in front of him. He needed to go slow, not push her away by rushing whatever was forming between them. Suddenly, a small grin formed on his face. "Do you need help changing?"

He just couldn't help himself.

A brief flash of panic crossed her face. "No...I think I can manage."

"You think? So, you're not exactly sure." Ben suddenly remembered something Zeke once said to him concerning Zoe. *She gets weak by my touch. Can't resist me. I use any weapon necessary to get my way.* Wise words. Very wise. With slow, deliberate steps, he walked toward Rina instead of heading to the living room.

He grabbed her hands, weaving his fingers through hers, and pulled her closer. "I would love to help you change."

Her heart started to pound in tune with his as a light blush tinged her cheeks. Good to know she was just as nervous as him.

"I think I should change by myself."

He lightly touched her lips, gaining a soft moan from her. "You sound so unsure. You keep saying you think. Trust me, I know. I'm very good at changing clothes. I've mastered it very well."

She chuckled, then rested her head against his chest as he squeezed her hands a little harder. "It might seem like I'm experienced, like I know what I'm doing when it comes to guys...but I'm not. I've perfected how to brush them off because it wouldn't do well anyway, not with how I know my father would react. I've dated before, very small, fleeting relationships. Really, only ones approved by my father. This, right here, with you, is new. This banter back and forth. I want you, Ben, but I'm scared."

She shivered in his arms. Not in a good way either. It broke his heart to know what sort of hell Rina had been living in. To think she couldn't even date whom she wanted because her father might not approve. He couldn't imagine ever dealing with that.

His sister Erin dated a loser a few years ago. His parents never liked the guy, but they didn't interfere. Maybe they should have. Maybe she wouldn't have gotten pregnant. Yet, he wouldn't wish his little niece away for anything. Little Isabella was too precious.

Ben lifted her head. The sorrow and slight fear he saw broke his heart a little more. "Rina, I'd never hurt you. I'd never force you. I was just teasing a bit. We can take this as slow as you need it to go. I care about you too much to screw this up. You're giving me a chance and I want it to stay that way."

"I feel like the one screwing up. Since the beginning. I don't want to lose you. And the worst part is, I already have."

"I'm right here. You didn't lose me." He kissed her lightly just to show her as well.

"Not for long. You'll see," she whispered, burying her face into his chest again.

"No, Rina, you'll see. If you think I'm going to give up easily, you're wrong. I know how wonderful you feel in my arms. I'm never giving that up. I'll fight for you. You better get used to the idea right now. You're mine. Nothing in this world is going to change my mind. Absolutely nothing."

## 5

Ben looked up as a pencil bounced off his chest, rolled toward him, and fell onto his lap. "Why did I earn a pencil thrown at me?"

Zeke leaned back in his chair, shoving his hands behind his head. "You've been quiet all morning. I hate it when you're quiet. Are you still pissed at me?"

"Did you talk to the captain?" Ben countered.

Zeke dropped his hands, as if he were going to slam them on the desk. "Geez, man, I'm not going to talk to the damn captain."

Ben twirled the pencil he picked up from his lap. "I like the relationship you have with Zoe. That you tell her everything. Isn't there some sort of bro code, though?"

Zeke sighed heavily. "I'm sorry she went to Rina. Whatever you say from now on about her stays between us. I swear."

A small smile emerged on Ben's face. To tell or not to tell? Everything with Rina was so new. Would telling Zeke what happened last night jinx him?

"What's with the smirk?"

"I stopped by Rina's house last night. I just...I needed to see her. These cases..." Ben whipped his hand at the papers covering his desk regarding the two recent murders. "They're messing with my head. Her date was dropping her off. A real jerk. A damn lawyer."

Zeke groaned, running a hand over his face. "I tried to tell you, buddy."

Ben shook his head. "It doesn't matter. He won't be bothering her again. I know why she doesn't want to date me. No...why she felt scared to date me."

Zeke leaned forward, the confusion marring his face. "Why in the hell would she be scared?"

A muscle started to tick in his jaw as he clenched his teeth. "Her father. By the few words she spoke, he's pretty demanding and controlling. She seems to think as soon as he finds out we're dating that he'll put a stop to it. I don't know. Buy me off, or hell, even threaten me. She said he's never physically harmed her, but I could see how scared she was. Her own father, man."

Zeke slowly grinned. "Dating? So, she changed her mind?"

Ben grinned back. "Until her father talks her out of it. She's worth any fight. I just hate to think of her getting hurt through the process."

"Makes some sense now."

"What makes sense?"

"Her demeanor. Her soft words. Never hollering or raising her voice." Zeke shrugged. "She probably learned at an early age how not to upset her father. He sounds like someone who wouldn't tolerate any backtalk."

Ben blew out a breath. Damn. What sort of childhood did she have? She always appeared happy, so he hoped it hadn't been that horrible. "Oh, yeah, I threw your dad out there. Anthony, the jackass lawyer, muttered something about his dad being the best criminal lawyer out there. I said your dad thought of me as a son and he's the best judge out there."

Zeke busted out laughing. "Oh, he'll love to hear that. What is it with these damn lawyers?"

Ben turned around as Zeke's eyes trailed behind him. "Oh, man, what is she doing here?"

"This is going to be fun. She's going to rip your balls off like she did to me every single time when I first started dating Zoe. If she knows about you and Rina, that is," Zeke said with a laugh as Dee made her way over to them.

Dee stopped in front of them and glanced back and forth, her lips pursed in a harsh look.

"Rina seemed much happier today, Ben. She didn't tell me much. Just that she decided to give you a chance. I was very happy to hear that," Dee said, changing her look with a genuine smile.

Ben started to smile wide when Zeke busted in with an annoyed tone. "Wait. What the hell is this? You're happy to hear that. Why aren't you threatening him? You never let up on me."

She brought her smile from Ben's face, dropping back into a scowl as she landed on Zeke. "Buddy, you still haven't worked your way into my good graces. Especially when I heard you wanted to return that lovely red dress I bought for Zee-Zee. Ben has always been a gentleman, never acting the way you do. He fell off the douche list a long time ago."

Ben chuckled softly as Zeke tried to keep an amiable expression on his face. Dee had been brutal to Zeke when he started dating Zoe. Ben had expected the same kind of treatment. That's just how Dee operated. She never made anything easy for anyone.

"That's just not right. And damn right, I wanted to return that dress. Only my wife gets to wear red dresses. Stop buying Brina dresses. She has enough. And what's with calling her Zee-Zee?"

Dee threw a hand to her hip. "You call her Brina all the time. Which, when you think about it, sounds close to Rina. There's no reason she can't be close to her other auntie. It's only fair. I will buy her dresses until the day I die. Get over it."

Zeke leaned over his desk, getting closer to her. "Get over it? I'm her dad. I have the last say."

"If it makes you feel better to think that..." Dee said with a wicked smile.

Ben chuckled again, interrupting the byplay between them. "I needed this good laugh. Thanks, Dee. What brings you by? Or was it just to say Rina's happy? She didn't say anything to...anything about..."

Dee placed a hand on his shoulder. "You're a nervous little nelly. How cute. I'm here about Zoe's surprise party on Sunday. We were going to have it at the bar downtown, but after we realized Zee-Zee would be in attendance we decided to change it. Last minute, I know, but it was more Rina's idea. She's starting to get a little bolder. I didn't want to test the waters and tell her no."

"Zabrina's not coming. My parents will have her," Zeke said, confused.

"Wrong. We invited your parents as well, so they're going to bring her. You know how your mom hates to be left out of anything. Geez, Zeke, get it together," Dee said, priming her hair a bit.

Ben tried to hold in his laugh as he could tell Zeke's irritation rise with each word Dee spoke. "So, you're here...for what?"

"Rina wants to have it at her house. We already started to spread the word at the change of location. I'm getting the cake and a few little gifts. Rina's going to take care of the other food and hang up some decorations. I thought she could use a little bit more help. Water, pop, beer, those things can get heavy," Dee said with a devilish smile.

His brows dipped in confusion. Why was she looking at him like that?

"You're practically playing matchmaker here. Yet, not once did you have a nice thing to say about me. Still don't sometimes," Zeke said with a grumble as he slumped back into his chair.

Dee rolled her eyes. "This, whatever it is, jealousy, maybe. Just stop it, Zeke. You're only adding to my enjoyment. That's me being nice and telling you that." She smiled. "I'm not doing this for Ben. I'm doing this for Rina because she's a little too shy. I might give you a lot of crap, but I know you're good for Zoe. I only do it because it's so easy. I also know that Ben is good for Rina. So, what do you say, Ben?"

"What am I supposed to say?"

"Are you still in shock?" Zeke slapped his hand on the desk as he chuckled. "She wants you to help Rina set up the party. Basically, give you time with her without trying to find another excuse. Am I right, Dee?" Zeke said, leaning back in his chair as if he were the king.

"Right," Dee replied dryly. She switched her focus to Ben. "You can handle that, can't ya?"

"Most definitely." He couldn't be happier that she thought of him, or even considered helping him out. He got along fine with her, but never really thought she would go out of her way to help him win Rina's heart. "I'll call her then."

"No. Don't give her a chance to decline your help. Just show up. Trust me. I know what I'm talking about here." Dee gave him a wink. "Gotta go, boys. Have a pleasant day."

She turned around, took a few steps, then whipped back toward him. "I see the way her eyes light up when she talks about you, even when she's trying to hide it. Just keep doing whatever you did last night. By the way, don't bother surprising her tonight. I have plans with her."

Zeke waited until Dee left, then pinned his gaze on Ben. "That's just not fair."

"Jealous?" Ben asked, the joy still plastered on his face that he was making headway with Rina.

"She never let up on me."

Ben laughed. "What can I say? I guess I'm cooler than you."

"Whatever. Her opinion doesn't matter that much," Zeke grumbled, even though his eyes said it did.

Another laugh escaped as he stood up and grabbed his jacket from behind his chair. "Come on. Let's go talk to some of Ashley's co-workers. Maybe they can give us some insight on her relationship with her husband. Not that I think he did it."

"I hate to agree, but I think you're right." Zeke stood up and grabbed his jacket as well. "How soon until the next body pops up? Because if we don't solve this today, we'll have another body."

There were no words to respond with, except he wouldn't let it be Rina. She matched the description of the two victims so well. A bad feeling had already started to worm its way inside, festering, building, staking a claim. It wouldn't be going away until they solved this case. He couldn't lose her—to anyone.

An hour later, Ben was losing his patience as they tried

to wrap up an interview with Donna, the office manager, at the doctor's office where Ashley had worked.

"No problems...with patients, other co-workers? Anything?" Zeke reiterated for what seemed like the twentieth time.

Donna shook her head. "No, detective. She was a nice woman, great worker. Sure, we get a few uppity or grumpy patients, but nothing that sticks in my mind worth mentioning. Ashley had a nice way about her. She was pleasant to everyone, even when they were acting like jerks."

"How about her husband, Gene. She ever say anything about their relationship? Do you know why they were fighting?" Ben tried not to frown, but he couldn't help himself. Frustration at every corner.

"Look, I know they had some issues to work out, but I seriously don't think Gene killed Ashley. He loves her." Donna put a hand on her hip, her irritation prominent.

"What issues did they need to work out? Why can't you just say it?" Ben didn't keep the annoyance out of his voice this time. He refused to be jerked around.

"He loves her." Donna fiddled her fingers on her hip, her lips pierced tightly. "He made a mistake. He slept with another woman. He told her himself. She wanted space from him, to think things through. But he loves her."

Zeke snorted with disgust. "Do you know who he slept with?"

"He would have never harmed her in any way," Donna insisted.

"Yet, he did. Emotionally. Why can't people figure this shit out?" Ben snapped. "Just because he didn't touch her physically doesn't mean he didn't hurt her emotionally."

Zeke glanced at Ben. "Ms. Delvine, do you know who he

slept with? Clearly, Ashley trusted you enough to confide in you about her marital problems."

Donna glared at Ben for a moment longer before shifting her attention to Zeke. "Her sister, Caroline. She had lunch with her sister just yesterday. She came back appearing happy. They talked it out. She was going to let Gene back into the house, into her life."

"Wow..." Ben muttered.

"We need a list of everyone Ashley had contact with yesterday. Do you by chance know where she went to lunch with her sister?" Zeke asked.

"The café down the street...a little mom and pop place. Ashley worked with some patients. She also handled the front desk for a while, like normal. We all take turns doing things in the office. She spoke to a few consultants that came in with different products. And she signed for a package that came in with the mail."

"Well, we'll need names to go with that list." Zeke gave her a thousand-watt smile.

The same smile he used to use when he flirted with a woman. Now he just used it to get his way. Ben didn't have time for that crap. Why couldn't people understand emotional pain?

"I'm not sure I can give patients' names out to you without a warrant." Donna smiled back.

This woman was a pain in the ass. Ben couldn't stand it. "So does that mean you won't divulge this information without a warrant?"

"Yes, detective."

"Be back in an hour." Ben turned around without another word.

An hour later, he walked back into the office just like he'd said. With a smile, the sort Zeke liked to give in doses when he really wanted something, he barely contained the urge to slam the warrant on the desk.

"We'll take that list now."

Donna stared at him for a brief moment before looking over the warrant. "I find it hard to believe anyone who walked into this office killed Ashley...or her husband."

"You'd be amazed who is capable of violence. I'm here to find a killer who brutally murdered your friend. You've already wasted an hour of my time. Please don't continue to waste any more of it."

Donna snatched the warrant from the counter. "I'll be right back."

Zeke shifted his feet as he crossed his arms and leaned against the desk as they waited. "You okay, man? I figured you would've been in a better mood since you worked things out with Rina. You're normally not grouchy with people. I am."

Ben shrugged. "This case...I don't know. It bugs me." He whipped his hand toward the direction Donna walked off. "And seriously, she thinks Gene didn't hurt Ashley. Sure, he confessed to cheating. She was hurting, though. You don't need bruises to wound somebody."

Zeke sighed. "So this is about Rina."

"I didn't say that."

"Come on, Ben. It's bugging you about her father. You know Rina hurts from the way her father treats her. You really jumped down Ms. Delvine's throat about getting emotionally hurt. You can't let that affect your job."

Ben gave him a mock laugh. "Yeah, okay, I'll work on that, partner. Just like you do so well."

"Yeah, yeah, we both suck at it. Let's just solve this case."

Ben nodded, hoping like hell they did. Soon.

A few minutes later, Donna walked back with the list

they wanted an hour ago. A very long list. At least twenty people they had to interview. Not to mention cross-referencing to see if anybody on the list knew Beth, their first victim. Beth and Ashley had to be connected somehow. Finding the connection was proving to be very difficult.

Beth worked at a salon. She had a different network of friends. She was recently single. Ashley worked at a doctor's office. She was married. She didn't go to the salon Beth worked at. Nothing tied them together. Except the one thing he hated thinking about. How friendly, how soft-spoken and generous they were to others.

The more they dug into their lives, the more Ben hated the similarities he saw. They sounded like Rina. They looked like Rina. While he had no evidence to suggest she would be a victim, he worried that she would be by these simple similarities. He wanted to voice his concern to Zeke, but he didn't. He knew Zeke would just say he was worried about Rina because of their new developing relationship. Maybe that's where his worry came from.

Crossing off the list of patients took all day. After speaking to each patient, no new insight was gained. Collecting twenty alibis hadn't been fun. Verifying those alibis had been even more painful. Focused and determined. He had to keep Rina safe.

Tired to the bone, he pulled into his driveway wishing he could've pulled into Rina's instead. It didn't matter how tired he was. Seeing her face would brighten his shitty day with ease.

Every patient had been interviewed, but they hadn't tracked down the two consultants and the delivery guy that Ashley dealt with. They also spoke to her sister, Caroline.

His stomach rolled with disgust at the way she treated Ashley, how she slept with her husband, and how Ashley graciously forgave her as if she borrowed a dress and didn't return it in the time frame she asked of her. Caroline told him and Zeke about the small argument—and Ben figured it had to have been small—that occurred between the two. She expressed her regret to Ashley, her remorse, and she said Ashley, after a few choice words, forgave her. She even told them how Ashley planned to let Gene stew a few more days and then let him come back home. She was forgiving him as well.

Ridiculous. The entire situation. A cheater was a cheater. He couldn't imagine doing that to anyone. Speaking to Gene again, he couldn't figure out why he did it in the first place. His pain from losing his wife was real. Heartbroken. Torn. But to Ben, he hadn't loved her enough to keep it in his pants.

They found him at his brother's house. He couldn't stand his own home anymore. He couldn't stand the fact his wife was murdered and he wasn't there to stop it. If he never would've cheated, he never would've been kicked out, and she never would've been home alone that night. The guilt was eating him alive.

While Ben thought he was a class-A jerk for cheating on his wife, he still didn't think he killed her. He was an idiot, like Susan originally said. He divulged everything to them. That he cheated, the things he said to Ashley, and that he confessed the next day after it happened. He explained how he drank himself into oblivion, got into the car and drove to their home and banged on the door for her to let him in before he finally realized he had his own key. He even told them to arrest him for drinking and driving. He deserved the punishment he said.

Ben actually contemplated doing it before Zeke shook his head with a smirk, knowing exactly what he was thinking. Yeah, the guy was in enough pain for losing his wife so brutally. Seemed punishment enough.

Dr. Everly put Ashley's time of death to about ten o'clock that night. Gene hadn't arrived to their home until around 12:30 in the morning. His brother corroborated his story, saying he sat with his brother drinking until midnight when he finally went to bed. He didn't even know Gene left. Otherwise, he would've stopped him. He knew how wasted he had been.

No more. Thinking about the case wouldn't help his mood, only lower it further. He stepped out of his car and hit the garage door button. Listening to the strumming noise of the door descending did nothing to dispel the thoughts of the case. One big fat mystery. No suspects. No leads. Just nothing.

One thing could distract his mind. The one thing he couldn't do tonight. Dee said Rina had plans with her. He wanted to thwart the plans with a passion. All he wanted was to see her face.

Walking inside the kitchen from the garage, the light made him jerk in place as he flipped the switch. Loneliness. A deep wrenching loneliness. He felt it every so often, but at the moment, it hit him squarely in the chest. He wanted Rina here and everything to work out. He wanted her in his home, in his life, forever.

Damn, if Zeke wasn't right. He loved her.

How did he tell her? Should he wait? She was scared to begin with. She would probably run screaming from him if he said those three little words already. They were barely dating yet. Not that it mattered. He knew enough to know his feelings weren't just lust or something crazy like that. Nothing but pure love. He had an entire year to get to know her.

The way she smiled at the simple things in life. Like a flower blooming in a garden full of weeds. He couldn't get that smile out of his head the first time he saw it as she and Zoe worked in the yard at Zeke's house. Zoe had instantly insisted some beautiful flowers be planted around his house the minute she officially moved in. She hadn't considered moving in official until her house sold. It hadn't taken long either. Zeke made sure of that. Ben had laughed at the playful bickering between the two as Zeke always insisted she was officially living in his home even though her house hadn't sold yet. She always countered that it wasn't official if she could walk out of his home and go back to hers. Until she had nowhere to go but another room in his house whenever he upset her, it was not official. He could still remember the looks he and Rina shared as those two argued about it. The smudges of dirt lining her cheeks as she dug in the dirt, Zeke and Zoe squabbling in the background. He loved her smile.

She always spoke with the voice of reason, as Dee liked to call it. Dee had a nasty habit of saying she was always right, no matter what they were talking about. Between Zoe and Dee, they sometimes couldn't come to an agreement. Especially how Dee needed to stop buying dresses for the baby before she was even born. Zoe had always reminded her they wouldn't know the sex of the baby until she went into labor. She didn't want Dee to waste money buying dresses when it should be trousers. Dee had shaken her head, not caring about the money. Rina had stepped in, smiled, and suggested with her soft voice that Zoe keep the receipts in case it wasn't a girl. Problem solved.

She always smiled politely, even when people were being rude. Ben had seen rudeness displayed many times, especially when they all went out for a few drinks. Some men—especially the men—just didn't know how to respect women. Rina always gave them an elegant smile and brushed them off as if they were nothing more than an irritating gnat. He rarely had to step in and help her. Sometimes it irked him because he wanted to. He wanted to be her hero and she never gave him a chance to be one.

She always helped anybody with anything they asked of her. No matter the time or day or how busy she appeared. If you needed help, no matter the problem, she dropped what she was doing. Before he had the courage to ask her out, and she ultimately turned him down, he had plotted many ways to feign any sort of help just to spend a little time with her. He never went through with any of his plans, but he sure made some good ones in his head.

She loved kids. He knew that by the glowing happiness that spread across her face anytime she held Zabrina. He wanted kids one day. He could already see Rina as the mother to his children. He was ready to take that leap.

No matter how mad she got, she always held her temper and voiced her displeasure with a quiet ease. He had to admit, that made him uneasy. She could break him in two with her quiet, soft voice. She already had. Not too long ago.

It didn't matter. She could break him all she wanted. As long as she always put him back together afterwards. Just a simple, soft touch on his shoulder always managed to glue him back together. When he thought about it, she did touch him a lot like that. Simple gestures here and there. So many little signs he should've seen.

Who cared about the past anymore? She was his. She was in his life.

He loved her. He wanted to shout it out to the world. Declare it to any person who asked. How couldn't he love someone like that? She made it easy.

How could he tell her he loved her? It had to be done in the perfect way. She could go running in the opposite direction if he didn't.

He pulled a container of meatloaf his mom sent him the other day from the fridge and shoved it into the microwave. Maybe the best way would be to lay it all out for her. Every little thing he felt. No waiting to tell her. She needed to know. Otherwise, he could lose her. Maybe he still would.

At least she would know how he felt. If she still wanted to keep him at arm's length, then it would be with the full knowledge of his feelings. It would be her fault and her choice. Or his fault for being a coward. He wasn't positive he could voice those three words.

The seconds ticked down as he waited for the signal his food was warm. He was no coward. He'd tell her.

Five...four...three...

The doorbell echoed throughout the house.

A small smile touched his face. What were the odds Rina decided to stop by his house? She did it once before. Angry, of course, but she stopped by. That had to count for something.

Opening the door with hope, his smile vanished. A man in an expensive-looking black coat stood in front of him.

"Can I help you?" Ben kept his hands by his side, his gun hidden, but ready to reach for it if need be. Threatening vibes swarmed him as he stared at the man. Distinguished looking, regal even, but something about the man made him feel threatened.

"Detective Benjamin Stoyer?"

"Who's asking?"

"Reginald Chastain. You know my daughter, Rina."

It all made sense. While Rina's father didn't show any disgust, anger, or disapproval in his facial expression, it was written in his eyes. He could see the resemblance to Rina as well. She had her father's eyes, a deep brown, full of depth. When she was upset, she always poised her lips in a straight line that betrayed none of that anger. Just like he did now.

His hair was perfectly combed to the side with one fell swoop, not a piece out of place. He wore black gloves that looked as expensive as his black coat. The wind held a slight bite, but he wouldn't classify it as cold. Why the gloves? Perhaps he wanted to conceal his fingerprints.

Ben already hated the man. Yet, he was Rina's father.

"What can I do for you? We both know that you know I am Detective Stoyer. Please, don't beat around the bush here."

"Good. I'm glad you see the issue." Reginald adjusted his glove on his left hand.

"I don't see an issue. I'm sorry that you do."

"Your behavior towards Mr. Tollhorn and my daughter was uncalled for. You should be lucky he's not filing a complaint with the department against you. Rina would like you to leave her alone."

Ben tried to keep his face just as expressionless. He found it very difficult to do. He imagined Reginald had a lifetime to perfect it. "She told you that, did she?"

"My daughter doesn't need to tell me anything. I'm her father. I know what's best for her. You are not what's best for her. Anthony is better suited for her."

"So you're okay with a man physically harming your daughter? Is that what you're saying?" Ben cocked a brow. "Because he had no problem grabbing her and squeezing her shoulders hard, to the point where I saw her grimace in pain. I guess I'm not surprised."

"Excuse me?"

"You hurt her just as much as Anthony did."

"I have never in my life laid a hand on my daughter. You'll do well to watch how you speak to me." Reginald pierced his lips in a thinner line, yet his voice didn't rise in volume.

Ben wasn't surprised in the least. He now fully understood how Rina never lost her temper. She learned it all from her father.

Ben leaned closer so Reginald could hear and understand every word. Not that he probably would. "You don't need to touch a person to hurt them. You hurt her every day by treating her with the words you use."

"Stay away from my daughter, detective. You have a nice job to occupy your time." Reginald adjusted his other glove, his eyes never wavering from Ben.

"Don't threaten me," Ben said through his teeth. He wouldn't raise his voice, no matter how much he wanted to. His hands clenched. *Don't hit the man. Don't do it.* Rina would hate him for sure.

"I had dinner with the chief of police just last week. We're very good friends. My daughter is dating Mr. Tollhorn, not you."

"You can say all you want about my job, about knowing the chief of police, but you will not scare me away from your daughter, Reginald. You're despicable for even doing this to her. Let her live her own life. She's not a child anymore."

"Do not address me as Reginald. It's Mr. Chastain to you. I don't repeat myself, but since you don't hear very well, I'll say it one more time. Stay away from my daughter."

"Learn how to respect her. Don't come to my home again unless it's to apologize. Good night...Reggie." Ben shut the door, grinning at what he saw in the man's face after he called him Reggie.

He may be an expert at controlling his emotions, but

Ben managed to surprise him and pull a bit out. His jaw had ticked, emphasizing his annoyance at his name being shortened in such a manner. Ben felt triumph in that.

Damn it! He shouldn't feel that. He was Rina's father. He could ruin everything. No matter how horrible her father treated her, he knew Rina loved him. Getting in the middle or making her choose a side would tear her apart. He could lose her in the process.

His hand stopped from opening the microwave. Food didn't sound so appealing anymore.

Ten o'clock. It was late.

Dee said not to bother Rina tonight.

Panic welled inside, weaving together with fear. Why did her father have to show up at his doorstep? So soon as well. He barely had any time with Rina to call her his and her father was already trying to ruin things.

He had to see her tonight. Putting a wedge between her and her father was the last thing he wanted to do. He had no choice. Her father just declared war.

## 6

Dee scratched deeply onto the notepad, more vigorously than was necessary. "Okay, so we don't need that much cheese. I mean, I like cheese, but I guess we don't need that much."

"Yeah, ten pounds seems a little excessive." Rina glanced at the pad. "Are you okay, Dee? You're always making sure Zoe and I are okay, but I guess we forget to ask how you are."

Dee waved her hand. "I'm fine. I'm glad to see you're happier."

"Yeah, I am." Rina looked away.

Dee dropped her pen. "Okay, what's with the big sigh? You were happy this morning, but honestly, the longer the day goes on, you just keep dropping into whatever the hell this attitude is."

"Why aren't you happy?"

"Quit dodging my question." Dee primped her hair, rolling her eyes at Rina's insistence that lingered in her eyes. "How do you do that?"

"Do what?"

"Have an argument without raising your voice?"

"Are we arguing?"

"It sure feels like it." Dee flicked the pen away with her finger. "I wish Zoe was here."

"That would defeat the point of giving her a surprise welcome back party."

"I know. It's just...never mind." Dee reached for the pen, her hand becoming stiff when Rina closed her hand over hers. "I'm not going to break down. I don't need coddling."

Rina withdrew her hand. "My father's very demanding, very controlling when it comes to...everything. That's why I wouldn't date Ben and why I'm still scared to."

Dee left the pen in its place, slowly bringing her eyes to meet Rina's. "He's a good guy. Your father should piss off."

Rina chuckled. "You always have a way with words."

Dee smiled back. "You always have a way of putting someone in their place. Even better than me."

"He's my father. How can I ignore his feelings?" Rina glanced down at the table. Tracing little circles on the table helped distract her. The concern in Dee's face was hard to look at.

"How can he ignore yours?"

Her finger froze like a statue. "I really like Ben. I don't know how I've managed to keep such a wonderful friendship with you and Zoe as I have. I imagine it's only because you both aren't men. He's always trying to find the perfect match for me. They never are. My feelings never matter. I think Ben's the perfect match. He'll hate Ben and ruin everything."

"You're a grown-ass woman, Rina. I know he's family, but he should know better. You deserve a man who will treat you like you need to be treated. Ben's worth it."

Her finger relaxed as she turned her eyes to Dee. "I am a grown-ass woman, aren't I?"

"Hell yeah. Are you gonna start acting like it?" Dee brushed her hair back as she smirked.

"Are you going to get that stick out of your ass and tell me what's going on?"

Dee raised her eyebrows in shock, then started to laugh. She laughed so hard that tears started to stream down her face. Her laugh became so infectious that Rina began laughing with her. The laughter filled the house, lifting Rina's heart.

Dee held her hand up, the laughter still coming out. "Give me a minute." She wiped her eyes from the happy tears and tried wiping the smile from her mouth. It was useless. "I wish Zoe was here."

"You already said that. I do, too." Rina wiped her face a little as well, as a few tears had escaped.

"No, I don't think you understand. I was having a mini pity party. We don't get together as much since Zoe found Zeke and had Zabrina. I get it. She's happy. I want that for her. And now...now you have Ben. I'm the lone wolf standing, without a pack anymore. I'm too loud. I'm too harsh to snag a good man. Not that I want one." Dee rushed the last bit out, then sighed dramatically. "Okay, I want one. Just not a douche. They're all douches."

Rina chuckled. "You don't really believe that. A man really raked you over, didn't he?"

Dee shrugged and grabbed the pen, squeezing it tightly. "I just don't want to lose you guys. You're all I have right now."

Rina glided her hand toward Dee's hand that held the pen. "You'll always have us. I'll speak for Zoe in that account."

"I know. I'm over my pity party." Dee took her hand

back, primping her hair again. "I'll just have to strut my stuff a little harder."

Rina grinned lightly. "You strut your stuff very well. Perhaps you should strut your stuff in front of Donaho."

"Eww, no." Dee rolled her eyes. "Look, don't let your father screw this up with Ben. If you break it off with him, make sure it's because that's what you want."

"I promise. I will."

Rina kept that promise, meant it with all her heart, until later that night when her father stopped by her house unannounced. Her courage wavered as he spoke to her about Ben and how she needed to stop seeing him. Telling her how rude Ben acted.

Stress overwhelmed her. She couldn't stop her eyes trailing to the few things scattered around her house. Her coat she slung across the back of one of the dining room table chairs. Or the two cups left on the counter from having a drink with Dee. Even the book just resting on her coffee table. Little things that would have no impact on most people. To her father, it was a clutter, a mess uncalled for.

Then, his words started to penetrate through that stress. Ben acted rude to her father. When in the world had her father seen Ben?

"Did you hear me, Rina? You'll join me at the country club on Sunday. You'll apologize profusely to Anthony for your behavior. I will not tolerate this nonsense."

"Where did you see Ben? How do you even know about him?" Rina said everything with a soft tone, almost as if she whispered the words. She saw the small shock in her father's eyes that she didn't readily agree to his demands, that she had the audacity to question him—on anything.

"It doesn't matter. What matters is he has no manners."

Rina took a step back, distancing herself—in more than

just physical space. She knew the moment her feet moved she was distancing herself emotionally from her father. "It matters to me. What did you do?"

"Honestly, Rina, your attitude is ridiculous. Accusing me of doing something. I am your father."

"Yes, you should respect what I do. Not constantly question it. I'm an adult. I'm thirty years old. I can take care of myself. When did you see Ben?"

"I will see you at the country club on—"

"No," Rina said with quiet confidence, cutting off her father's words.

His look would've told others that she screamed at the top of her lungs. "Excuse me?"

"I have plans on Sunday. I told Anthony that. I also told him there wouldn't be a second date and I meant it. I'm seeing Ben. Don't tell me where and when you spoke to him. It doesn't matter, you're right. It's not going to change my mind. He's a wonderful man who treats me as I should be treated. I won't let you ruin this like you have every other relationship I've ever tried to have."

"This is why this man is horrible for you. Look at the way you're speaking to me. I am your father."

"Then start acting like you are. Because all I see is a man trying to control somebody into doing something they don't want to do."

"Clearly, you're not feeling well right now. I'll call you in the morning."

Her father left her standing in the middle of the living room. He didn't say another word.

What happened? She expected more berating, more spewing of words to change her mind. There had been no mistaking the surprise in his eyes, the awe in her outspoken words. She never spoke to her father like that because she never had the courage to do so.

The moment her mother died, when she was four years old, her father changed from a wonderful, loving man to a hard, difficult one. Knowing he was in pain, she tried to make his life easier by being the dutiful daughter. Never disobeying. Never falling into trouble. Never living her life like she wanted.

As time went on, she slowly started to do her own thing. Within reason. She still tried not to do anything that would upset him. Not until she felt threatened for the first time in her life. She finally found a man she wanted with everything in her heart, and her father wanted to take that away.

She promised Dee she wouldn't let Ben go unless that's what she wanted. Well, she didn't want that. She felt liberated, and a small amount of peace absorbed into her veins for finally standing her ground against her father. Sadness and heartache slowly melded into one as well.

She'd perfected holding in her emotions, learning it all from her father. Today was the first day they both let their emotions slip. She saw the hurt in her father's eyes. She didn't want that. She just wanted him to be happy for her, to be proud of her, to support her for once in his life. Would she ever get that? Probably not.

After what felt like hours, when in reality mere minutes went by, she finally turned toward her bedroom. She stood there for so long contemplating everything that happened in those brief minutes, she realized he hadn't been in her home long.

Long enough to criticize, to make her feel small. Long enough to change the dynamics of their relationship. Long enough to know Ben held her heart in his hands.

She changed into pajamas—a light shirt and a pair of

shorts—and curled under the sheets. She figured her father had to have approached Ben somehow. His house, maybe. What did Ben think now? Her father probably didn't say anything nice. He was so spirited and determined last night to make a relationship work between them. Did he still feel the same way? Not one man ever did after dealing with her father. Should she call Ben?

Bolting upright, her stomach dropped to the floor. She should call him. Learning the truth would be better than sulking about it until tomorrow.

Sinking back under the covers, she yanked the covers to her chin. Calling would be very bad. Hearing the rejection over the phone would probably break her heart. Even hearing it tomorrow, perhaps in person, would shatter her to pieces. Sulking was the way to go. Ignorance, while foolish, didn't make her feel like her entire world was ending. Pretending. That's all she had to do. Pretend it was all okay.

The courage to drive to his house a few nights ago was about the extent of bravery she had anyway. She had been so angry that he told Zeke she turned him down. She expected it to come out much sooner. When it didn't, she just assumed it would to stay between them. She didn't want everyone else to know how weak and pathetic she had acted.

They knew now.

Yet, she didn't get the impression anyone thought of her as weak. Just her father.

She tried to close her eyes and fall asleep. Her rebellious mind wouldn't let her. Images kept swirling around. Images that made it all seem like everything was okay. Ben's gorgeous smile. The way his face lit up with delight when she finally said yes to his question. His sweet voice. The tender words he delivered that he would fight for her. A desperate knock.

Wait, what?

Bolting upright again, she listened intently.

Someone was knocking at her door. At eleven o'clock at night. Who would be at her house so late?

Her father would never come back, especially this late. Ben—well, she didn't want to think about what he really thought about her anymore. It couldn't be anything good. No man could ever stand the brutal look and words from her father.

That left Dee. She must still be in her funk, which was quite unusual for her. She never displayed that type of insecurity and loneliness like she had tonight. It had been a very welcome surprise.

She could use another girl heart-to-heart. She threw the covers to the side, happy that Dee came back. Without grabbing her robe or tossing on her slippers, she shuffled quickly to the front door and whipped it open.

Ben stood in the doorway. He didn't look happy. So much for delaying the heartache.

"Hi, Ben." Her voice sounded shaky even to her. Not a good time to sound so insecure.

"Can I come in?"

Nodding, she stepped aside. He walked past her without a word, the anger still prominent on his face. She took her time closing the door. Pretending again. That's all she had to do. Just pretend that she didn't see such anger from him.

"Rina?"

Turning around, unable to pretend further when he said her name, she almost stumbled by the heat in his eyes. Not the good kind either. He was still upset.

"I'm sorry."

"What the hell for?" He ran a hand through his hair.

"For my father. I know you're mad. If you're here because you want nothing to do with me, I understand." Rina whispered it so quietly, she wasn't sure he heard her. She couldn't even look him in the eye.

A warm hand touched her cheek, gently lifting her chin. "I'm not mad about your father."

"But you're mad?"

He brought his other hand to cup her face, tenderly rubbing her skin with light caresses. He held her gaze, then kissed her lightly before dropping his hands.

"I'm a little mad. Didn't you lock your front door? You opened it so fast I didn't hear a lock disengage."

What? Why was he concerned about her front door? "I... maybe forgot to lock it."

Ben brushed his eyes up and down her body, cringing. "You look like you were in bed. Damn it, Rina, were you in bed?"

"Yes."

"And you didn't lock your front door?" He pointed at the front door, the anger clear in his voice.

"Why are you yelling at me about my door? Yell at me about my father. I don't understand."

"I don't give a damn about your father. I give a damn about you," he said right before he pulled her into his arms and kissed her fiercely.

---

HE HELD her tightly as he demanded her mouth to open, her body to submit to his delicious assault. She did exactly what he wanted. She melted into his hard frame, clinging to him as he kissed her with all his pent-up passion that he held inside for almost an entire year. He glided his tongue everywhere, imprinting his taste so she would never forget. His hands went from grasping her cheeks, to running through her hair, to stroking her back, to cupping her ass, where he pulled her into his body to let her feel the way he felt. To show her what he wanted, almost needed with a deep pain.

He hadn't realized he moved her against the door until he heard a soft moan escape from her lips. He instantly backed away.

"Don't ever do that again."

"Don't do what again? I'm so confused, Ben. What did I do wrong?"

A rough breath escaped. *Keep calm.* Frightening her was the last thing he wanted to do. He grabbed her hands, kissing each one lightly before bringing them back down with a tight grip.

"Rina, you went to bed. You didn't lock your door. I get this feeling you didn't even look through the peephole before you opened the door. There is a lunatic out there killing women...women that look...lock your door, please. Just, please, lock your door at all times."

"I just forgot. So much happened tonight. It'll never happen again."

Damn these cases. He couldn't tell her, though. His fear was enough to handle. There was no way he could handle hers as well. One issue at a time.

"I don't even want to think about your door being unlocked again. Please, Rina, please, don't forget." He squeezed her hands so tightly he knew she felt his fear.

He pulled her away from the door and walked to her couch. Without waiting or thinking about it, almost as natural as breathing, he sat down and pulled her onto his lap. "Now, I guess we should talk about your dad."

"What did he do?" She stared at their hands linked together.

"Look at me."

Rina took her time raising her eyes.

"He stopped by my house. He—"

"I am so sorry." She tried to get off his lap.

Gently but firmly, he wrapped his arms tightly around her and inhaled the sweet scent of vanilla that, anytime he smelled it, made him think of her. He kissed the top of her head, then cradled her head against his chest.

"I love holding you. You fit perfectly in my arms. I love your sweetness, your kindness. Hell, I even love when you talk in that soft, calm voice when you're mad. Do you get what I'm saying?" he whispered, hoping she understood what he was trying to say without actually saying the words themselves.

"You should just tell me what my father said," she whispered back, clutching his shirt into a crumbled mess.

"He made it clear he doesn't want me dating you. He's your father and I will try to show him respect. I'll struggle with that, especially when he treats you the way he does. But for you, I'll try." He tightened his arms as he kissed her hair again, inhaling a bit of her essence as well. "He can say whatever he likes, but nothing will ever change my mind. I want to be with you."

"Maybe I'm not worth it. He's relentless."

Ben reached for her hands clutching his chest, slowly disengaging her fingers that were entwined in his shirt. He folded his fingers within hers, bringing their hands back to his chest.

"You're worth any fight in this world. I only want you to be happy. I would hate it if this caused you pain. It obviously already has."

"I try so hard to make him happy and nothing ever really does. I haven't seen him truly happy since my mother was alive. She died when I was four." She glanced down, sighing. "It feels good in your arms. I want to be with you, Ben."

"I'm sorry about your mother. Anytime you need to talk, I'm here. I hope he'll come to understand that I just want to make you happy."

"Don't hold your breath. He'll never understand." She rubbed her thumb over the top of his hand. "Thanks for coming over. My father stopped by earlier. I was worried he might've changed your mind."

"I couldn't decide whether it was a good thing to come over. I'm sorry it's so late. Although, not that sorry. I love holding you like this."

"Me, too."

They sat in silence for a while. No words were needed. Ben couldn't get enough of her in his arms. Damn the time. Leaving sounded like the worst idea ever, but it was inevitable. He couldn't rush her. At the moment, his body vehemently disagreed with that idea.

Her body started to relax. Too much. Her head drifted down his chest. "Rina?" he whispered, even knowing she fell asleep.

He shifted her body enough to where he could stand up at the same time he held her cradled to his body. Venturing down the hallway, he figured out which room was her bedroom and gently put her down. The thought of leaving ripped him to shreds. The covers looked inviting, half rolled up her body. He should cover her a little more. The picture in front of him was very enticing. He couldn't just crawl in the bed, no matter how much he wanted to, ached to.

The front door. He couldn't leave without the deadbolt being flipped. Such a dilemma. He sat down on the edge of the bed, brushing a warm hand down her cheek. His beautiful Rina. Never in a million years did he think he would be able call her his. Now he could.

One kiss. Just one and he would think of how to get the damn door locked without waking her. Although, he should say good-bye. Or not at all, just crawl into bed with her. He liked that option the best.

Leaning down, his lips brushed her cheek. All options flew out of his hands when she turned toward him, wrapping her arms around his neck.

"I fell asleep. Sorry," she whispered sleepily.

"It's late. My fault. You need to lock the door behind me, even though I know you're very comfortable."

"Lock the door for me." She scooted closer, pressing her head against his chest.

"I can't get the deadbolt unless you give me a key." His heart beat a little faster at the thought. Would she really give him a key?

She wrapped her arms tighter around him. "No..."

"Well, then, you have to get out of this comfy bed and lock the door behind me." She could still manage to break his heart with her words.

She sat up, looking him straight in the eye. "I didn't mean lock the door for me on your way out. I meant...lock it and come join me in bed."

The fire in his eyes lit up instantly. "Rina, if I stay, I won't be able to control myself. I want you so badly."

"I would love to see you lose control." She smiled coyly, blushing as the words slipped out.

A slow grin grew. He snatched a kiss and stood up quickly. "Be right back."

ANTICIPATING his warm hands on her body, the excitement of having him as she'd been dreaming of for so long, she tossed her shirt off along with her shorts and panties. So brazen to get naked without him in the room yet. Why not, though? She wanted him for almost an entire year. There was always something about the way he looked at her, the way he spoke to her. No more waiting or hiding behind her emotions, her fears.

She stood up to her father, and now she would live the way she wanted. She wanted Ben with every breath in her body. She wanted him to know she had no regrets or hesitations when he walked back in. He would know the minute he climbed under the covers.

She tossed the blankets over her, snuggling within the warmth. Her eyes started to drift close. What was taking him so long?

The bed dipped. She opened her eyes to see his handsome profile.

"Are you sure, Rina? I don't want it to feel like I'm rushing you."

"I've never been more sure in my life. I'm getting cold without you."

Ben nodded with a smile. He stood up, took his jacket off, and tossed it over the chair near her bedroom door. He removed his gun and badge, laying them on the nightstand. He almost hesitated on taking off his clothes, but a sultry grin from her removed that uncertainty.

Nervous.

Was he as nervous as she was? The way he unbuttoned his shirt with jerky movements made her think he was. Nice to know she wasn't alone with that feeling. As he went for his belt buckle, she needed a question answered just to make sure they were on the same page.

"What took you so long to come back? Are you sure this is what you want, Ben?"

He left his belt hanging as he leaned onto the bed, grabbing a delicious, yet quick kiss from her. "There's nothing I want more."

He stood back up, unbuttoning his pants. "I ran to my car for the extra bag of clothes and toiletries I carry in the trunk for emergencies, so I have it for tomorrow. With these murders, Zeke and I are working a little tomorrow morning. I also walked around your house, just double checking the locks on the doors and windows."

She glanced at his gun lying on the nightstand. "You really do worry about me."

He removed his pants and sat down, climbing under the covers. "I'll always worry about you. These cases...I can't even describe what they're doing to me. I just worry like hell about you all the time."

He pulled her into his arms, his eyes widening in surprise as he roamed his hands up and down her silky skin. "I think I'm a little over dressed under here."

She smiled shyly. "A little."

He tugged his boxers off, then pulled her back into his arms.

She snuggled her head into his chest, suddenly afraid. "Ben?"

"Yeah." He rubbed her back gently.

"I want this. I really do, but it's been a long time for me."

"We'll take it slow. I would never hurt you, Rina."

"I know you wouldn't. Dee and Zoe say I can rebuff men with ease. I don't think so. I always feel nervous around men. You're not like other men. But I'm still nervous."

He kissed the top of her head. "I've already said it, Rina. I'd never force you into anything you don't want. Not even now. If all you want is for me to hold you, I can do that. I love doing that."

"I'm afraid I won't do anything right...that I..."

"Rina," he whispered into her ear, his hot breath tickling her senses into overdrive, "you're an expert. The little circles you're drawing on my back right now are driving me insane."

Her hand stilled, unaware she had been doing that.

He chuckled. "Don't stop."

Sensuous doodling recommenced. What should she do next?

He took the wonder out of her mind when he pulled her head up and her lips to his. The kiss started out slow, just like her hands smoothing around his back. She went from drawing small circles to caressing up and down.

The kiss heated up, more demanding, more uncontrollable, as did her hands on his back. Losing focus of everything, his hands started to weave their magic around her front, claiming her breasts with soothing caresses. His taste intoxicated her. His hand started to glide down to her soft mound when he jerked away from her.

"Shit, Rina, when I came over, I never expected this. I just needed to make sure we were okay, especially with the visit from your father. I don't have any condoms on me. Do you?"

Deep, slow breaths. Focus on the question. What was the question again?

Condoms.

That was a problem.

Biting her lip, she shook her head. "I'm on the pill."

His brows puckered, the indecision clear. "Do you feel comfortable with this without a condom, just being on the pill?" He hesitated, then coasted a warm hand down the side of her ribcage, brushing the edge of her breast. "Because I do."

She smoothed the contours of his face, wiping his frown away. So good to know he was as nervous as her. "I know what I want, Ben. That hasn't changed. I don't want to wait."

"Good." He pushed her to lay flat on her back, shoving the covers away. "Let me make you feel comfortable. If it's been a while for you, I don't want any part of this to hurt. It's been a while for me, too, if you were wondering. You won't be thinking about anything but me by the time I'm done."

"Done doing what?" she whispered with anticipation as she watched him slide down her body.

"This."

## 7

Rina's body ignited with erotic tingles the minute his tongue touched the most intimate part of her body. She had kissed other men, had tame sex, but she had never let a man touch her in such a way. Never knew it would feel like this.

Like soaring to the top of a mountain, the adrenaline rush of looking down in the valley below, the beauty of it taking her breath away. He took his time coaxing that beauty out of her, swirling his tongue in delicate strokes, almost knowing beforehand what way she would like it.

Nerves had overpowered her before, but not anymore. She couldn't even remember why she had been nervous. Soon the tingles started to sizzle in her skin, turning to pulsating zings. Each time he moved his tongue, she craved more. The minute she felt a finger slide inside, she bucked off the bed, moaning with tender delight.

He continued his magical work with his tongue and finger, filling her body with so much desire she never knew she possessed. Moans drifted around the room. The ecstasy he created made her wonder why she had pushed him away for so long. The minute she felt another finger added with the first, she clenched the sheets with fury. She wanted more. More of him. All of him.

The words teetered on her lips for him to shove deep inside her, but her voice broke before a sound could escape. He suddenly started suckling hard, moving his fingers a little faster, creating a sensation she didn't know existed.

Her fingers slipped from the bedsheets and grasped his head. The pleasure tore from her lips as she squeezed strands of his hair. The sensations consumed her, wrapped her in a cocoon of bliss. Completely immobile. No energy to move a muscle. It was too much.

His hands lightly settled on her thighs as her body tried to come down from the high. His mouth pulled away, yet still so close as his hot breath warmed her with continued pleasure. She should move. Say something. She did neither.

Small peppering kisses started from her belly to her neck until his warm breath tickled her ear, sending more delicious shivers down her spine.

"You are so beautiful," he whispered.

CENTERING HIMSELF OVER HER BODY, he gently entered her with slow precision. The kisses wouldn't stop. His lips needed to touch her everywhere—her neck, her ear, and then a small path down her chest to suckle on her nipple. Sweet, sweet Rina. He wanted to claim her as his in every possible way.

He kept his movements small, light, making sure to take his time. She felt so tight around him. It took all the constraint he ever possessed not to just plunge deep inside.

Not a moment of this would hurt her. Not one part of her would feel pain. It seemed like a difficult quest.

Although, he never heard her moan in pain or cringe away from him with discomfort. If anything, she clung tighter to him, moving her hips to meet him each time he pulled out and gently back in, a little farther each time.

He never knew he had such patience. Never knew he could love a woman more than he did now. He now understood the worry, fear, and pain Zeke went through last year when he thought he would lose Zoe to a crazy stalker. He never wanted to experience any of those worries, but he did. They still had so much to overcome. And overcome he would. She was in his arms, in his body and soul, and he would never let that go for anything.

Moving to her other breast, suckling hard on that nipple, she lifted up from the pleasure of his touch. Needing full connection as her wetness teased him, he pulled back one more time and pushed gently, yet firmly.

She inhaled a sharp breath and clutched his back fiercely. He stilled his movements, letting her body get used to him deep inside, and placed a tender kiss on her cheek.

"Are you okay, Rina?"

"I never knew it could feel so...so...beautiful. Please don't stop."

He gazed into her eyes and smiled with pride to go with the desire in his eyes. She never lost connection with his gaze as he moved slowly. Perfectly in tune, they created a rhythm that felt like old times. He moved, she moved with him. It didn't matter how slow he went, or how fast, she moved with grace each time he did.

Laughter wanted to escape at the ridiculous notion that she thought she didn't know what to do. She knew exactly what to do. Hell, he figured she could've laid there with no movements whatsoever and it still would've felt incredible.

Slow and steady, the magic continued to build between them. Needing more, craving more, he claimed her lips in a blistering kiss. She clutched the back of his head the minute his lips touched hers. He felt the ferocity, the passion in her hands, mirroring his exact feelings for her. Yet, he continued to slowly plunge in and out with desired patience.

Her tiny little moans got louder, her hands got tighter, almost yanking on his hair. She was climbing closer to a climax. She did the same exact thing when he was down loving her with his mouth. Something he ached to do again. She tasted so delicious.

Increasing the pace would draw her pleasure out right away. But the moment didn't call for that. Didn't speak to him that way. He kept thrusting at the same pace, wanting to savor every beautiful second. As he dreaded, she finally clenched around him, ending the glorious pleasure. He groaned with elation, his climax joining hers.

Moving away from her seemed impossible. The only sound to perforate the air was their heavy breathing. Why were they both breathing heavily when they moved with such slow care?

To think he had been nervous as hell. He had wanted her for so long, and to finally have her seemed surreal. It was like having a dream—a sweet dream he never wanted to end. As if he would wake up, realizing that's all it was—a dream. Even with her body pressed lovingly under his, he wanted to pinch himself to make sure he was really awake. God, what a true nightmare if it were all a delirious dream.

"I'm no expert myself, but this...what just happened...it's never felt so right in my life. I never want to leave this bed," he whispered in her ear, lightly taking a nibble.

"I'm so glad I have you in my life."

He lifted his head, kissing her deeply. "Me, too." He rolled to the side. "Let's clean up and get some sleep. I really am exhausted."

She nodded with a sleepy smile. Before long, after they used the bathroom, she was curled in his arms. Right where she belonged. It didn't take long for sleep to come. Not one nightmare existed for the first time in a long time.

---

RINA WASN'T sure what to expect in the morning. Everything between them was so new, so fresh, and so confusing. What she didn't expect, for whatever crazy reason, was Ben to start moving his hands every which way on her body and take her again with such sweet, slow passion. She decided she liked the unexpected.

He still couldn't get enough, to which she enjoyed, and joined her in the shower where he loved her one more time. By the time she dressed, her body almost protested to walk to the kitchen. So relaxed. So ready for more. She wanted to climb back into bed with him and stay there all day. He looked delectable as he leaned against the counter waiting for the coffee to finish.

"I tend to make my coffee black. Hope it isn't too strong for you."

She walked into his arms and rested her head on his chest. "I'm sure it'll be fine. Thanks for making it." She kissed him before leaving his warmth to grab two mugs from the cupboard.

"Do you have a travel mug for me? I hate to just run out on you, but I told Zeke I'd meet him at the precinct around nine."

"Of course."

She put one mug away and reached higher to grab one of her travel mugs. Her shirt inched higher as she stood on her tippy toes. A soft groan escaped behind her. "You okay, Ben?"

He cleared his throat. "Yeah. Just praying the day goes fast. I miss you already."

She turned around, smiling shyly. "So, you're coming back after you're done working?"

"If that's okay. I heard Zoe's party was changed to your house for tomorrow. I thought you'd like some help setting it up."

"I'd love that."

"Good. I'll definitely have a better day knowing I get to see you tonight. What do you plan on doing this morning?"

She grabbed the coffeepot and filled their cups to the rim. "I have some errands to run. Things to get for the party."

He walked toward her, taking the mug she offered. "Don't do too much without me. I want to help."

"Have a good day at work."

He sighed. "Call me if you need me."

He grabbed a quick, searing kiss that made her ache for him to carry her back to the bedroom instead of walking out the front door. But that never happened.

---

BEN SAT down at his desk as Zeke put the phone back on the hook.

"Just talked to Claradessa Phantosia, one of the consultants. She's going to meet us at a coffee shop so we can talk to her." Zeke leaned back in his chair as he looked at Ben with a critical eye. "You look different."

"Not really."

"You had a pep in your step when you walked in. Did you see Rina?"

He shuffled a piece of paper and grabbed a pencil. "Yeah, I saw her."

"Shit. You finally got laid, didn't you?" Zeke started to laugh.

"What makes you say that? And I'm not talking to you about Rina like that." Ben finally tore his eyes away from the meaningless papers in front of him and glared at Zeke.

"Mm-hmm, sounds like the shit I always said when you picked on me about Zoe. Payback is a bitch, buddy. I'm going to have fun with this."

"You annoy me." Ben threw the pencil at Zeke. He couldn't help but chuckle when Zeke wouldn't stop laughing. "Seriously, I'm not saying anything, but I spent the night at her house. It was hands down the best night I've ever had. That's all you're getting from me."

"Oh, I'm gonna dig and dig and dig until you talk a little detail. Until you're squirming in your little seat. Just like you always did to me."

Zeke's cocky grin should've annoyed him. It didn't. He deserved it and would gladly take the ribbing because Rina was finally his. "Let's get to work. When do we meet Claradessa? Such a weird name."

"Yeah, wait until you hear her voice. High-pitched like a singing canary. It was somewhat brutal talking to her on the phone. Hopefully, it's not as bad in person. In an hour. Let's call the other consultant and the delivery driver, or we can pop in unannounced."

"Stoyer. My office...now!" Captain Ganderson said,

coming from behind him. He didn't stop as he passed their desks. When he heard two sets of chairs move, he turned around. "I didn't say you, Chance. I said Stoyer."

Zeke slowly sat down, giving Ben a confused look. Ben shrugged, having no clue why the captain wanted to see only him. Whatever it was couldn't be good. The captain looked pissed. He followed the captain to his office and shut the door when the captain hollered at him to do so.

"Have a seat, Stoyer."

Ben took the seat and waited for the captain to sit down. The urge to tap his leg in a nervous gesture consumed him, yet he controlled the impulse by placing his hands on his legs. What the hell could he have done? The captain looked irate.

"What sort of mess have you landed in?" Ganderson asked slowly.

"None, cap. I have no idea what you're talking about."

"Were you disrespectful to Susan Wells at a crime scene?"

Ben jerked slightly, then sighed. "I was slightly rude for a moment. I apologized right after. These two cases are brutal...It won't happen again, cap. I'm sorry Susan thought I was that rude to tell you."

"She didn't tell me. You pissed someone off, Stoyer. A lot. You're one of the best damn detectives I have. I can't afford to lose you. Do you have any idea who the hell you pissed off?"

Shock. Confusion. Anger. It all devoured him in an instant.

Reginald Chastain.

Didn't the man basically threaten his job last night? He didn't waste any time. Why the hell was he surprised?

"I do, sir. I don't really know how to fix that problem. You do what you have to do. I'd hate to lose my job when I always do the best damn job that I can. But if it happens, it happens. I'm not caving in to anyone's demands." Ben leaned back in his chair and smoothed out his pants. Wrinkles had formed when he clenched his legs.

Screw Reginald. He wasn't letting Rina go.

"Just what sort of demands? What the hell is going on? I had the chief of police calling me at home, telling me to get my ass into work to talk to you about your attitude. Apparently, you also had an altercation with Anthony Tollhorn, Attorney at Law," Ganderson said with a drip of sarcasm on the last part. "Start talking, Stoyer. I can't help you if you don't tell me what the problem is."

"You could call it an altercation all right. He put his hands on one of my friends. Rina. You've met her. Not enough to where I could consider it an assault, but enough for me to tell him to back the hell off. Their date didn't end well. She's now dating me. Her father, Reginald Chastain, doesn't like that. He showed up at my house last night, and he didn't come right out and say it, but he said enough that he would make problems with my job if I didn't stop seeing his daughter. Not gonna happen, cap. She's too important to me. Take my job away. No one's taking Rina away, unless that's what she wants."

Ganderson leaned back in his chair and sighed. "That's a helluva mess, Stoyer. You're a great detective. Try to make peace with him. I'll do my best to ignore any demands coming my way, but I can only do so much."

"I appreciate it, sir. It is what it is. I tried telling the man last night what his daughter meant to me, but his ears were clogged. Zeke and I have an appointment with a potential witness. Are we done here?"

Ganderson waved his hand toward the door. "Try not to

make any more waves. I don't like coming into the office on a Saturday."

"Will do, cap." Ben stood up and walked out. It took all his willpower not to slam the door. It wasn't the captain's fault. He was just following orders.

Zeke stood up as he neared their desks, but a simple hand in his face halted any words from leaving his mouth.

"Let's go. I need some air. We'll talk in the car."

Zeke nodded, grabbed his jacket, and threw it on. The minute they got in the car, Zeke was on him. "What the hell was that about?"

"Rina tried to warn me that her father would be relentless. That he'd do everything in his power to make me stop dating her. That's one of the main reasons she would never give me a chance: her damn father." A vicious curse slipped out as he ran a hand through his hair.

"What did the captain say to you? I don't understand."

"Her father came over to my house last night. He threatened my job if I didn't stop seeing her. The words exchanged between us weren't pleasant. He just followed through with his threat. I got questioned about being rude to Susan, which the captain didn't hear from Susan herself, so how the hell did Rina's father even know about that? I was questioned about that damn attorney, Tollhorn. I was told to be on my best behavior, or bye-bye job, basically."

"You're shitting me?"

"I wish I was."

The scenery passed by in a blur as his mind whirled everything like a tornado on a rampage. Should he tell Rina about this? Would she leave him just to save his job? That seemed like a very Rina-like thing she would do. Screw his job. He could find work somewhere else. But, boy, he would miss it.

"I don't know what to say. I can't believe her father is that crazy. Or has that much influence."

"Let's focus on the case."

The rest of the drive remained silent, except where Zeke told him he called the other consultant and delivery driver. They could get each meeting knocked out within two hours.

Not particularly thirsty, but needing something to occupy his hands, he ordered a coffee with Zeke and sat down at a table to wait for Claradessa. Two minutes later, she walked in.

She wore high, high heels, the back heel so thin Ben almost worried she would fall. In addition to that, she wore a black pencil skirt with a red suede coat wrapped tightly around her. A white, delicate hat covered her hair as long blonde curls rested onto her shoulders. Simply beautiful. He knew she knew it as she walked up to them with a bright smile and an almost come-hither look in her eyes.

Regardless of her beauty, she didn't hold a candle to his beautiful Rina. Especially when she opened her mouth.

"Detectives? You have to be the ones waiting for me. You're the only two dashing devils in this place. Wonderful coffee, don't you think?" she said with her high-pitched voice, her eyes trailing to their coffees, then up their bodies slowly.

"Coffee's great. We just have a few questions about Ashley Patterson. You interacted with her at Dr. Conway's office on Wednesday morning. She was murdered later that night." Zeke gestured for her to take a seat.

She pulled a chair out and smoothed her skirt as she sat down. "I heard. Just horrible. Such a nice woman. We always had a little girl talk on the side before I left. She loved my scarf I was wearing that day. I told her I bought it at Little Red's Boutique, on clearance, too. Can you believe that?"

*Try not to make any more waves.* Words to live by lately. But damn if he didn't want to roll his eyes and answer with sarcasm. "What sort of scarf?"

"Oh, a green silk one that went just delightful with the white coat I wore that day. I wish I was wearing it today to show you, but it would clash horribly with this coat."

"Did Ashley make a comment as if she was going to go there after work?" Zeke asked.

"Well, she did ask where I got it from. Yeah, I think she made a comment how she wanted to stop there, but wasn't sure if she would have time. She said she already had other plans."

"Do you know what they were? Or if she was meeting someone?" Zeke asked.

"Oh, no, she didn't get that detailed. She just gushed over my scarf, we talked a little about that, and then I did my business and left."

"Where were you that evening? Any particular plans you had around ten o'clock that night?" Ben asked.

"Are you asking, as in, am I available? Or as in an alibi?" Claradessa asked, her eyebrow rising in wishful anticipation.

Ben cleared his throat. "An alibi, Ms. Phantosia. Just doing my job and being thorough."

"Of course. You look like a man who is very *thorough* in everything." Claradessa bit her lip, her eyes trailing up and down in a very blatantly sexual way.

"Right. So, where were you?" Time to go. This woman scared the hell out of him.

"I was home alone. I had a very busy day at the office,

and I put my feet up before going to bed at...well, ten o'clock."

"Is there anything else that sticks out to you about Ashley?" Zeke asked.

"No. She seemed like her normal self. Happy, friendly, and just anxious for her plans that night." Claradessa stood up. "Is that all?"

"Yes, thank you." Zeke stood up as well. "We appreciate your time."

"Anytime." Claradessa gave Ben one more secretive smile and left the place.

"She is one scary-ass woman." Ben stood up, shrugging his jacket on.

"Very. She sure wasn't holding back on you." Zeke snickered as they walked outside.

"Shut the hell up. I have Rina now. I don't need that woman." Ben turned around and shoved his finger in Zeke's face. "Not that I want her. She was too much of...everything. And her voice..."

"I know. Screeching, high pitch. Just nauseating." Zeke patted him on the back. "So, you have Rina now? How does it feel to say that? Details. Lots and lots of details."

Ben shrugged him off his shoulder. "Don't go there."

"Oh, but I am."

## 8

Erin bounded off his porch with agitated footsteps. Slamming his car door did nothing to dispel the hole in his stomach from growing larger. His sister never called him in a panic. Never. Not even when she found out she was pregnant with the loser she dated for far too long.

"You have to fix this, Ben. I'm scared." Erin stopped just short of giving him a hug.

Normally, she gave him a hug in greeting. Having four sisters, he was comfortable with affection. His family was a tight-knit group. They shared everything. Maybe he didn't as much as his sisters did, but he shared enough. Erin refusing to give him a quick hug did not bode well. He definitely saw it as refusing. She always flung her arms around him in zealous energy. It could get annoying at times. Now it just unnerved him further.

What had put her in a panic, demanding he meet her at his house? Telling Zeke he had to leave didn't sit well with him. These cases needed to be solved. Especially for his peace of mind. Zeke completing the interviews on his own made it seem like he was avoiding his job.

"What's the matter? Is Isabella okay?" Ben reached out to grab a hug. He needed that hug.

Erin took a step back. "Some man came around from child services. Child services, Ben! He said he received a report of child neglect. I'm a good mother, damn it."

"That makes no damn sense." Rubbing his jaw, he took a step toward her. "Why do I get the feeling you're mad at me?"

"He mentioned your name. And not in a good way. Why am I on the verge of losing my little girl because of you?" Erin slapped her hands on her hips, the anger clear in her eyes, as well as the fear.

"I would never do anything to hurt you or Isabella. Seriously, Erin, do you think I would do anything to jeopardize your family? It hurts that you do."

"What's going on?"

Ben ran a hand through his hair, pulling on the ends, then shoved a hand toward the house. "Let's go inside."

He walked past her without another word. He generally wasn't abrupt to any of his sisters. He knew the wrath they would dish out for such rudeness, but he didn't give a shit right now. Enough was enough.

Damn Reginald Chastain! Because he was the exact reason why Erin was suddenly getting visits from child services. She was a good mother. She would never hurt Isabella, or neglect her in any way.

He unlocked his door, disarmed the alarm, then closed it with more force than was necessary after Erin stepped inside. He stared at the door. Erin stood behind him waiting for answers that he didn't know how to explain. Losing Rina would be unbearable. He also couldn't live with himself if Erin lost Isabella.

A small hand clasped his shoulder. His anger, irritation, and fear slowly dissipated with that light touch. Maybe she would finally give him the hug he wanted when he first laid eyes on her.

"Talk to me. That man said someone reported Isabella was left alone for several hours while you were watching her. That you left her alone. That, as her mother, that neglect fell on me. You watched her two weeks ago for me. They—"

He punched the door. "I would never leave Isabella alone. I *didn't* leave her alone. Never have and never will. She's only four years old." He whirled around to look at Erin, his hand stinging from the blow to the door.

"I know that. I even told the man to talk to Isabella, who told him everything you two did that day. He seemed satisfied after that, but he said he would be keeping a close eye on the case. He said they take matters like this very seriously."

"I'm sorry, Erin. Shit. I'm so sorry."

He hung his head as he walked past her to the living room and sat down on the couch. Pulling on the ends of his hair again did nothing to ignore the pain in his heart, or the pain in his hand. Why couldn't life go right for him just once? Was that too much to ask?

The couch dipped. Familiar arms wrapped around him. Erin rested her head against his shoulder. "Why would someone lie? I'm sorry for acting pissed at you. I'm just scared to lose Isabella."

"It's complicated. It's bullshit. And I guess he knew right where to hit me."

She lifted her head from his shoulder. "Who?"

"Rina's father." He glanced at her, then went back to staring at his clasped hands. The pain in his hand was slowly ebbing away. He wished the same could be said about his heart. "I asked her out. She turned me down. That was three months ago. She turned me down because she knew her father would never approve. Clearly, he doesn't."

"You're a great guy. Any woman would be lucky to snag you."

He tilted his head toward her. "Thanks, Erin. I guess not everyone agrees."

"She turned you down. I don't get it. Why would her father bother you?"

"Because she just decided to give me a chance, regardless of what her father thought. He came here yesterday and threatened my job if I didn't stop seeing her. Looks like he's also threatening you. I will never let you lose Isabella. Never."

She slapped the back of his head, a normal action she committed whenever she thought he was acting like an idiot. As the youngest in the family, she thought that a lot. In her mind, the youngest one was always right.

"What the hell, Erin? So you're still pissed," Ben mumbled, rubbing his head, even though the slap hadn't hurt.

"You're going to break it off with Rina, aren't you? Because of what happened today."

"I don't want to. Isabella doesn't deserve any pain from this. If they took her away from you for even an hour that would be painful. I don't know what to do. He got to my job this morning, and now this. He's relentless. Rina said he would be. What's the big deal I'm dating her? Why is he so vicious?"

"Is she worth it? I have this strange feeling she is. Out of everyone in the family, I've dated the most. I like to consider myself an expert when it comes to dating, besides Damon. I don't know what happened there."

"Momentary lapse of judgment that created the best thing in your life." Ben nudged her shoulder with a grin.

"He did give me Isabella, you're right." She nudged him back. "Anytime you talked about Rina, just a simple thing like she was at Zeke's with you guys, I heard the longing in your voice. You hid it well, just not from me. I don't want you to lose her."

"Well, we have a problem then. I don't want you to lose Isabella because of me."

"So fight back. Since when is my big brother afraid of someone? Since when would my big brother ever let anyone get the better of him? I like Rina. I don't know her that well, since I've only been around her a few times. But, I'll ask again, is she worth it? Because I just can't imagine my big brother backing down."

"I love her. I want to tell her so badly. I don't want her to be hurt either. I'm a wedge between her and her father. That hurts her. But she's worth any fight in the world."

"Then forget I ever came over here mad. You didn't leave Isabella alone. In the end, we would win that fight. He's being vicious, but he's also lying. Everyone has dirt. He obviously can't find any on you, so he lies to get his way. Don't let her go. I'll be mad at you."

Ben laughed lightly. "You were mad about what happened. Now you'll be mad if I let Rina go. I can never win with you."

"Geez, why would you? I'm the queen of everything. Listen, learn, obey. I'm the youngest, which makes me the wisest."

"So you've always said." He grinned and pulled her into

his arms. "Love you, brat. I really am sorry for the scare today."

"I love you, too, knucklehead. Go back to work. I'm sorry for pulling you away. Dad said you're working a tough case when I talked to him yesterday."

"Yeah, it's a rough one. Make sure you're always aware of your surroundings and all your doors and windows are locked."

"Ten-four." Erin stood up. "Isabella wants to see you now. You're front and center in her mind since that guy showed up. You know how she acts when she gets something in her head."

He chuckled as he stood up as well. "Yeah, just like her mother. A nuisance until you get your way."

"I'll pretend you never said that. When are you going to come over?"

"How about tomorrow morning? I have a ton to do today. Zoe's party is tomorrow evening. Tell her we'll have a tea party. I'll bring the cookies."

"You're the best brother ever. She likes—"

"Yeah, yeah, chocolate chip are her favorite. I'll never forget that, especially when she freaked out the one time I brought peanut butter cookies over. I love peanut butter cookies. I can't believe she doesn't."

"She loves everything else you love." She grabbed a quick hug, kissed him on the cheek, and opened the door. "See you tomorrow."

Ben set the alarm and walked out behind her. He waved good-bye as she pulled out of his driveway.

Back to work. Solve this case. Solve the issue about Reginald. So much to solve. Grabbing his phone to call Zeke felt like an anchor pulling him down. Not yet. He couldn't call him yet.

It was time to fight dirty. Not that he wanted to, but it was time.

Twenty minutes later, he pulled into a driveway. His sister was right. When in the hell had he ever backed down from something? Reginald Chastain thought he could threaten him, threaten his job, threaten his family, and he would just put his hands up and walk away. Think again. He would fight until the end.

Rina getting hurt was inevitable. She would be hurt if he walked away, because while she didn't profess her love, he felt a strong connection last night. She would also be hurt if he stayed, her father remaining angry with that fact. He'd rather her be hurt that way. At least she would be in his arms where he could help soothe the pain away.

He knocked on the door before he lost his nerve and waited patiently. Without warning, all of his nerves suddenly washed away. This was the right decision. The minute the door opened, he knew.

"Ben, what a surprise? Is Zeke with you?" Richard, Zeke's dad, said as he smiled wide.

"No, Your Honor, it's just me. It's sort of a personal matter. Do you mind if I come in?"

Richard opened the door wider, curiosity written on his face. "Of course. Lose the 'Your Honor'. I'm not in the office. You know that, Ben."

Richard closed the door, nodding down the hallway toward his study. "You're lucky Deborah isn't home. She'd want to whip you up something to eat and be curious as hell why you're here without Zeke."

"Well, I do enjoy her meals. I'm sort of disappointed she's not here."

Richard chuckled as he sat down behind his desk,

gesturing for Ben to take a seat. "What's going on? How can I help? I have to say, I'm a bit surprised to see you."

Deep breath. Definitely the right decision. Ben gave Richard a brief description of the last few days. Suddenly, the weight on his shoulders lifted. Drifted away. The pain was still there, but he didn't know how to get rid of it.

Slamming his hand on the desk, the pain that radiated up his arm couldn't hide the pain in his heart. "I just want to make Rina happy. I don't want a war between her father and me, but he's started one. If he thinks he can bully me into walking away from her, well, it's not going to happen. Nobody is taking Isabella from Erin. Nobody."

"Where did child services get that information from?"

"I have no idea. I have to look into it."

"Don't. Leave it to me. If you're the one being accused of leaving Isabella alone, then it's best you stay away from it. That's why you came to me, correct?"

"Not really. I could've had Zeke look into it."

Richard leaned back in his chair, sighing. "Then what do you need from me? I'm always here for you. You're like a son to me, you know that."

"Any talk around the courthouse about me? I mean, I didn't expect any of this, and look how fast it all happened."

"Nothing. I would've squashed it immediately had I heard anything. Who is Rina's father? He has to have some sort of power, influence to get at you this quickly."

"Reginald Chastain. That's all I know. Rina really hasn't told me anything else about him. He came to my home, threatened me, I spat back, and he left. I called him Reggie just to piss him off. And it pissed him off. Rina's going to hate me after this is all done."

"You picked the one woman with a powerful father,

that's for sure. I never made the connection before that he was her father."

Ben jerked in his seat and leaned forward. "You know him?"

"I've met him a time or two. He's big in the political scene. Comes from money. His father was a senator. He didn't go into that avenue, but he still donates to certain campaigns, keeps his hands in certain pockets. He owns a company, something to do with biomedical engineering. He built that company from the ground up. He's smart. He knows a lot of people."

"He's also a pretentious ass."

Richard chuckled. "That he is."

"Why does he hate me so much? I just want to make Rina happy. Why am I not good enough for her?"

"You are good enough for her. Don't ever doubt that. I'm sure he has his reasons, albeit, dumb ones. What is it you want me to do, Ben? Spell it out, because I'm just not sure here."

"Erin said he's making waves for me because he can't find any dirt. I walk the straight and narrow, so he won't find any dirt." Ben hesitated. Did he really want to fight back dirty with Rina's father?

"You know a lot of people yourself, Judge. Perhaps you've heard things about him that...I don't know what I'm saying here. I don't want this. I don't want to be the man's enemy." Ben sighed and rubbed his jaw as he slumped into the chair.

"Let me see what I can find out. You have a few nasty cases to solve. Focus on that. Focus on Rina."

"What should I say to her?" Ben stood up. Why the hell was he asking Zeke's dad this? What about his own dad? Maybe because the question kept whirling around his mind and he needed an answer now. At least before he saw her again. The night would come eventually.

"Is it ever good to keep secrets? If you remember, because I heard some stories, Zeke and Zoe didn't communicate very well in the beginning. Communication is key in any relationship, Ben. You think Deborah lets me get away with crap? No, she communicates right away what the problem is."

He smiled as Richard grinned back. "You're always right, Judge. Thank you."

Richard met Ben in front of the desk and clapped him on the back. "Tell Zeke that. He never believes me that I'm always right."

Ben couldn't help but laugh. "Yeah, right. He never believes that when I say I'm always right either."

"Don't worry about any of this. I'll look into it. How are these latest murder cases coming along?"

"Like shit, Judge. You heard about them?"

"I hear everything. Let me know if you two need anything. I'm a knock, call, or drive away."

"I appreciate it...for everything."

Ben said good-bye. Weight lifted. Definitely lifted. Not by much, but enough to get him through the rest of the day until he saw Rina. What should he tell her? Did she know how despicable her father could truly be? He wasn't sure he wanted to ruin her illusions. The man *was* her father.

## 9

Her finger barely grazed the doorbell, yet the soft rings echoed behind the door. She stepped back to create space and lots of needed air. True freedom wouldn't be had until she hopped back into her car and drove away. Of course, that wasn't an option. Except her foot took another step back thinking she could almost get away. The door swung open.

"Rina, always a pleasure to see you," Thomas said, moving away from the doorway and gesturing her in. "Why did you ring the bell? You know you're welcome to come in at any time. I opened the gate, so I knew it was you."

"Of course, Thomas. How are you?" She gave him a quick hug before stepping back, looking for that freedom again. The walls appeared to be inching closer, the air swallowing her whole. God, maybe she couldn't do this.

"I'm always wonderful when I see you. Although, the day could be better. Your father is in a mood. I hear the date with Anthony didn't go so well."

"Do they ever when it's up to my father?" she said very quietly. Heaven forbid her father hear her voice something like that. His sharp tongue would make sure that never happened again. Best to whisper.

"He means well. He just has a funny way of showing it."

"If you say so, Thomas." Rina sighed. "Is he home?"

"He's in his office. Come on." Thomas gestured for her to follow him with the same friendly, loving smile he always used with her.

Rina smiled at her father's longtime butler and confidant, falling in step behind him. If a problem needed fixing, Thomas to the rescue. A party needed to be planned, Thomas set it up with ease. The house needed to be cleaned, Thomas always made sure it stayed in tip-top shape. There wasn't one thing that Thomas could do wrong. He was perfectly matched for her father in every way. He could take one look at her father, know exactly how he was going to react, and plan accordingly. He was the best butler she had ever known. And they'd had many. None of them lasted very long. Her father was a harsh man. He didn't forgive, nor forget. Ever.

Thomas had been with her father for the last ten years. The longest to last in the household without getting thrown out to the streets without so much as a fare-thee-well. Her father never stood for insolence or incompetence. One minor display of that and you were dismissed immediately.

Rina had liked Thomas the instant she met him. Twelve years older than her, she always saw him as her other father, giving advice when her father cut her down. Of course, that was something her father did frequently. She hadn't been living at home when Thomas was hired, but she had visited her father often. No matter how many times she came to find some sort of approval from her father, she never received it. She would be on the verge of tears, unable to hold them in. Thomas was always there to dry them, to offer kind words of encouragement.

He always stood up for her father, insisting he cared in his own way, showing his feelings in the only way he knew how. Just because he was harsh didn't mean he didn't love her. She wanted to believe that. Thomas always said it in a way that made it believable.

There were times when she wished Thomas had been her real father. He always gave supreme advice, showed her love that she craved to have from her real father, and had the look of pride in his eyes for her. Then, after that longing spread throughout her heart, she'd hate herself for it. Her father, rare as they may be, had tender moments that she treasured.

She could still see him standing up in the middle of the auditorium, clapping the loudest, no one else around him able to overpower his sound. She had been in fourth grade, just finishing her solo for the choir. He had been so proud of her. His smile, beaming like fresh rays of sunlight, lit up the room for all to see. That's all she ever wanted to see from her father. Pride. Happiness. Love.

She had no idea where it all went wrong. Why he turned into the man he was today. The only thing that made sense was when her mother died. He had died that day as well.

"Chin up, darling. Don't go in there looking like that. That permanent frown will be a dead giveaway. Care to tell me your woes before you step in?" Thomas asked. His eyes shined with tenderness, his brows crinkled with worry.

She always thought he had a world of wisdom, wondering about the kind of life he led before he came into their world. He was a very private man, never revealing much of his past. While he wasn't that old, she could see the wisdom in his eyes. His hair, sprinkled with gray, gave the appearance that he was older than he truly was.

"No, I'm fine, Thomas. Here's my smile." She could offer a smile any day. It was the part where the happiness reached her eyes that was the problem.

"He won't bite, you know. He loves you."

"Thank you, Thomas." She placed a soft hand on his shoulder, then lowered it to the door with a gentle knock.

A loud booming voice from the other side said, "Come in."

Steeling her shoulders, her armor was in place. A deep breath and the anxiety washed away. She opened the door and took a few steps before speaking. "Hello, Father. I hope I'm not interrupting."

Reginald stood up from his desk, his face expressionless. "Of course not. I always enjoy a visit. I'm glad you came."

"I'll make it short," she said softly.

"Do I take that to mean you're not here to apologize?"

"I have nothing to apologize for. I'm not the one who spoke to my boyfriend, and if I'm not mistaken, threatened him. I have no idea what you said because Ben wouldn't tell me. I think I'm the one who should hear an apology."

Reginald stepped around his desk, shoving his hands inside his pockets. His eyes narrowed into thin slits, his brows puckered, and his lips straight-laced with precision. "I don't like it when you speak to me that way. That man is no good for you."

"Why? Tell me why, Father. What has he done to make you dislike him so? Because, no matter what happens, he just wants me to be happy. He doesn't want any tension between you and me. He doesn't want to be the cause. He's not. You are. You've never been happy for me. You constantly tell me what to do. That hurts. I'm always afraid to tell you that it hurts. Not anymore."

Her eyes started to itch, the water brimming to the edges like a dam wanting to burst. She would not cry in front of her father. "I love you. I always will. But I can't have you acting this way anymore. It hurts too much. I love Ben. He's the one I want, not Anthony. If I know you, which I think I know you pretty well, you're already planning ways to get Ben to go away. Don't. You're probably already planning ways to get Anthony back in my life as well. Don't."

She wrung her hands, dropping them when she realized what she was doing. "I came here for one reason. Leave Ben alone. I don't want to write you out of my life, but I will if you make me. I want Ben in my life, and he's staying. Don't interfere like you always do."

"Don't be ridiculous. It's not my fault you always pick men that walk away from you."

"You're going to lie to my face. You're telling me that you never had a hand in making those men walk away." Her hands clenched into fists. The audacity to lie. How could he?

"It's not my fault when a man chooses to walk away from you. I have no idea what you see in this detective. You're ruining your life."

"No, I'm living it for once. He's kind. He's loving. He respects me. He treats me the way you used to treat Mom. Why is that bad?"

"The door will be open when you come to your senses. I have some work I need to look at now, Rina. Thomas will show you out." Reginald turned around and sat down in his seat.

"I do believe we came to an understanding, Father."

"An understanding? I don't think so." He looked up from his paperwork with the same arrogance he always wore.

"But we did." She couldn't hide the pain anymore. A tear trickled down her face. She turned her back to her father and gently closed the door when she really wanted to slam it shut with frustration.

"Either you knew how long that conversation would be, which wouldn't surprise me," she said with a weak grin, "or you were waiting right outside the door."

Thomas's lips turned up with mischief. "That's my secret. I could tell right away when you came into the house that this wouldn't be a good conversation. I'm sorry he can never see what's right in front of him. A beautiful, talented, wonderful daughter. It's about time you stood up for yourself."

"What happened to always saying, 'He loves you'? You always take his side."

"I don't choose sides, Rina. You're both my family. He does love you. I hope you don't stay away long. We'll both miss you."

She stepped closer and touched his shoulder. "That's up to him, Thomas. Maybe you can talk some sense into him. I can walk myself out. No time like the present to talk to him."

---

BEN PARKED the car and took a deep breath. Leaving Richard's house, everything felt fixed. Better. Now, the anxiety and tension was back full force.

He met Zeke in front of the building. Running home to Erin had cut time in their day. Time that he wanted to spend with Rina. Now he was nervous to see her. He had to tell her about her father. He just didn't know how to.

"So, what happened?" Zeke held his hand on the door to

the apartment building, but made no move to open it. Ben could tell he wouldn't until he got answers.

"Child services bothering Erin because of Rina's father. Now he's messing with my family, creating lies. I will never let Isabella get hurt."

Zeke's mouth dropped as his eyes rounded with surprise. That's exactly how Ben felt when Erin spilled the news. He shuffled his feet, then glanced at the ground. "I paid a visit to your dad."

"Why?" Zeke dropped his hand from the door and rubbed the back of his head. "Please tell me he hasn't heard anything around the courthouse. I can't believe her father is this ruthless. I thought I had it bad last year. I only had Zoe to convince to love me."

Ben raised an eyebrow. "That makes me feel so much better."

Zeke let loose a small laugh. "Sorry, man. I didn't mean for it to sound like that."

"He hasn't heard anything yet. He heard of her father, though. Power, money, contacts everywhere. He's going to poke around and see if he can find anything out about him. Feels wrong. I just want a chance with his daughter. I just don't get it."

"Me neither. Thinking about it isn't going to help. Do what you gotta do and that's it. If there's something to find, my dad will."

"That's why I went there. You're...you know, not pissed or anything, are you?"

"No. Not sure why you'd think that." Zeke clapped him on the shoulder. "Let's interview this delivery guy, Jones Maverick. I already talked to the other consultant and she wasn't helpful at all. Her husband was home as well. He gave her an alibi. Are you ready?"

"Yep. Thanks for doing the work without me."

Zeke walked inside the building, searched the board for the apartment they wanted, and pushed the buzzer when he found it. "You do it for me other times. No biggie. I just wish this shit with Rina's father would stop."

"Me, too. You have no idea."

The door clicked loudly, indicating Jones had allowed them entry. Ben grabbed the handle and let Zeke walk through first. Three floors later, they were standing in an apartment that reminded Ben of his bachelor days in college. Although, the more he glanced at everything in sight, he decided he hadn't been this messy.

Movies, magazines, and newspapers were scattered around the living room. The coffee table situated in front of the television was covered with cups, a few plates, and a pizza box that looked like it should've been thrown away a month ago. Clothes hung on the couch and recliner, a small trail lining a path down the hallway. Ben didn't even want to know where the trail would end.

The place was disgusting. The smell—not even sure what he smelled—was enough to make him want to gag. They needed to make this quick. Very, very quick. The bile was rising at the back of his throat.

"Mr. Maverick, thank you for seeing us," Zeke said, trying to sound normal as he tried not to breathe through his nose.

"Yeah, sure. I heard about that lady. How can I help?" He started grabbing clothes, piling them up in his arms, as he tried to clear a section on the couch. "Just...it's the maid's day off." He laughed lamely as he threw the pile at the wall and started to gather more crap from the couch. "Oh, shit, I've been looking for that." He dropped everything, grabbing for the controller that was tucked between a seat cushion and a porno magazine.

"Mr. Maverick—"

"Oh no, call me Jones." He held up the controller with pride after interrupting Zeke. "Been looking for this thing forever."

Zeke nodded and inhaled a breath. "Jones, we need to ask you some questions about Mrs. Patterson. No need to clear a spot for us. We won't take much of your time."

"Okay. Shoot. What do you want to know? Nice lady. Always a smile on that broad's face...oh, I mean lady." He shuffled his feet. "Ask away."

"You delivered a package to the office on Wednesday. Did you speak to Mrs. Patterson?" Ben asked.

"Yeah. She signed for the box and I went on my merry way. Didn't say much to her. 'Sign here.' 'Thanks, ma'am.' That sort of stuff. Not sure what you're looking for."

Ben imagined he really didn't understand. No sense of cleanliness, lack of manners. This guy was clueless. "Did she seem happy, mad, sad? What was her mood? Did she say anything to you?"

"Nope. She seemed fine. It wasn't much of an interaction. She said 'thanks.' Oh, and 'have a nice day.' I don't always get her when I drop stuff off there, but anytime I get her, she's always nice." Jones smiled as he tossed the controller back and forth between his hands.

"Where were you Wednesday night?" Ben asked. His voice betrayed no irritation, annoyance, or disgust at the smell that was really starting to make his throat itch. Captain Ganderson would be so proud.

"Oh man, playing that new game that just came out. Shoot 'em Up Heavy, you know, that new shooting game. It's sick, man, just sick. Hard as hell. I can't seem to get my shot right. I've been trying to get headshots, but I always miss." He shook his head as if he couldn't believe how bad his aim was. "I bet you guys would nail that game. I mean, you shoot your gun all the time, I bet."

Ben shared a look with Zeke. This guy was worse than an idiot. "So, you were home alone all night is what you're saying?"

"Yeah. Wanna see it? It's so cool." Jones went toward the gaming device when he heard a throat clear behind him. "Oh, right, you're here to talk."

"Yes, we are," Zeke said, sharing another look with Ben that they needed to wrap this up. "Where were you last Saturday night?"

"Here. I work, come home, and play my games." His eyes fell to the couch, cringing when he saw the porno magazine still displayed out in the open. He unobtrusively, or at least he probably thought so, picked up a shirt and tossed it over the magazine. "I like my games."

"Everyone should have a hobby." Ben lifted his eyebrows with a smile. He pressed his lips together. Laughing would be very bad. "Thank you for your time, Jones. We appreciate you seeing us."

"No problem. Sorry I couldn't be more helpful."

They left, trying not to laugh until they were out of earshot.

"What the hell was that?" Zeke said with a crazy laugh. "He's, like, thirty-five and still living like a twenty-year-old."

"He likes his games," Ben replied with a chuckle.

Zeke's laughter died. "His games. Could his behavior be an act? Those scarves and notes hidden underneath the bodies scream games loudly at me. Do we think that crackpot could be our guy?"

Ben stared straight ahead as he thought about it. "He

didn't seem like the type. Maybe, just maybe, he was over-doing it to throw us off. No alibi for either night. Let's check him out further. See what we can find. Then I say we call it a day. I have a lot to talk about with Rina."

"Good luck."

Ben nodded. He needed that, and a whole lot more.

## 10

The world shifted back into its normal equilibrium the moment Rina opened the door. Her face lit up with happiness, mirroring the exact look on his face.

"It's late. I didn't think you guys were working this late tonight. I even talked to Zoe, who was surprised." She stepped back as Ben walked in.

He closed the door, locking it right away. "We made some headway. Neither of us wanted to quit. A few other things popped up as well."

She bit her lip. "Nothing serious, I hope."

"Nothing that can't be fixed. I'm hungry. And then I did want to talk."

"You have me worried now, Ben. Is it about last night, because I—"

He grabbed her gently by the shoulders and planted a kiss on her lips that told her it wasn't about last night. His tongue dove in without hesitation, taking, claiming, searing his taste everywhere. She groaned when he pulled away.

"I didn't mean to scare you. Last night was the best night

of my life. It's just, we need to talk, and I don't know how to say it. I didn't mean to throw it out there like that." His stomach took the opportunity to grumble in protest.

"And you're hungry," she chuckled.

He gave her a charming grin. "I am. I missed lunch. It was a crazy day."

"Come on then, I'll feed you." She grabbed his hand and pulled him into the dining room. "Have a seat. What do you want to eat?"

"I didn't come over here for you to feed me. We can order something."

He sat down after she pointed a finger to a chair that issued no arguments. He liked her like this. Demanding. Assertive. It was adorable. So un-Rina-like.

"I have lasagna in the freezer. When I make a pan, it's always too much for just me. I freeze a lot of it. I can heat that up."

"Sounds delicious."

He couldn't help himself. His eyes roamed over her body as he said it. She wore loose black drawstring pants and a semi-tight pink cotton shirt. Nothing extravagant, but enough to get the blood flowing in his veins. Perhaps they could skip the food and the talk, and head straight to the bedroom.

"Ben?"

Nothing but temptation stood before him. He had to tear his eyes away. "Yeah?"

"If you don't stop looking at me like that, you're not going to get any food."

His grin widened. "I can't help it. You're beautiful, Rina. I've had to hide how I felt for so long, I just can't contain it any longer. If I want to look at you like I want to rip all your clothes off and love your body from morning 'til night, I'm going to. I want you. I could take you right here on this table."

The surprise in her eyes at his candid words didn't stop him. He stood up and took a step toward her. If he reached out, he could grab her hand and pull her into his arms. Instead, he stood frozen. Why had he decided to skip the food and head straight to the talk?

"Rina..."

"Are you about to ask me if we can have sex on the table?" Her voice sounded frightened, yet mixed with anticipation.

He shook his head, biting his lip to keep his laugh from escaping. "I wouldn't ask. I'd just grab you into my arms and have my way with you."

"Oh." She took a step back, but her eyes glossed to the table with desire.

"Rina," he said with a chuckle, "I'm not going to grab you...yet."

Her eyes went round with shock. "Meaning...that...it's a table...Ben..."

"I love you."

Heart pounding like a jackhammer, she had to be able to hear it. See it even. It felt like his heart could explode at any moment. His hands were clammy—almost where he needed to wipe them down his pants, but that would make his nerves even more obvious. She stared at him, her eyes still wide with shock, maybe even wider than before. Her silence frightened him the most. He expected her to say something, even keep her stammering going. Why wasn't she saying anything?

"I think I fell a little bit in love with you the first time I met you. You spoke so softly, yet fiercely to Zeke about leaving Zoe alone, it was impossible not to love the way you commanded the situation. Each new day, I find something new to love about you. You just make it so easy." He sighed heavily. "I had a rough day. You told me your father would be relentless. He has been."

He put his hand up when her mouth started to open. No way did he want to hear one word from her if it had to do with her father. Anything else would be fine. Like, I love you. Yeah, he'd love to hear the sentiment returned.

"We never talked much about him. I found out he knows a lot of people. I've been told at work to be on my best behavior, or bye-bye job. You're worth more to me than my job. Then, my sister Erin, she had a problem with child services concerning her daughter. Isabella's only four. They say they received a report that I left her alone while she was in my care. They said that reflects badly on Erin as a mother."

He ran a hand through his hair, pressing his lips together to keep the vulgar words from leaving. Rina didn't need to hear that. "Nobody messes with my family like that. I would never leave Isabella alone. If your father wants to play dirty, I will. I don't want to because I don't want you to get hurt. I would never hurt you, Rina. I love you too much. I just want to make you happy."

Silence filled the room. Ben looked at Rina with his heart displayed for the world. If she chose to walk away, she would walk away with the full knowledge of his feelings. That's the only way he wanted her to leave him. She looked back at him with confusion, shock, and something else he couldn't decipher. He didn't know what else to say. So he didn't.

"I'm sorry." She took a step toward him.

"Sorry?"

"For the trouble my father's causing. Normally, I don't

even know what he does. The guy always disappears from my life with a lame excuse."

She took another step and placed a soft hand on his chest directly over his heart. "You're the only man to care, to keep pushing forward, to keep fighting for me. I don't even know why my father does what he does. I've never been brave enough to ask."

She raised her head, meeting his eyes. "I love you, Ben. I have for a long time. For the first time in my life, I'm willing to go against my father to keep what I want. And I want you. Do you still want me?"

"That was never in question." He claimed her lips in a blistering passion and pulled her roughly against his hard body.

SHE SANK INTO HIS BODY, wrapping her arms around him. Home. She felt perfectly at home in his arms. His hands slid down her back and grabbed her bottom, eliciting a moan from her lips. One minute she was standing, the next he lifted her around his waist. Locking her legs around him, holding on as he continued to kiss her, her heart soared to a new place. One so filled with happiness she was afraid to let go of him.

His gun wedged into her thigh, but she didn't care. The delicious fever burning in every limb of her body as she pressed tightly to his hot shaft took away every other thought. She wanted him deep inside her. Cradled perfectly to his body made her crave that sensation to the brink of madness. He turned her around, moving a few paces. Even after he set her on the edge of the table, she kept her legs tightly clamped around him.

"Ever since you asked me about having sex on this table, that's all I can picture. I want you, right here, right now. Unless you say otherwise. Unless you want me to walk you to the bedroom instead," he whispered against her lips, nibbling, waiting for her answer.

She shivered once. Sex on the table seemed so naughty. She never considered doing anything of this sort. His hard erection still pulsating between her legs made the consideration very easy. The rebel in her pushed through.

"You said you wouldn't ask, that you'd just have your way with me. That's what I'm waiting for."

Ben cradled her cheeks, rubbing his thumbs back and forth. "I'll never ask again. I plan to have my way with you in as many spots as I can think of."

Her cheeks flamed with heat, but she said nothing as she raised her arms when he pulled up her shirt. He tossed her shirt behind him, tackling her bra next. He unhooked it with ease, tossing that behind him as well. He dropped his eyes to her breasts, taking his fill. He reached for one, caressing her nipple.

"There isn't a spot on your body that I don't love." He bent down, taking her nipple into his mouth, suckling hard.

He took his time, switching back and forth between both nipples, suckling, nipping, and doting on them as if he just won first prize in a contest. She leaned back, resting her palms on the table to stay upright. She hung her head back, eyes closed, as she delighted in each time his tongue swirled around or his teeth nibbled. She could let him feast on her breasts all day. Each time his tongue hit a new spot, elation pricked her skin, making her hungry for more.

She looked at him when his mouth left her body and watched patiently as he unhooked his gun and badge. He had to move her left leg to do so. He caressed up her thigh, lifting it slightly, taking his time as his hand moved up. He grinned, her face flushing by the movement. He set his gun and badge plenty away from where they were. She enjoyed the way he had to reach, her legs still wrapped tightly around his waist, his hard erection pressing farther into her as he did. His phone also joined the pile, making each of his movements drive her crazy with need. He reached for the buttons on his shirt when she stilled his hands.

"Mmm, no, let me."

She took her time undoing each button, scraping her knuckles against his skin as she did. His body trembled each time. "Are you cold?" she asked with a sly grin.

"I'm dying of heat, and if you don't hurry up, I'm going to die of starvation. I need you."

"I do believe you took your time removing your gun and badge. Why the rush now?"

He leaned closer, giving her a quick kiss. "I like teasing you. Not so much on the getting teased back. You drive me insane with your light touches. It just makes me want you more."

She stilled her hand, one finger touching his chest. She lightly moved it back and forth. "And you think your touches don't drive me insane. Oh, Ben, a simple look from you drives me insane. I have no idea how I managed to keep my true feelings from you for as long as I did."

"Shit, Rina, I have no idea either. Don't ever do that again. I love you in my arms. I always will."

His look scorched her to the bone. Her hands trembled as she finished the last few buttons a little faster, albeit, a little clumsily. The heat between them had reached new heights. She did the last button and let the shirt fall open. Smoothing her hands up his chest, she relished in the shiver that engulfed his body. She slid her hands underneath the shirt near his shoulders and let it drop to the floor as she guided it off.

"My turn." He didn't wait for a response. He grabbed her tightly against him, kissing her lips with a renewed passion. His kiss was hotter than before, fiercer, more frenzied. His tongue dug deep, swirling in a dizzying pattern as she tried to keep pace.

---

THE KISS never broke as he trailed his hands down her back, hooking his fingers inside her pants. He lifted her up, pulling her pants and panties along as he trailed his hands downward. His hands slid down her thighs as he guided it all to the floor. The minute he felt it all hit his feet, he pulled her closer, his lips still connected to hers.

He cupped her ass, sliding his hands up her back, skimming the sides of her breast. He brushed them back down, moving them to her front, and continued to tease her as his hands ran down her thighs.

Up then down, several times.

She moaned as the kiss became stronger. He knew she was almost there, almost ready. He wanted her wet. So wet, that he slid in with ease. The minute she ran her hands up his back and clenched his hair tightly, he knew.

He kicked his shoes off, then reached for his belt, unbuckling it quickly. Next, his pants were unbuttoned and zipper flying down with a speed he never displayed. She helped shove his pants down along with his boxers, his clothes joining hers on the floor. Then he guided her down on his hard shaft and nearly growled with pleasure when he could feel how deep he was.

He broke the kiss, grabbing her face tightly. "I love you,

Rina. Nothing is ever going to change that. I hope you always believe that. Never doubt me, never doubt this."

"I never will. I love you, Ben."

"Then hold on, sweetheart, I'm about to love you on this table." He smiled brightly, claiming her mouth again.

He brushed his hands across her cheeks, over her hair, down her back, and cupped her ass tightly. He started thrusting slowly at first, savoring every moment, every movement she made. This would be a night to remember. To sear into his brain until the end of time. The moment he confessed his love and she confessed back.

He still couldn't believe she said it back. The three little words he had dreaded to tell her. The shock wouldn't dissipate. His heart still pounded like crazy. What made it better was hers pounded in tune to his.

He honestly didn't believe the day would get any better. But it had. It didn't matter what problems they had to sort out. As long as she was in his arms, nothing else mattered.

He jerked slightly when her hands grabbed his ass and squeezed. Smiling against her lips, he lowered her to the table and took one more kiss before he lifted his head. "Hold on, sweetheart."

She grabbed his ass tighter and held on as he pumped in and out of her. There wasn't any slowness, any lingering doubts. This was raw love. He held onto her sides, gliding in and out of her, rocking the table as he did. His hands shifted up, grabbing her breasts, fondling a bit. He wanted her harder, though. He wanted to consume her. Last night, he had taken her with a slow passion that spoke of his love. Today, professing it, he wanted to brand it on her.

He moved his hands back down, gripping her hips tightly as he thrust in and out with a desire he never felt before. Suddenly, a mixture of passion and pain consumed him when she squeezed his ass so tightly he could feel her nails dig in. Her body convulsed into a blinding ecstasy when her climax hit without warning. He watched as her face bloomed a deep red, her moans singing within the room. Smiling like a man in love, which he was, he pulled her tighter to him as he thrust three more times before his chest fell onto her body.

Waves of ecstasy flowed over his body. His head lay in the crook of her neck. Trailing small, light kisses to her ear, he whispered, "I think I love this table."

She giggled. "More than me?"

He lifted his head. "Never, but it's a close second."

He scooped his hands underneath her and pulled her close to his body, still deep inside her. "How about a shower and then some food?"

She nodded, clutching his back. "Maybe you should let me down. I can walk there."

"I'm not letting you down, sweetheart. I think I'm going to love you against the bathroom wall now. You feel too damn good to let down yet."

## 11

He closed the door quietly, then spoke loudly. "Honey, I'm home."

Zoe popped her head out of the bedroom, her face stern with annoyance. She shuffled down the hallway with quick footsteps.

"Mister, you're in trouble. If I hear one peep from our little girl because you're too loud, well, big trouble. That's all I'm going to say."

He chuckled and pulled her into his arms. "I like being in trouble. Will you spank me?"

She laughed, pressing her face into his chest to keep her laughter down. She lifted her head back up when she could manage it. "No. Your punishment will be no spanking."

"That is punishment. Let's go to the bedroom. Food can wait. Your body under mine can't."

She held her feet steady as he tried to walk her backwards to the bedroom. "We can't right now."

"I don't care what things you need to get done. They can wait. I can't. I hate being deprived. If I start crying like Brina, will I get my way?"

"Nice try, but no."

"Is it because I'm late? I'm sorry we had to work so long on a Saturday. We're getting closer. Sort of."

She brushed a hand across his cheek. "It's not that. You can't have your wicked way with me because your father is here, in the kitchen. I don't think he wants to wait while we engage in that sort of activity."

She smiled brightly as his eyebrows rose in surprise. "Why didn't you say that to begin with? I guess I didn't see his car parked outside. Shit, sure hope he didn't hear anything I said."

She laughed, walking out of his arms. "Since when are you shy about that?"

"Umm...since it's my dad." He pulled her back to him, kissing her hungrily on the lips. "Get naked and wait for me in bed. Wait, not naked, put on my favorite dress. I'll make it quick with my dad. No arguments. Or I'm going to spank you for not listening."

"I haven't lost all my baby fat, Zeke. I don't think that dress is going to fit me."

Zeke twirled her out of his arms, holding her hand outstretched as he looked her up and down with a sensual eye. "It'll fit, honey, trust me. The best part is peeling it off you. The tighter it fits, the harder it makes me. I love seeing all your delicious curves. Now quit arguing with me and just do it."

She winked, let go of his hand, and turned toward the bedroom. "I like arguing with you. We shall see who wins this argument."

Zeke groaned as she walked away, swaying her hips in an enticing way. Torturing him. This visit with his dad would be short. He wanted his wife so much he was almost tempted to make his dad wait while he had his way with her.

So tempted, he found himself moving his feet toward the bedroom until he heard Zoe lock the bedroom door.

A laugh escaped. His wife knew him so well.

He headed toward the kitchen where his dad sat on a stool at the counter drinking from a coffee mug.

"Hey, Dad, what's up?"

"I won't keep you long," Richard said with a grin and gestured his head toward the coffeepot. "Join me for a cup."

"I drank way too much of that today. I'm good. I might heat up some leftover food while we talk." Zeke opened the fridge, rummaging around until he found a container of the chicken dinner Zoe made a few days ago. "So, what's the visit for?" He moved closer to his dad, whispering, "Can't you watch Brina tomorrow? The party was moved to Rina's, you know."

"Heat up your food. It's not about that." Richard nodded to the microwave and waited until Zeke shoved the container inside the machine and hit the start button. "Tell me about the progress on your case."

Zeke turned around and leaned against the counter. "What for? I haven't asked you for anything."

"I know. Don't know why."

Zeke groaned. "Dad, you know. I just hate coming to you for work-related stuff. I hate that critical look you always give me."

"You think you'd be over that by now." Richard laughed. "How's Ben?"

"Okay, I guess. He told me he paid you a visit. He's really worried about Rina. He was heading over to her house tonight to talk to her about everything. I'm hoping I don't get a call that he needs my shoulder or anything. It'll break his heart if she turns him away. I haven't helped with the way I goad him about her."

"I'm glad he told you about seeing me, I don't feel as bad coming here."

The microwave beeped loudly behind him. Instead of pulling out the food, he stood up. "Something I should know?"

"After his visit, I made a few calls. Ben's name has been thrown around the courthouse. Judge Deiters said he heard a complaint or two on how Ben arranges his warrants. As in sketchy, maybe even false information thrown in there."

"That's bullshit."

Richard threw his hand up, waving it up and down. "Calm down, Zeke. I know that. So does Judge Deiters. He was quite surprised when he heard that. For the time being, though, until things are settled, I think it's best if you come to me."

"Like that won't look suspicious. Who made the complaint?"

"I don't care what it looks like. Ben's a damn good detective and has never crossed the line. I know who made the complaint. I'll take care of it."

"Dad, I want to know," Zeke said as he advanced toward the counter.

"Trust me to handle this my way. Ben came to me for assistance, and I'm going to help him. I already started looking into Reginald Chastain's life. I haven't found much. I was thinking a one-on-one with him would be better."

Zeke shook his head. "I don't know, Dad. Ben probably wouldn't like that."

"I'll think about it, but if I think it's the best route, I'm taking it. Now, update me on this case. No arguments."

Zeke ran a hand through his hair. "No suspects at this time. We ran through Beth and Ashley's life and we're not seeing anything that links them together. They're as different as can be, except for their temperament. Everyone we talk to says they were nice, sweet, soft-spoken."

Zeke fell against the counter and released a heavy sigh. "Shit. No wonder why Ben's been on edge lately. He always thinks of Rina when we work on these cases. She fits the profile."

"But you have no idea how he chooses his victims?"

"No. I keep telling him there's nothing to worry about when it comes to her. He still worries like crazy. You know how we joke around. It's our way of staying sane while we work. We haven't been doing that lately."

"What else do you have?"

"We interviewed two consultants today that Ashley dealt with the day of her death. One wasn't helpful at all. The other, Claradessa Phantosia, she gave us a small lead. She wore a scarf that day and Ashley made a comment about it. She informed her where she purchased it—a small boutique, Little Red's Boutique."

Richard's face perked up. "Ah, yes. I know the place. I've purchased a few things for your mother. A little high-end. They aren't cheap."

"No, they aren't. We called Susan, who met us there with the two scarves used to strangle the women. They came from that store. The tags on the scarf hold a unique design, marking them as a Little Red's Boutique item. A small red hat, fedora looking, with a black feather sticking out from behind. I'm sure with that identifying mark we would've figured it out sooner or later, but Ms. Phantosia did help us make that connection faster."

"I'm getting the impression it didn't matter."

"Yeah, they sell a lot of scarves. An array of colors, like a damn rainbow. The store manager, Shawn Pitts, was nice enough to give us a list of their employees. We ran out of time today, so we still need to check everyone out on that list."

Zeke sighed, rubbing the back of his neck. "We also interviewed a delivery guy that interacted with Ashley the day of her death. Jones Maverick. He was definitely weird. No alibi for either murder. He didn't seem like our guy, but we're not discrediting him yet. We ran his record. A few marijuana possessions, thefts, and one burglary back when he was twenty. I'm still wondering how he was hired for the delivery job. Who's to say he won't steal any of the packages he delivers? He's definitely weird."

"How about Ashley's husband? She was married, wasn't she?"

"Clean. His brother is his alibi the night of her murder. No record, no problems other than cheating on his wife."

"Keep me posted. Let me know if you need a warrant for the boutique. Perhaps pulling credit card records of everyone who purchased a scarf will help. It'll probably be a helluva list, but it's somewhere to start. You can cross reference the names on the list to possible names associated with Beth and Ashley."

Zeke grinned. "We thought of that. Makes me think we'll have a warrant to you in no time. That list will be a bitch to go through."

Richard stood up. "I'll leave you to eat and enjoy the rest of the evening with your beautiful wife. I'll let myself out. See you tomorrow."

"Bye, Dad. Thanks." Zeke waved as his dad nodded at him and walked out of the room.

Zeke grabbed his food and gobbled it down in record speed. He tossed the dirty dishes in the sink, leaving to clean it later. Now to devour his wife in the most delicious way. He was dying to see her in that dress.

Zoe was nowhere to be seen when he walked inside the room. He frowned, yet thankful she hadn't kept the door locked. He needed his wife and he needed her right this second. He stepped into the bathroom that also remained Zoe-free.

Where could she have disappeared? Sometimes these tortuous games were fun, but not right now. He walked out of the bathroom, figuring she went to Brina's room when he stopped dead in his tracks. Zoe stood leaning against the wall near the door in the delicious red dress that always made him salivate with desire.

"I guess it does fit. It feels really tight, though," she whispered, smoothing her hands down her sides to her thighs.

"You look perfect." He advanced at her, pinning her body against the wall. "I can't wait to peel it off you."

"What are you waiting for?" She ran her hands up his chest, grabbing his face. She kissed him, gliding her tongue in with ease.

He pressed into her, his hard shaft craving to be inside her. He yanked his mouth away. "I hope Brina's sleeping well because I'm going to devour you from head to toe. But first, I'm going to love you against this wall in this dress. I love this damn dress."

---

BEN INHALED, letting Rina's sweet aroma fill his senses. He wrapped his arms tighter around her, grateful the night had ended in his favor. The way the day had gone, he didn't have high hopes it would.

"Thanks for helping. I appreciate it," Rina said softly, tracing a finger around his chest.

"No problem. Sorry it took so long. I just couldn't help myself."

He smiled. She distracted him easily. It had taken quite a while to set up the party. She would reach high to grab something from the cupboard, a hint of skin showing as she did. That small view was enough to make him forget what they were doing and take her into his arms instead.

Or how she bent down to grab napkins hiding in her cupboard near the floor and her little bottom swaying in the air. He couldn't help but come up behind her and loop his arm around her, which led to more than that.

His favorite distraction had been when she asked him to carry her extra folding chairs from the spare bedroom to the living room. He heard her holler from the bedroom to come help. He walked in prepared to use his muscles to carry the chairs, only to find her struggling to grab them from the closet, her body waggling in his face in the most delicious way. He couldn't help himself. He grabbed her from behind, scooped her into his arms, and carried her to the daybed where he lost all train of thought. It took a long time before the chairs were carried into the living room.

"I don't care it took so long. You can help me anytime."

He kissed the top of her head. "I will always help you."

"I'm looking forward to the tea party tomorrow. I can't wait to meet Isabella. Are you sure your sister will want me there? It's my fault that—"

"Stop." He squeezed her tightly, then rolled her to her back and leaned above her. "Nothing is your fault. Whatever your father does is on him, not you. Erin likes you. She said she'd be mad at me if I walked away from you. You have nothing to worry about."

"I don't want her to hate me."

"She doesn't. Isabella will love you. She's a little pistol, so watch out. She likes to play tricks and make silly jokes."

She chuckled. "Sounds like you."

He gave a wounded look, although his eyes shined with laughter. "Me? Never."

He touched her cheek, rubbing his thumb back and forth. He held her gaze as he brushed his hand down her neck to the center of her chest. Smooth. Soft. And his for the taking. Back and forth between both breasts, he teased, caressed, trying to decide which one to give his full attention to.

"Ben?"

He twirled a finger around her left nipple, lightly blowing. "Yes."

"I thought we were going to bed."

He took her nipple into his mouth, sucking hard, then tenderly swirled his tongue to soothe. Lifting his head, a sly grin formed. "We are...as soon as I'm done here."

"Okay," she whispered breathlessly as his mouth continued the sweet torture on her body.

Thirty pleasured minutes later, they curled together and fell asleep. Ben normally liked his space, sprawling out as he slept. But the feel of Rina in his arms overpowered that. He couldn't get enough of her soft body cradled next to him. It secured the knowledge that she was in his arms and she couldn't walk away. Perhaps after the drama settled down he wouldn't feel that way.

As she turned slightly to her left, he didn't think so. He turned with her, curling an arm around her stomach. Every time she moved, he moved with her. His body subconsciously knew when she moved, needing to move with her. It didn't matter if it was a simple hand touching one part of her body, he needed contact. He needed the reassurance she was right next to him.

Bolting upright, his heart pounding, he glanced around the dark room. Damn, was that a nightmare? Yet, he couldn't remember what he had been dreaming. Nothing in the bedroom looked out of place. The bedroom door was still securely closed. His hand touched Rina's arm. His heart started to calm a fraction, knowing she was perfectly safe.

Perhaps that was it. He hadn't been touching her while he slept. Damn the fear that overwhelmed him at the thought of her leaving him.

He slowly laid down, his hand still resting on her arm. A strange muffled noise bounced around the room. Eyebrow cocked, his eyes shifted to the wall to the left where the kitchen was. This wasn't about Rina then. He must've heard the noise in his sleep.

He shoved the covers off, reached down for his pants, and quickly scrambled into them, grabbing for his gun next. He looked over at Rina as she sat up with a confused expression. Before she could ask what he was doing, he put a finger to his mouth.

Leaning onto the bed, he cupped her cheek. "I heard a noise. Lock the bedroom door behind me and don't open it until you hear my voice. Understand?"

She shook her head as the fear in her eyes poured out in waves. He kissed her hard, then headed for the door and slowly made his way down the hallway. The minute he heard the lock click on the door, he moved a little faster.

A quick peek into the spare bedroom noted nothing off. The bathroom came next, still noticing nothing astray. Gun clenched firmly, he continued down the hallway. At the end of the hallway, another noise filtered through the air. Definitely coming from the kitchen. It sounded like scraping, as if someone was trying to get in via the window above the sink.

Dashing around the corner, he moved lightly through the dining room. A dark figure stood outside the window jimmying the lock. He didn't make a sound, but somehow the person instinctively knew they weren't alone. The person looked at Ben, disappearing in a flash.

Ben cursed, running for the front door. He unlocked it quickly and took an extra second to close it before he dashed down the steps and ran to the left side of the house. Shit! Nobody was there. Running back the way he came, he sprinted toward the road just in time to see the person jump into a dark-colored medium-sized car and drive away.

Cursing viciously, the words swirling into the dark night air, he clenched his gun tightly. It was impossible to make out a face. The person had worn a black mask. Even more irritating, he couldn't identify the make and model of the car. It was parked too far away, which made it impossible to get a look at the plates.

The window. The bastard had tried to break into her house. As he neared the window, he froze. Lying precariously on the branches of a bush near the window was a green scarf. His worst nightmare had finally come true. The potential intruder went from a punk breaking and entering to the sadistic killer he was searching for. His steps back to the house were slow and measured.

How? Why?

It suddenly seemed too crazy that Rina would become a victim. Was the killer watching him and Zeke? Did the killer see how much Rina meant to him? How she matched the description of the other victims?

He opened the front door and flipped the light on, needing the darkness to disappear. It wasn't helping to keep the nasty scenarios out of his mind. He walked to the bedroom and knocked lightly on the door.

"Rina, sweetheart, let me in."

A second later, she whipped open the door and fell into his arms.

"What was the noise?" she asked in a tiny whisper.

"Someone tried to break in." He pulled her tighter to his body when shivers overtook her. "They got away from me, but don't worry. I'm here and I don't plan on leaving."

He wanted to crawl back in bed and hold her tight, let the dreadful night disappear as if it never happened. He kissed the top of her head and shifted her away. "I need you to get dressed. I have to call Zeke and Susan."

"Why? They didn't get in."

"Get dressed. I'll make the calls and we'll talk."

He guided her into the room and snatched his shirt from the floor. Without one word, unsure of what he'd say anyway, he grabbed his phone and headed out to the living room. Both calls were made quickly, berating himself when Rina, who had taken a seat on the couch, overheard the last part of his call with Susan.

"What's going on, Ben?"

He ran a tired hand across his chin. "I found a scarf on the bush near the kitchen window where the person tried to break in. He dropped it, or maybe left it on purpose. I don't know."

She grabbed his hand when he wouldn't stop rubbing his chin. "He? You saw the man?"

"No, he was wearing a mask. I didn't get a good look at a damn thing."

"Then how do you know it was a man?"

"Rina..." He paused, trying to formulate the right words. Her eyes were filled with worry. "The scarf outside, it's a sign that it's tied to the murder cases Zeke and I have been working on."

She shook her head in confusion, her eyes swimming with concern. "I don't understand."

"Remember when I came over that night, just needing to see you, to make sure you were okay?"

She nodded but didn't say a word.

He squeezed her hand. "I was worried and going out of my mind because...because you look like the victims. Same body type, same hair color. The first victim, Beth, when her hair covered her face, for a moment, it reminded me of you."

Rina gasped.

"I pictured so many things in my mind, but I never thought it would touch your life. Do you know how many women match that description? Tall, slender, auburn hair. Too many."

"Then how is it possible? Are you sure?"

"I'm positive."

"But, Ben, how can you be sure? It's a scarf. It's cold out. Maybe—"

"There's no doubt in my mind. He used a scarf to...to kill both women. It's his signature."

"Oh my God, if you hadn't been here... If I had been alone... If I—"

He let go of her hand and grabbed her face fiercely. "Don't go there. I was here. I am here. I'm not leaving you."

A kiss wouldn't erase the terror, but he had to try. She resisted at first, her nerves unable to let him in. But he refused to let her hold him back. He pushed his tongue through, opening her mouth wide. She sunk into him, finally kissing him back. He took his time to explore, to coax out the tremors taking over her body.

When he felt her body relax, the trembles cease to exist, he pulled away, his mouth mere inches away from her. "Zeke and I will figure this out. Until we do, I'm not leaving you. Consider me your new roommate. Nothing will happen to you, I swear."

He claimed her lips again, wiping out the renewed fear that came back from his words. Images of scooping her into his arms and taking her back to bed swamped his mind. He wanted to kiss away each tremble that touched her body. It would take all night to vanquish each one. He felt them everywhere. In her arms, her legs, her hands. The frustration that he couldn't do anything to stop it made his blood boil with anger. He couldn't even kiss her longer. The doorbell went off.

A groan escaped as he pulled away. "It's probably Zeke. Be right back."

He checked the peephole, then unlocked the door and stepped back to let his partner in.

Zeke didn't pretend to make the situation better. He didn't joke. He didn't tease. He didn't even offer a smile. "You okay?"

"I screwed up. He was right there. I saw him. We looked at each other. And I let him get away."

Zeke clapped a hand on his shoulder. "No, you didn't. You tried. He had a head start running. Don't think about it, man. How's Rina?"

"She's scared but holding it together. You got here quickly."

"It concerns Rina, so, of course, I moved my ass. I didn't even stop to tell Zoe the reason. She'll freak when she finds out."

"Come on." Ben tossed his head toward the living room. He walked quickly to the couch and sat down next to Rina.

The need for any sort of connection had him grabbing her hand.

Zeke took a seat on the chair next to the couch. He sat on the edge, his hands clamped together as he leaned forward. "I talked to Susan on the way. She'll knock on the door when she's done processing outside. She said she'd head to the window right away. Did he get the window open at all?"

"No. He was still trying to jimmy it open when I walked into the kitchen. The minute he saw me, he ran."

"How did you hear anything? We had the bedroom door closed. I didn't hear anything," Rina said quietly.

"Light sleeper, I guess. I don't know. I woke up and just felt...panic. I looked around the bedroom wondering what the hell woke me up. That's when I heard something," Ben replied, kissing her hand. He blew out a breath, gathering the energy to go down the road he wished to avoid. "You said you had errands to run today. What kind?"

"Why does that matter?"

"Rina, we need to figure out how you connect with the other victims. Anything you can tell us will help," Zeke said.

"You could be wrong. Maybe it was just some kid. You're wrong. You have to be," Rina whispered with a tremble in each word. "Why would someone want to hurt me, Ben?"

He cradled her body against his, bending his head to rest on hers. "I don't know, sweetheart. That's what we're trying to figure out. We have no idea how he picks his victims, or why. We've been trying to find a connection between Beth and Ashley. That's why we need to know your habits, places you frequent. I swear I won't let anything happen to you."

"Me, too, Rina. Nobody is touching you. I can't handle

the hospital. I hated seeing Zoe there every single time. I sure in the hell don't want to see you there," Zeke replied.

She sat up straighter, took a deep breath, and nodded. "Okay. What do you want to know?"

Zeke smiled, sharing a look with Ben. Pure relief. She wasn't falling apart like it appeared she was about to do.

"Let's start with today. Ben said you ran some errands. What kind? Every place you went," Zeke said.

"I ran to the grocery store, Racker's, off Division Street."

"Is that where you always go?" Ben asked.

"Yes. They always have good sales. The pop and water I bought for the party was a steal." Rina rubbed her finger against the back of his hand. "I ran to the bank, not far from Racker's. I almost ran to the party store, but remembered that I had napkins, plates, and plastic utensils in my cupboards at home. So I passed that. I need my haircut, so I called my stylist. She was booked for the day, but I made an appointment for next week."

Ben's hand became stiff. "Where do you get your hair done?"

Rina stared at their hands, then glanced up to the worry etched on his face. "Style Me Salon. I always go there."

"Shit. When's the last time you had your hair done?" Zeke asked.

"A month or two, maybe. Why? What's wrong?" Rina asked as the fear returned full force, oozing out in each word.

"Our first victim, Beth Darlington, worked there. Do you know her?" Ben asked, loosening the death grip he had on her hand. *Stay in control.* He couldn't afford for both of them to lose it.

"I always have Tina Beckers as my stylist. I've never

heard of Beth. Is that the connection?" she asked breathlessly.

"Don't know, maybe. We can't connect Ashley there, but I don't like it that you go there to get your hair done and then this happens," Ben said, releasing a heavy sigh. He pulled his phone out of his pocket, taking care not to let go of her hand as he did. He scrolled through a few pictures until he landed on the one he wanted. "Do you recognize her?"

Rina glanced at his phone. Her eyes went round with shock. "No. Wow, we don't look alike in the face, but her hair...I don't remember ever seeing her at the salon. I'm not always focused on my surroundings."

"Start to be. Take note of everyone around you. If you get a funny feeling, take an extra look to see who's around you. Every little detail counts," Zeke piped in. "Show her some more pics."

Ben scrolled through his phone showing Rina pictures of Jones Maverick, the delivery guy, Claradessa Phantosia, the consultant, Steven, Beth's ex-boyfriend, and Ashley Patterson, the second victim. Rina recognized none of them.

"Well, it was worth a try. Any other places you went, Rina?" Zeke asked.

"Um...well, just one more place. It'll be no help to the case," she replied in a whisper.

"Let us determine that. Where else did you go?" Ben asked with a delicacy he never displayed. He didn't like the way she whispered, the fear that escaped in each syllable.

Rina turned her head to the side, her eyes screaming of sadness and pain. "I went to visit my father. It was my first stop, actually. Like I said, it doesn't really pertain to the case."

"It didn't go well?" Ben asked, even though he meant it

more as a rhetorical question. Of course, it didn't go well. "You didn't tell me."

"What can I say? I asked him to leave you alone, and clearly, he disregarded my wishes. You had a horrible day because of my father...and me. I just hate thinking about it all."

Her fingers became loose in his hands as she tried to pull away physically, and to his horror, emotionally. The way her eyes shifted, her posture, the way she bent her body back away from him. He refused to allow her to push him away. They had an uphill battle, thanks to her father, and he would fight every step of the way. She loved him. He knew her true feelings and he wouldn't let her forget that.

He grasped her hand tighter, clinging to it desperately as he tossed his phone beside him. He grabbed her waist to turn her more toward him, his fingers splayed as if he were digging in like a stake to the ground. Claiming his possession, his strength in the love he felt for her. He was never letting her go.

"My day wasn't horrible because of you. None of this is your fault. He's your father, but the blame isn't transferred to you. We'll get through this together. I promise. If you visit him again, perhaps I should come with. We didn't exactly have a pleasant conversation the last time we talked, but I'm willing to try again."

A smile tinged her face, snuffing out a hint of her sadness. "I'd like that. That means a lot to me. I'm afraid that visit wouldn't go well, though. I know my father."

"And I know Ben. If he wants to try and talk it out, he'll try his damndest. He can have a way with words, on occasion. Not very often. Not like me. I'm a master at words. I could help him with some pointers," Zeke said.

Two heads turned toward him, almost as if they forgot he was still in the room. "Just my two cents on the situation, that's all."

"Yeah, a real way with words there, partner," Ben said dryly. Although, the small ticking in his cheek near the corner of his mouth said he was trying not to smile.

"That's a nice offer, Zeke," Rina said softly. "Let's not worry about it right now. I believe we have more pressing matters at hand."

"You're right, Rina. We'll have to dig deeper into the other places you frequent. It's pretty damn late, though. Let's talk more tomorrow. You need sleep. You look exhausted," Zeke said, a hint of a smile in his eyes. Only Ben noticed.

"I don't think I'll be able to sleep. I don't know how I'll get any of this out of my mind." Rina shivered.

"Oh, I don't know, I think you will," Zeke said, a small smirk forming this time.

"Knock it off," Ben muttered quietly to Zeke.

"Knock what off? I didn't do anything."

"You know what you're doing."

"What am I doing? I didn't do anything," Zeke said, holding in his laughter as he placed a hand on his chest, feigning innocence.

"You are too doing something and you know exactly what you're doing. You're purposely doing it to get on my nerves like I always did to you. Knock it off." Ben lifted his eyebrows, displaying a look that said he'd pop Zeke a good one if he didn't.

"Yeah, buddy, ol' pal, that's not happening. I'm going to torture you until the end of time, and even then, for a little bit longer." Zeke smiled wide, turning his attention to Rina, who looked confused as she glanced between the two of them. "Don't worry, Rina, you'll be able to sleep. Ben will make sure of it. Won't you, Ben? Or do I need to give you tips on how—"

"I'm good, Zeke. Knock it off," Ben said, smiling this time, enjoying the triumph in interrupting him when Zeke glared.

"Tips?" Rina asked with her soft, lovely voice. A small smile hid behind the worry lining her face. "Are you talking about what I think you're talking about?"

"Probably, unless you have a dirty mind, Rina," Zeke said jokingly. "I was talking about unwinding with a glass of wine, or maybe even a strong shot of whiskey. Get you relaxed a bit. Then a bedtime story to get your mind off everything. Bedtime stories do the trick. I read Brina bedtime stories all the time."

A bout of laughter escaped from her lips. "You're so full of it. I can say that Ben doesn't need any tips from you, Zeke. He tells bedtime stories just fine."

Ben coughed, trying to clear the embarrassment. He looked over at Zeke, who looked stunned that Rina said something so bold. She never spoke like that. He went from embarrassment to pride.

"Yeah, Zeke, I tell wonderful bedtime stories. Maybe I need to give you tips on telling a few good stories to Zoe." Ben wrapped his arms around Rina, snuggling her against his body.

"Nope, I tell wonderful stories as well. I bet mine are better," Zeke shot back.

"Highly doubtful. I can weave a wonderful tale, anytime, any place."

Rina laughed louder. "Okay, boys, enough with the tales of glory. Thank you, Zeke."

"For what?"

Rina bit her lip, yet the happiness still lingered. "For

making me feel better. I always enjoy listening to you two banter back and forth. It always brings a smile to my face. You're right, I'm sure I will sleep fine tonight, as long as Ben is by my side."

"I'm never leaving your side," Ben rushed in.

"I'm fine, both of you, really, I'm fine. You both made me feel better."

"We'll figure this out. We have a few things to do tomorrow instead of waiting until Monday, but you have nothing to worry about, Rina," Zeke said.

"Then I'll try not to." Rina turned her head toward the door when a loud knock sounded.

"That's probably Susan. We'll be right back," Ben said, kissing the top of her head, and stood up.

"I'll wait here." Rina didn't need to be told that he didn't want her to follow.

Ben and Zeke walked to the door and let Susan in, who held an evidence bag. Ben nodded for them to follow him into the dining room.

"Did you find anything useful?" he asked the minute they all converged in the room. As his hand rested on the table, the sudden image of Rina laid out on it piercing his mind, her passion filling the room. What a delicious image. He removed his hand to help dispel the image. It only helped a fraction.

"Besides this nasty scarf? No. There were scrapes on the windowsill, but no prints. Did you catch if he was wearing gloves? I'm assuming he did," Susan said as she handed the bag to Ben. "Same identifying tag on this scarf, indicating it came from Little Red's Boutique. Maybe I can find something on the scarf itself, but don't hold your breath."

He looked the scarf over, resisting the urge to flee the room and throw up. "Did you happen to find a note?"

"Nope. Just the scarf." Susan shrugged. "Does your friend match the description of the other victims?"

Ben nodded but didn't say anything.

"I understand now why you were so upset. We'll get this bastard, Ben," Susan said confidently.

"I'm sorry about that, Susan. I never meant to take any anger out on you. I actually got a firm talk from my captain about that," Ben said, fishing for any sort of clue how Reginald found out about the incident. Maybe Susan had gone to the captain herself and the captain withheld the information from him.

Although, the surprise was evident on her face. "I never said anything. I might've made a passing comment to Jill, another co-worker, about how you acted. I thought it was strange. You never act like that. I can't imagine Jill would go behind my back and make a complaint against you on my behalf."

"Well, my captain found out somehow. Don't worry about it, Susan. I was in the wrong. I apologize again," Ben said.

"Apology accepted. I understand." She smiled, nudging Zeke in the shoulder. "You don't look like you got enough beauty sleep."

Zeke gave a strained laugh. "That'll be difficult until we solve these cases and Brina learns how to sleep through the night."

"Well, I'll get this scarf to the lab. We've been busy as hell. I'll try to move everything from these cases up, but I can't make any promises. Does Rina have an alarm?" Susan asked, taking the evidence bag back from Ben.

"No. I'll talk to her about it," Ben replied.

"You do. She could just stay with you for a while. It could

take a few days for an alarm company to come out," Zeke said.

"I'll talk to her. Thanks, both of you, for coming so quickly. What the hell is with the different colors of scarves? What is this sick bastard doing? I feel like he's now playing games with us. I feel like he's targeting Rina because of me. You think he's been following us, Zeke?" Ben finally decided to throw it out there, what he'd been thinking from the beginning since he eyed the scarf.

"Well, shit, I certainly hope not. Zoe doesn't have auburn hair, but now that you said it, she's going on lockdown. I refuse for her to get hurt. I can't go through that again."

"If that's the case, maybe you're getting closer than you thought. Maybe you came across him during your investigation," Susan said.

"Maybe we have come across him. Slick son of a bitch. I can't wait to get this bastard. Damn it, I let him get away!" Ben slammed his hand on the table.

"I told you to not think like that. It's not going to help. Tomorrow I'll get a warrant for the credit card records at Little Red's Boutique. It'll be a damn long list, but we'll get this asshole sooner or later. My dad already said he would sign the warrant."

"He's definitely playing games. I'd love to know why he leaves creepy notes and always uses a different color scarf," Susan said with a sigh.

"Yeah, like a damn rainbow. Red, orange, yellow, green, bl—" Zeke stopped speaking.

"Oh, shit," Ben said.

"The scarf tonight was green. Beth's was red. Ashley's was orange. Why wasn't tonight yellow, if he is playing a sick joke and following the colors of the rainbow?" Zeke said.

"Because he already used yellow. We have a dead body

out there and we just haven't been notified yet. Nobody's found the body," Ben said.

He knew they were right in their thinking. Now it was a waiting game. Waiting until the call came in for another victim. He prayed they were wrong.

His eyes glossed to the evidence bag stuffed with the green scarf dangling from Susan's hands, knowing he wasn't wrong. Rina was supposed to be victim number four tonight, not number three.

## 12

Her skin prickled with unease as she blew out a breath to calm her sporadic nerves. She glanced around. What would her best plan of escape be? The area was deserted. The street, quiet and peaceful. If she ran, she'd have no one to stop her. All she would have to do was run fast and run hard. Or she could simply get back in the car and demand to go home.

"Rina, what's the matter?" Ben asked, grabbing her hand that was clenched tightly to her side.

"I don't think your sister will want me here, especially with a crazy psycho out there wanting to hurt me."

Ben lifted her hand to his lips, gently placing a tender kiss. He wrapped his other arm around her waist, pulling her closer. "My sister likes you. You're not going to worry about any crazy psycho. Only I am and how I'm going to catch the bastard."

He produced a small grin, gingerly brushing his fingers on her back in a small pattern. "I'd be helping Zeke right now getting that warrant and pursuing a few leads, but I promised Isabella a tea party. If there is one thing you never do, it's break a promise with that little girl. She never forgets anything. Someday she'll have some man bending over backwards to do her bidding without lifting one finger. Sort of the power you have over me."

"I do not." She bit her lip to hide her smile.

"Oh, sweetheart, you do." He snatched a kiss. "I don't mind one bit."

She stared into his eyes and forgot about all the escape routes. Not that she found many. Run like hell, or hide in the car. Not very effective escape routes.

A sudden image of last night when Ben made her forget about the horror that entered made her blush fiercely. It was selfish, she knew, but she wanted to go home and have her way with him. It didn't particularly help with the way he held her either. His hard body pressed to hers in the most intimate way. Curve for curve, fitting perfectly.

"What is that beautiful mind of yours thinking? Because if it's what I think it is, you better stop," he whispered, dropping his lips to her neck as he pressed tiny kisses along the curve up to her chin. His lips continued a small path to her lips, sinking his tongue in for a few brief seconds. "We should go inside before I suddenly break a promise to a little girl and whisk you back home."

"Stop distracting me, Benjamin." She stepped out of his arms to gather the strength to walk to the front door. She would never make it there otherwise. He felt too wonderful, too tempting.

"Hmm, Benjamin, huh? You make it sound like I'm in trouble."

"You will be if you don't keep your hands to yourself during this tea party. I need full concentration. I lose my focus when you touch me."

"Good to know. Now I'm curious what sort of punishment you'll dish out."

Her eyes glided to the funny way he walked as he ventured toward the door, knowing the exact reason why, and laughed deliriously. "Behave. Adjust yourself before you knock. You don't want them to see how uncomfortable you are, do you?"

"Adjust it for me?" he asked hopefully as he turned around.

Her eyes went round with shock, her hand covering her mouth as more laughter wanted to escape. "You are a devious man. I don't think I ever truly knew how much you like to tease. It's not nice. I don't think Isabella would appreciate me touching you in such a manner. She's peeking out the window."

Rina pointed to the window on the left, a curtain pulled slightly, and a small blonde-haired girl poking through. Ben's eyes trailed that way, his face turning beet red. He offered Isabella a small wave and turned toward Rina to hide the huge bulge in his pants. Another laugh escaped as Rina watched him adjust his pants.

"Okay, let's put our mind into tea party mode. Otherwise, I'll never survive. Stop enticing me." He pointed a finger in her face, telling her he meant business.

Not one to normally start their sexual encounters, but unable to resist, she clamped her mouth around his finger and slowly drew back as she swirled her tongue around.

"Don't put your finger in my face...unless you want me to do that again." Her face lit up with excitement. "Tea party mode commence."

She walked around him and continued on the pathway to the front door. When she noticed he hadn't followed her, she glanced at him and asked in a sweet, soft voice mixed with mischief, "Ben, are you coming?"

He adjusted himself one more time, then walked toward her with determined strides.

"You're going to pay for that," he whispered in her ear and knocked soundly on the door.

Before she could respond, the door whipped open, and a petite, blonde-haired little girl stood with her hands on her hips.

"What you doing, Uncle Ben-Ben? It took you a really, really, really long time for you to come to the door," Isabella said. Her eyes zoomed to his hands. "Where's my cookies? You promised."

"Keepin' you on your toes, darling. Just wanted to make sure you remembered." Ben winked. "I left them in the car. This is Rina. Why don't you escort her inside?"

Isabella squinted her eyes, assessing Ben like a suspect. "I think you forgot. Lies are bad, Uncle Ben-Ben. You say so."

Ben looked sheepishly at her. "You got me, Bella. I plain forgot. This beautiful woman next to me distracts me so easily. Forgive me, angel."

"As long as you brought chocolate chip cookies and not peanut butter." Her eyes never wavered, glaring at him for all she was worth.

"I would never bring peanut butter cookies. You're gonna make a great detective one day, angel," Ben said with a charming smile.

"I learn from the best." She smiled wide, her glare instantly disappearing. She snagged a quick hug from him, then pushed him backwards. He barely moved an inch from her little push. "Get the cookies. We can't start until we have them."

She turned to Rina. "Uncle Ben-Ben's right. You're bootiful. I wanna show you Princess Dolly." She grabbed Rina's hand and pulled her inside.

Rina followed obediently, grinning at Ben as he winked at her and made his way back to the car. She had a feeling this would be the best tea party she ever attended. Isabella would make sure of it.

She was dragged with a tiny hand until they landed upon a white table with different colored legs. Pink, purple, yellow, and orange. Each color standing out brightly and decorated with splatters of crayon and marker. The table was set with four place settings. One plate, one cup and saucer, a napkin, and a spoon all nicely displayed in an arrangement that made Rina smile. She wondered if they would be drinking real tea and if she would have to raise her pinky as she drank. That's how she always drank her tea when she had her lovely tea parties as a child.

Although, she never had four place settings for real people. It was always her dolls that made up her list of guests. It was a rare moment when her father would join her, even as she begged and begged him to just have one sip.

Here was Ben, making sure nothing got in his way to have a simple tea party with his niece. He would be a wonderful father. He was the total opposite of her father. How sad. Her father could use some tips from Ben on how a father should act.

"You can't be sad at a tea party. Why you sad?" Isabella asked, holding a bedraggled doll in her hands.

Rina turned her eyes away from the table to the little girl standing next to her. She pulled a smile out of nowhere and pushed those depressing thoughts away. "I was just thinking it's been a long time since I was invited to a tea party. I miss them. Thank you very much for letting me join you today."

"I like you. You very nice." Isabella beamed with excitement as she held up her doll. "This is Princess Dolly. Can she sit on your lap? She wants to."

Rina took the doll from Isabella's offered hand. The doll looked to be handsewn, made with a strong fabric. Her face was painted on, or whatever Rina assumed you used on cloth, with a button for a nose. Her hair was made with braided yarn; a dark-brown color that she could see was getting worn. She wore a pink dress with white stars sprinkled all over. On her feet, black booties, also made with fabric, were sewn on with care. She wondered who made it for her, suddenly jealous. No one ever made her anything with such delicacy, such love, such care.

"I would love to have her sit with me. She's beautiful. Just like you."

"I knew you'd love her. See, Momma, I told you." Isabella turned her head to smile proudly at Erin, who shrugged with laughter.

"You sure did. Like you always do." Erin walked over to Rina. "It's nice to see you again. I'm glad you're joining us."

"Are you sure?" Rina had to ask. She wouldn't want herself here if she were in Erin's spot.

Erin laughed. "I'm sure." She bent down toward Isabella. "We need our tea. You're our hostess. Why don't you grab it from the refrigerator?"

"But of course," Isabella said in her most debonair voice she could manage. Which, to Rina's ears, was quite well. Isabella ran off toward the kitchen.

Erin watched her run, then turned her attention to Rina. "I'm not mad at you, or Ben, really. Hell, I don't even hate your father for what he did. After the anger wore off, only sadness entered. My dad's always been there for me, guiding, teaching, explaining the ways of life. He's never done anything like your father did, but I understand. He's protecting you in the only way he knows how."

Erin sighed, her eyes glancing at the table that was set so perfectly. "He doesn't need to protect you from Ben, obviously. But he doesn't know that. I wouldn't wish Isabella away for the world, but sometimes I wish my dad would've protected me from her father. He really destroyed me." Erin glanced back at Rina. "Nobody is taking my little girl from me, especially when it's a lie. I'm not worried anymore and neither should you."

"Friends?" Rina asked tentatively, holding her hand out. She wouldn't worry if Erin wasn't going to.

"Friends." Erin grabbed her hand and squeezed with a huge smile. Her smile dimmed for a moment. "You make Ben happy. You hold his heart like no woman has before. Don't hurt him, please. I'd hate to have to hurt you."

"It's the last thing I'd ever do. I promise."

---

BEN STOOD IN THE FOYER, hidden behind the wall. He was the protector, the one who made sure his sisters were taken care of. He'd never in his life had one of his sisters try to protect him. At least, not that he was aware of. The sad reality was he felt like he needed it a bit this time.

Rina loved him, expressed it in every way she knew how. With her words. Every time he said the three little magical words, she would repeat it. With her actions. Moving her hands over his body that said she loved him without having to say the words. With her looks. The way her eyes glanced his way, the love shining within their depths.

Yet, she never said the words 'I love you' first. She waited patiently for him to speak them. She never initiated contact in an intimate way with him unless he started it, except their first time together when he climbed into the bed and she was already gloriously naked. She tried so hard to hide her looks, to hide the love she felt for him. Just like she held her feelings from him for over three months. Three months lost because she was scared to let go, to do something for herself for once.

He had Rina, but he didn't know for how long. He still worried when the day would come and she'd give in, walk away because she was just too scared to keep fighting.

He needed to show her why they were worth fighting for. He wouldn't make walking away from him easy. If she did, he'd make damn sure she struggled doing it.

BEN OPENED the door and let Zeke in. "How'd the day go?"

"Busy. How'd the tea party go?"

Ben closed the door, then walked into the living room. "Good. You know Isabella. She always throws an excellent tea party. Rina was tense at first, but she quickly relaxed. Isabella doesn't let anyone be sad at a tea party. Rina and Erin got along well."

Zeke sat on the couch next to Ben. "Good to hear. I made a little headway."

"Did you get the warrant and the records?"

"Yeah, I saw my dad first thing in the morning. I went to the boutique, got the credit card records, which, let me tell you, is going to be a pain in our ass. It's long. Too long. I made the manager go back six months, just to be safe."

"Whatever we have to do. What else did you do?"

"With the help of Officer Spencer, we interviewed some of Rina's neighbors about last night. A neighbor two doors down, a night owl or something. She happened to be awake when the man ran to his car. She caught the last three digits of the plate as it sped off. One, five, six. It's a start."

"Better than I did." Ben sighed. "Anything else?"

"Quit beating yourself up. That's all I got done today. I figured we can start fresh tomorrow. We should talk to Rina later about her habits and go from there. Dee's going to bring Zoe over in another hour or so for 'girl time.' I'm pretending to be at work still." Zeke grinned at the ploy to get Zoe over to Rina's. "I hope she's not too exhausted for this party."

"Is she okay? Here I am, always worrying about Rina and not asking about Zoe."

"She's fine. She just overworks herself. She dotes on Brina while she's awake, and the minute she goes down for a nap, she's bustling around the house to get everything done she couldn't while Brina was awake. It wears her out. I don't want her going back to work. I think it's just going to add unneeded stress. Not to mention, I told her I'd be bringing her to and from work until this bastard is caught. Of course, that scared the shit out of her."

"With good reason. Maybe we should carpool. I'm driving Rina to work as well."

"We'll meet at their office, leave one of our cars there, and drive to the precinct together. How about that?"

"I like that plan. Have you told Zoe you don't want her working?"

"Not really."

Ben chuckled. "Remember all those misunderstandings you two had last year that could've been avoided with simple communication. Haven't you learned anything, buddy?"

"I remember," Zeke replied sarcastically. "I told her she doesn't have to work."

"Try telling her you don't *want* her to work. There's a difference."

"Okay, Mr. Know-it-all. I can see you've talked to Rina, yeah?"

Ben shifted on the couch, rubbing his knee with agitation. "Yeah, we're good. I just worry how much it's taking a toll on her, the tension between her father and her. I know it's still there."

"It will be until he comes to his senses." Zeke slapped him on the back and stood up. "It's a party for my wife. I guess I should pitch in and help. Let's see what Rina needs us to do."

"Good luck with that. She's already kicked me out of the kitchen twice for trying to help."

Ben couldn't hold in his smile. He knew why she kicked him out.

"I know that look. Perhaps with a referee in the kitchen you'll manage to keep your hands to yourself," Zeke said with a chuckle.

Ben clapped him on the back. "I don't know, man, it's pretty damn hard. I can see you calling a personal foul against me."

"Personal foul?" Zeke looked shocked. "What the hell you going to do, knock me on my ass if I prevent you from touching her?"

"You never know. She makes me want her, especially when she moves around the kitchen reaching for stuff or bending over. It doesn't take much."

Zeke laughed louder. "I know what you mean. It's a nice feeling, isn't it?"

Ben looked him in the eye. "It is."

They walked into the kitchen. Rina was busy at the sink washing fruit. Ben walked over to her and wrapped his arms around her tiny waist. "Can we help yet? Zeke really wants to since it's a party for Zoe. You're not going to deny him, are you?"

She leaned against his chest as she let the water run over her hands. "I think it'd be easier to get things done with you two out of the kitchen."

Ben lowered his mouth to her ear. "What can I possibly start with him in here with us?" He nibbled her ear and pressed a few kisses on her neck.

"That." She opened her neck to give him better access. Realizing what she was doing, she moved her head forward and turned to look at him. "Stop distracting me, Ben. You two can start moving the things from the fridge into the dining room. People should start arriving soon."

He sighed but gave her a delightful smile. "If I have to." He pressed another kiss to her neck before backing away.

"I almost called unsportsmanlike conduct there," Zeke said with a twinkle in his eye.

"Learn your football, can't call that when contact is involved." Ben walked to the fridge, pulling it open.

"Oh, yeah, personal foul." He couldn't stop laughing, even after Ben shoved a pasta salad bowl into his stomach.

"Rina asked that we set up the table. Go."

"Sure thing, Ben. After you. You know how I hate it when you make me go first all the time." Zeke shifted the bowl into his left hand, holding out his right hand for Ben to lead the way.

Ben grabbed a vegetable tray. Carrots, broccoli, celery, and cauliflower all separated in their own little corners. Neat. Perfect. Just like her.

He held it carefully, not wanting to ruin her perfection,

and closed the fridge door. "I'd be more than happy to go first. I like going first."

"Yet, I always seem to be walking first or talking first. You never take the lead."

"I am now."

They walked out of the kitchen, squabbling back and forth, as they liked to do. A small beautiful laugh rang in his ears. Ben loved hearing her laugh.

---

"You guys shouldn't have done this. I don't feel like I deserve such a wonderful gesture," Zoe said, her eyes glistening with tears.

"Girl, don't start the waterworks. You did that way too much when you were pregnant," Dee said, combing a hand through her unruly hair. "Oh, shit! Are you pregnant again?"

Zoe's eyes bulged out. "No. I just had a baby, Dee. For goodness sake's. Lower your voice. This was really nice."

"We love you. You're our best friend and we wanted you to know how happy we are that you're coming back to work." Rina wrapped her arm around her, squeezing lightly. "And, you know, if you're back to regular activity in the bedroom, it's not that weird of a reaction from Dee."

"Ha! See, even Rina thinks so." Dee raised an eyebrow. "Which is strange. You never say things like that."

"Voice of reason. That's me, remember?" She glanced away. Getting into her sex life wasn't something she wanted to do. But oh, what a sex life it had been recently.

"Right. Voice of reason, my ass. You're getting some. Zoe's getting some. I'm sitting here, thinking about it, hearing about it, yet, not getting any. Where's my hunky detective? You promised me one, Zoe." Dee made a pouty face.

"I really liked Newman for you, but he started seeing some woman from his high school days. I swear." Zoe held her hand up as if she were swearing on the bible. "What about Donaho? I'm surprised you guys invited him."

All three of them turned, eyeing Donaho across the room talking to a few other co-workers, Mr. Young included.

"I thought you'd be more surprised at Mr. Young being here, what with all that trouble last year. You know he's still seeing Mrs. Murphy," Dee whispered.

"Mr. Young had nothing to do with any of that, besides sleeping with Mr. Murphy's wife, Carly. She's really not Mrs. Murphy anymore," Zoe whispered back.

"Maybe the future Mrs. Young. I can see that happening. And you ignored the comment about Donaho," Rina added with a small smile that said she really wanted to hear what Dee thought. Anything to avoid talking about her life.

"Is it because you're with Ben that you're becoming more outspoken, more into the intrigue? You never press further when I dodge something, or hell, Zoe does. Where's the change coming from?" Dee asked, raising an eyebrow.

"Oh, Rina, I think she's still dodging the question," Zoe said with a laugh.

Rina leaned into her, laughing as well. "She is. What does that say?"

"It says I hate you two. I don't like that man." Dee glanced over again at Donaho. Neatly combed brown hair, his bangs swept to the right. Brown eyes to match his neutral mood. He never displayed any sort of emotion. Straightforward, to the point. He wore glasses that fit his face very well. Black square-like frames with a gold line trailing down the temples.

"Why not? He seems nice." Rina followed her gaze.

"He's boring. There's nothing nice about him. There's something off about him."

"Dee, why are you so cynical when it comes to men? Isn't it time you told us?" Zoe asked, the concern prominent in her eyes.

Dee shifted her glance to Zoe, just as quickly looking away. "This is your party. We're not talking about me. We're here to talk about you."

"Shifting again, Zoe. Let's leave her be for now," Rina said softly.

"Oh, all right," Zoe conceded.

"Good. Let's shift to Rina and how it's going with Ben." Dee looked at her with anticipation, scooting her chair closer to her. "I mean, you are getting some, right?"

"Dee," Rina whispered with shock. "Keep your voice down."

Zoe giggled as Dee shrugged. Rina watched them as they waited patiently for her to answer. She didn't want to answer because she didn't know what to say, or how to describe her feelings. They were so mixed up, swirling around inside. So much for distracting the conversation away from her. Their eyes never wavered.

"Oh, all right, yes, of course. He's wonderful. Truly wonderful. And I don't know what to do."

Zoe and Dee's smiles dimmed. Zoe laid a hand on her shoulder. "What do you mean? He's wonderful. You just said so."

"My father's making his life hell. It'd probably be easier if I—"

"If you're going to say it'd be easier if you walked away, we're going to have issues here, Rina," Dee said matter-of-factly. "Are you not a grown-ass woman? We had this conversation, remember?"

"I remember," Rina said softly. "He suggested going with me to talk to my father. That's a very bad idea."

"But worth a try." Zoe tilted her head. "Maybe your father just needs to see the two of you together. To see how happy you are with Ben. I like that idea. You should do that."

Rina turned her head toward the living room, her eyes zooming right to Ben, who stood talking with Zeke and his dad. "Maybe I will. He's worth the fight, even though it scares me."

RICHARD SAT with Zabrina on the couch, feeding her. The night went by fast. Almost everyone invited showed up, welcoming Zoe back to work, doting on Zabrina, and had a good time out of the office.

"You're a natural, Grandpa," Dee said, grabbing some plates from the coffee table as she looked at him with a sweet smile.

"Ah, thanks, Dee. She's too precious. Makes it easier. How have you been? I didn't get to talk to you much."

"I'm fine. Work and play. I know how to manage that just fine, unlike other people." Dee laughed.

Richard watched as she continued to pick up a few more plates, her eyes continuously glancing at Zabrina. "Did you want to feed her? I can help finish picking up."

Dee stood up straight, the light in her eyes at the prospect, just to shut down completely. "Oh, no, I'm fine. I'm not good with babies. They cry on me. Never stop. I'll just throw this stuff away now. Good talk, Richard."

"Yeah, it was, Dee," Richard said to her back as she walked away.

Strange woman sometimes. But the pain in her eyes as she walked away, he knew there was a story there. Not his business, of course. It did make him curious, though.

"Dad, how's Brina?"

Richard looked at Zeke standing behind the couch. "She's almost done. How's the clean-up going?"

"We have a problem."

Richard became alert, his body straightening. Brina shifted in his arms, clutching the bottle tighter as if she thought he was about to take it away. "What's the matter?"

"Our third victim was just found. Ben and I have to go. He's telling Rina and the others. I..." Zeke ran a tired hand through his hair. "Why does life have to get so difficult? I hate worrying about my wife. Honestly, I don't think I have to. I think it's Ben who has more of the worry."

"You two head out and do your job. I'll stay with Rina. Your mother can go home with Zoe and stay with her and the baby until you get home."

"Are you sure? It's getting late and I don't know how long we'll be or..."

Richard gave him a reassuring smile. "I'm sure. Go talk to them. Let them know. I'll get Brina ready to go."

Zeke nodded and walked away. Ten minutes later, Ben and Zeke were out the door. Five minutes after that, everyone else left besides him and Rina.

Richard locked the door and found Rina in the kitchen still fluttering around. Nervous energy. The kitchen was spotless. Yet, she kept rearranging everything and wiping down the counters as if it were covered in dirt and grime.

"Are you okay, Rina? Everything will work out. Please try not to worry."

She stopped wiping the counter, her head slowly rising to look at him. "I can see the worry in Ben's eyes. He tries so hard to hide it. It only makes me worry more. I honestly don't know how I feel right now. Thanks for staying."

"I don't mind." He leaned against the counter as he weighed his next words. "Can we talk?"

She looked at him again, clutching the rag in her hand. "What would you like to talk about?"

"Your father."

She grasped the rag so hard the water trickled down her hand and onto her shirt. "Why?"

"I would never do anything to hurt you. I love Zoe. She's been a wonderful addition to our family. You're her best friend. I wouldn't do anything to ruin that. I've known Ben a long time. He's almost like he's part of the family. He hurts, I hurt. I just want to help in any way I can."

"And how do you suggest you are going to do that?"

"I know your father. Not very well, but we're acquainted. If I felt like having a word with him, would that bother you?"

Rina bit her lip. "Could I stop you?"

"If you say yes, it would bother you, then, of course, I wouldn't do it."

She turned slightly, whipping the rag into the sink. It landed with a loud thud. Richard could see her mind churning like a rough current as she stared mesmerized by the rag. The indecision was clear, making it that much harder to keep silent and wait for her to say something. Perhaps he should've kept his mouth shut.

She finally looked at him. "The thought of you talking to my father scares me more than a serial killer trying to break in and kill me. That says a lot. I don't want to be scared like that. I don't mean to give the impression my father's a bad man. He's not. He's just very set in his ways. He loves me in his own way. I love him." A heavy sigh fell out. "I think I'd like to try to talk to him first with Ben. He asked to go with me. I like that he's thoughtful like that. He loves me. Sometimes, I don't feel worthy of that love."

"You are, dear. Ben's a good guy. He'll treat you right. I'll back off. Just know that I'm here for you." Richard smiled tenderly at her. "You can go to bed if you like. I'll keep watch until Ben returns."

"I'm not that tired. How about a movie?"

"Sounds like a plan. Come on. This kitchen is spotless." Richard gestured with his hand for her to follow.

She glanced at the sink one more time where the rag lay tangled in a ball instead of nicely folded across the middle portion of the sink. Such pain in her eyes when she turned back toward him. What he wouldn't do to take the pain away.

Hopefully, the talk with her father went well. Otherwise, he'd have to step in. Ben was like a son to him. Nobody messed with his family.

## 13

Ben took his time getting out of the vehicle. Stretched his legs. Rotated his head to loosen the kinks. Flexed his fingers. It did nothing to calm him down. He still felt tense in the core of his body.

Rina was safe. Richard offered to stay with her. He would make sure nothing, absolutely nothing, happened to her. Yet, the fear lingered. He wanted to be home with her. Not here. Not at another gruesome crime scene.

"Game face, buddy. Snap out of it. She's fine." Zeke gestured his head toward the house. "Night's not getting any younger. Come on."

Ben nodded and followed Zeke into the house. They walked down the long foyer, pausing when the wall gave way to the living room.

Sprawled on the couch lay their victim with a yellow scarf adorning her neck. She sat in the middle of the couch. Her arms and hands were stretched out, palms up. Her legs extended out, her ankles crossed. Bruises marked every inch of her skin.

"Did you look for a note yet, Susan?" Ben asked quietly,

wanting to walk out of the house already. This victim was the hardest to look at.

Susan looked over at them, kneeling in front of the body. "Not yet. I wanted to take pictures first. I need to document everything before I can move her. I just got here."

"What's with the change of scenery? Why the living room?" Zeke finally took a step inside the room, walking around carefully.

A multicolor afghan was folded nicely on the armrest of the couch. A large black TV stand was centered against the wall, movies all lined up in alphabetical order on the bottom two shelves of the stand. Behind the couch, two bookshelves filled with books, magazines, and pictures, all organized efficiently. In addition, a small coffee table, clear and free of any clutter in front of the couch.

Ben slowly followed Zeke, trying to look around the room instead of the brutality on the couch. "It's strange, for sure. The entire case has been strange. No signs of a break-in at the other crime scenes, no evidence to help us, no witnesses, just nothing. I hate nothing."

"We'll find something. Don't lose hope yet." Susan stood up. "We're backlogged in the lab for at least a month." She looked back and forth between the two, a wide smile on her face. "But, because I have a soft spot for you two, I pushed some stuff ahead of the pile. Like the hair I found in Beth's house."

"Well, I'm going to go out on a limb here and say you didn't get a hit, since you're not jumping up and down with joy." Ben smiled back.

"No hit in the system, you're right. DNA does confirm it's a male. Not much, but it helps. To be safe, since I know she was dating that Steven guy, I did a cross-check with his DNA. Not a match."

"I didn't take him for the killer type. He was really shaken up by her death." Zeke looked at Ben. "Let's have a look around the house. Did you have a chance to look around the house yet, Susan?"

"No. Have at it, boys."

Ben and Zeke went in opposite directions to search the house. Zeke started in the dining room and kitchen, while Ben headed toward the bedrooms.

He took his time in each room, starting with one spare bedroom and one room turned into an office. Nothing appeared out of place except for normal everyday living. He shuffled through her bills lying on the big oak desk against the wall, noticing a few past-due bills. The ones to really stick out were the medical bills. He grabbed the stack and kept moving on.

He walked into the master bedroom, sighing heavily. A perfectly made bed. No clothes littered on the ground. Closet doors neatly shut. No sign of any struggle. He poked his head into the closet, checked in her drawers, and anywhere else that might point out a clue.

He saw Zeke walking out of the bathroom when he stepped out of the bedroom. "Anything?"

"Nothing. No sign that he tried getting in through a window and the door leading to the garage was locked. The garage looked clear of any signs of a struggle or point of entry. You?"

Ben lifted the bills. "Past-due bills. Lots of medical bills. Maybe nothing. Maybe something. Windows were all secure and no scrape marks. So, he picked the lock on the front door, or she let him in."

"Medical bills, huh? We didn't find that Beth or Ashley had any medical issues," Zeke said, walking with Ben back to the living room.

"But, remember, Ashley worked at a doctor's office. Maybe...shit, we didn't even ask for the victim's name."

"After a while, I don't even want to know." Zeke sighed.

Ben nodded in agreement. That was the truth. They all blurred as one. Red hair, slim woman, battered body—dead. Having a name didn't change anything.

"Gentlemen, good evening," Dr. Everly said as they walked into the room.

"Dr. Everly. Do you have a time of death for us yet?" Ben asked hopefully.

"Rough, rough estimate, I would say last night. I'll give you a more specific time frame later when I've had a chance to perform the autopsy."

"Well, if it's before the attempted break-in at Rina's then we have the same guy," Zeke said.

"You're doubting we do." Ben frowned, unsure why Zeke would even doubt that.

"No. I just...I don't know why I said it like that. We do need a timeline of events. Why did he kill one woman and race over to grab Rina the same night? That's weird. Don't you think so?"

"Yeah, I do. But, again, the whole damn thing is weird." Ben glanced at Susan helping Dr. Everly. "Find that note yet?"

"Evidence bag on the coffee table." She nodded her head in the direction of the table. "He moved the table as well to position her as he did."

Zeke grabbed the bag and closed his eyes when he finished reading it. He turned around and handed the bag to Ben.

*Yellow for the sun, I just have one.*

"Sun? He has one. He says sun, like the one in the sky. Does he really mean son, as in a kid?" Ben said.

"Could be. Maybe he feels jilted by a woman. Did he lose a son? Does he blame the mother? Maybe these women act as a substitute for the one woman he hates."

"That's a possibility. Medical bills." Ben raised his hand again, showing the bills. "New area to look into."

"Thanks, Susan. Dr. Everly. Let us know if you find anything. Like, right away," Zeke said with a wink to Susan.

"Will do, Zeke." She winked back.

Ben and Zeke headed for the foyer. The minute they were out of hearing range, Zeke stopped Ben.

"Does Rina have any medical problems that you know about?"

Ben ran a hand over his face, sighing. "I don't think so. She hasn't said anything to me. I sure hope not."

"We need to talk to her about that."

"No, I will. If she does, the whole world doesn't need to know."

"Meaning I'm the whole world?" Zeke asked, the concern changing to hurt.

"That's not what I meant. It'll just be easier if I ask her myself. If she does, she probably doesn't want everyone to know. And by everyone, I mean everyone in our little circle. If Zoe knew anything, you would already know. So if Zoe doesn't know, then Rina doesn't want her to. Don't take it personally. It's not."

Ben walked around Zeke and out of the house. It figured he'd take it personally. But Zeke had failed him once in keeping things between them. He didn't want to take the chance Zeke would slip up to Zoe again if Rina didn't want people to know. God, he hoped she didn't have a serious medical issue.

Zeke met Ben outside on the lawn just as Officer Jeffers joined him.

"So what do you know?" Ben asked Officer Jeffers. He risked a glance at Zeke, who didn't appear to be irritated by his blunt words back in the house.

"Her name is Carol Johnson. Age thirty-three, single. She works at the law office downtown as a secretary. Tollhorn and Tollhorn, Attorneys at Law," Officer Jeffers said.

"Wait, what? Tollhorn?" Ben instinctively reached for his gun.

"Something about that bothers you. What part?" Zeke asked, obviously catching the way he curled his fingers around the holster. He had no idea why he reached for his gun when Anthony was nowhere near him.

"Tollhorn, Zeke. Same jackass that Rina went out with this week. Little odd the next victim is someone who works at his law office. And maybe that accounts for Rina getting attacked."

"Calm down, Ben. Loosen your grip." Zeke nodded at his hand and waited until he let go and hung his hands down. "She wasn't attacked. Attempted B & E, at the most. He's definitely someone we need to talk to. Late night visit?"

"Love to." Ben looked at Officer Jeffers. "Anything else you can tell us? Who found the victim?"

"Her neighbor. They were supposed to have supper tonight. She never showed, so the neighbor, Ms. Nelson, let herself in with the spare key she had. She's the one who told me where she works and that she's single. Now, mind you, she said she's single, but she had been on those dating websites. She had a few dates in the past few weeks."

"Thanks, Officer Jeffers. Call us if you find anything else out. We have a lawyer to go see," Zeke said.

They piled back into the car. Ben slammed the door harder than normal.

"Are you going to be okay, partner? The source of your

anger was nowhere in sight and it had you grabbing for your weapon. I'm a little concerned meeting him face-to-face will be a far worse reaction. Like actually pulling the weapon out."

"I'll be fine. I won't let that jackass get to me. Besides, Rina's with me now. She's safe. I'll be sure to remind him of that if his tongue gets a little loose."

---

"I'D CLASSIFY this as harassment, detective." Anthony held the front door firmly in his hand, just waiting for Ben's reply and the opportunity to slam the door in his face.

"Watch what you say very carefully, Mr. Tollhorn. I'm Detective Chance with the St. Cloud Police Department. I work with Detective Stoyer. We have a few questions about one of your employees," Zeke replied before Ben could release his anger and frustration toward Anthony.

"Excuse me? And just what employee are you trying to get in trouble?"

"Do you know a Carol Johnson?" Ben asked, ignoring the hostility pouring from the man's eyes. He could stay calm. Rina was the utmost, calmest person, even in the face of anger. He could be, too. Maybe. Hopefully.

"Of course I do. She's my secretary. Whatever sick game you're trying to play, it's not going to work."

"She was murdered last night. Her body was found a few hours ago. Where were you last night?" Ben asked, not losing a beat. He should feel remorseful for being so unsympathetic. Impossible, though. The man standing in front of him didn't deserve his remorse. Not after the way he treated Rina.

Anthony staggered back from the door. His face morphed into a sick pain that couldn't be mistaken.

"You were sleeping with her, weren't you?" Zeke asked, going for the jugular right away.

"I...I need a drink." Anthony waved his hand in a careless gesture. "Come in. I know you have more questions."

They followed him to his office where he proceeded to pull a bottle of scotch off the shelf behind his desk. He snatched a glass from the tray that sat next to the scotch and poured himself a full glass, then downed half of it before looking at them.

"Should I repeat my question?" Zeke asked, looking around the office.

A large, spacious room filled with a massive oak desk and a booming leather chair. A couch rested near the window, white blinds pulled halfway down. A small lamp sat on the desk, light spilling out on the papers splattered around. Another lamp, in the opposite corner of the room, stood lit up as well. It appeared as if they had interrupted him working.

Anthony refilled the glass, his hand visibly shaking. Placing the cap back on the scotch, he lifted the drink to his lips, downing the full glass.

"I slept with her a few times. Mostly at the office. Sometimes at a hotel." He traced a finger over the cap of the scotch. "How did she die?"

"We can't go into specifics. It's an on-going investigation. You seem quite shaken for a man who just took out another woman last week." Ben eyed the scotch bottle and the way he circled the top.

Anthony whipped his head toward Ben. "You mean Rina?"

"Yeah. I mean Rina. You seemed pretty strong about

your feelings with her. Did you know someone tried to break into her house last night?" Ben's gaze never wavered, the anger simmering to the top, yet not boiling over. He saw the pain in Anthony's eyes when he relayed the nasty news. He also saw the torture on his face to have another drink.

"Why do I get the impression you two think I had something to do with both things?" Anthony looked between the two, his finger trailing a path on the bottle. "I would never hurt either of them, especially..."

"Especially...who? Rina? Carol? Which one held the key to your heart? For some strange reason, I'm going to say Carol. Which is odd. Her neighbor said she was trying those dating websites out. We haven't looked into that yet. What will we find?" Zeke asked.

"You two, you look...like you're good at your job. But really, what else is there for you? Money is power," Anthony said as he yanked the cap off the scotch bottle again.

"Money is bullshit. So is power. A good woman in my arms, the love of my life. Now we're talking." Ben eyed the bottle as it tipped over, the warm amber liquid falling into the glass with a splash.

"A woman so good in your life that it makes you turn to the bottle in an instant," Zeke added.

Anthony stopped pouring, the liquid that would soothe all his pains only reaching halfway. "I saw something in your eyes that day, Detective Stoyer. The way you spoke to me, kicked me out of Rina's life. I played my part. I thank you for playing yours."

"Can you please stop talking in riddles and just start answering our damn questions? Because I'll be honest, you're looking like a wonderful suspect right now." The anger was simmering back to the surface. Reaching for his gun again sounded like a great plan. Maybe scare some answers out of Anthony. No more bullshit.

"I feel like this is where I invoke my rights to a lawyer and quit talking." Anthony slammed the glass back, downing the contents with one swallow. "But, because you're catching me in a moment, I'll talk a little."

Anthony grabbed the back of the leather chair, squeezing hard. "Carol and I had a thing. I'm sure if you look her up on those dating websites, you'll see her profile. Nothing much became of it. I think she dated a few losers. While I didn't take her out on glamorous dates..." Anthony paused, glancing at Ben, "Like I did Rina, I loved her. I suspect she loved me. But what can I say? Sometimes in life, your life is chosen for you."

"Why did you go out with Rina if you loved Carol?" Zeke asked.

Great question. He was dying to know himself. Holding in the anger was a testament to his patience. How in the world did Rina do it all the time? He could barely control not clenching his fists, although he still found himself doing it.

"Because I had to. My father wanted it. Her father wanted it. Really wasn't much choice. While I had Carol, and I wanted Carol, I can't say it was a horrible thing to go out with Rina. She is a knockout. Isn't she, Detective Stoyer?" Anthony's cool eyes turned to Ben, the devilish tilt of his lip mocking him.

"You know, for a minute, you had me. I really thought you loved Carol and were torn up about her death. Now I just see the original jackass I first met. You can keep giving us a spiel and I'm never going to believe a damn word that comes out of your mouth." Ben unclenched his fists. "Now, where were you last night?"

Anthony stared at Ben for a long moment, the piercing glare never wavering, the tilt of his lip frozen in stone. "Having drinks with my father and Rina's father at the country club near Sauk Rapids. We didn't leave until about 11:30. I got home around midnight. Check the alarm system. I didn't disarm it again until the next morning around eight. And yes, I was home alone the entire night."

"Seems convenient that part of your alibi is with Rina's father. Even your own father." Ben still hadn't blinked, refusing to back down on the stare directed his way.

"Do you really think I'm capable of killing another human being? A woman that I loved? Do I look like a cruel person?" Anthony asked, frowning deeply.

Ben didn't need to contemplate that question, not even for one second. "Yes."

"I believe I have nothing more to say. Contact my lawyer for any future communication, unless, of course, you're going to arrest me right this instant."

"Let me guess. Your lawyer is your father," Zeke said with a bit of cockiness.

"Wow, you're a smart man, detective. I can see how you earned your badge."

"Wow, still a jackass. If you had anything to do with Rina's break-in, or the murders of these women, you'll be sorry. You'll rot in prison. Have a pleasant evening, Anthony," Ben said with a smile, walking past Zeke and out of the room.

Zeke's footsteps trailed behind him. He had no idea if Zeke wanted to say more, but he couldn't stay in that room any longer. He called Anthony a jackass. Not once, but twice. If he wasn't concerned about his job, he should be now. There was no way that wouldn't get back to his captain. He'd be suspended, at the least. Fired, at the most.

It didn't matter one bit. He wasn't going to stand there and let Anthony talk like that. He didn't know what sort of power Anthony had, or even Rina's father. He had everything he needed. She was waiting at home for him. That's all that mattered.

"So, that went well," Zeke said, closing the front door. "What do you think? You really think he's good for it all?"

Ben stopped walking a few feet from the car and turned around. "I do. But, you know, it's still in the pit of my stomach, the doubt. We don't know the time of death yet for Carol, but I have a feeling it's going to fall in the same time frame when he was with his dad."

Ben whipped his hand at the house. "He's more than a jackass, he's...he's...shit! He's not an idiot. I think he's capable of killing. I really do. But he's not an idiot. I don't think he would kill his own secretary, especially one he was sleeping with."

"I agree. For a minute there, I thought you lost your edge, your common sense. He is a jackass, definitely. He's not our killer. We'll check his alibi, though. Who do we want to verify that with? His father or Rina's?"

"How about the damn country club? I'm not sure I'd believe a word of either of those men. Plus, the next time I see Rina's father will be with Rina. I promised her I would be cordial and try to make nice with him. Try to work things out. Going to his house and grilling him on an alibi for Anthony, the golden boy, is not trying to make nice."

"Good point. Country club it is."

## 14

B en leaned against the doorframe, taking in the sight. He could watch Rina all day, every day, in her element. She was always so delicate, so precise in her movements. One would think it would look robotic or monotone with the precision she displayed. To him, it was pure beauty and grace.

He especially enjoyed watching her dress. He liked it better when she undressed, completely naked for his taking. But watching her dress was almost as desirable. It made him crave to rip the clothes back off, to claim her body with a heated frenzy. Temptation sat on the tips of his fingers. Right this instant as he watched her slip on her skirt and button her blouse. He couldn't stand it anymore when she bent down to grab her high heels.

"Let me." He bent down before she could reach her shoes, her brow lifting in amusement. He tossed his head to the bed. "Have a seat. I'll put them on for you."

She glanced at the bed and shook her head. Yet, her feet moved to his bidding. "You're going to make us late, Ben. Won't Zeke be waiting for you?"

He knelt down in front of her, lifting her foot gently. "I don't care. Do you want to know how many times he was late? I know the reason for every single time. Just one look at his ridiculous face and I knew."

He started to softly rub her foot instead of sliding her shoe on.

"Are you planning on making us late so you can show him a ridiculous look on your face?"

"It crossed my mind." He placed a kiss on her foot, making a small trail from her ankle to her knee. "I've never been late for that reason. I think I want to try it out for once."

"Ben, I think..." Her voice trailed off when his hands slid up her thighs, his fingers brushing near her panties.

"You think what, Rina? Tell me," he whispered close to her lips.

"I think...think..." She couldn't seem to finish her sentence as his fingers dove in her panties.

"I think so, too, sweetheart." He chuckled against her lips, laying her back onto the bed.

He continued his assault with his fingers as he kissed her fiercely. He loved it when she always ran her fingers through his hair, grabbing on as if she were ready to hold on for the ride of her life. Sometimes, she yanked hard, making him want to cringe in pain. She could do anything she wanted. He never wanted her to stop touching him, loving him.

"Damn, Rina, I love you." He stood up, whipping his pants and boxers off with a quickness that said he suddenly needed her with a passion. She wasn't planning to stop him, either, when he saw her unzip her skirt and slide it off with her panties.

He climbed onto the bed, plunging into her without one

word. She clung to his shirt, wrapping her legs around his waist as he took her on a wild ride. He wanted to shout it to the world how much he loved her, how thankful he was that she decided to follow her own heart. And he hoped she continued to do so. Losing her would be like losing a part of himself.

He tried to show the depths of his feelings each time he thrust into her, each time his lips touched hers. Every time he placed a scorching kiss on her soft body, he hoped she felt the amount of his love. He needed her to feel his love. Because he dreaded the night wouldn't end in his favor.

It was a high probability he would be suspended, or even fired, when he walked into work today. Another reason he didn't care he would be late. His actions last night with Anthony would bring down the trouble. Rina wouldn't blame him. She would probably blame herself. He could see her walking away to save him, save his job. He refused to let her do that. Claiming her as he never had before would help show her why she was meant to stay in his arms.

Sweat rolled down his shoulder blades as he thrust deeply inside her. The heat swirling around them did nothing to dispel his hunger for her. If anything, he grabbed her face harder as he devoured her lips.

Her hands let go of his shirt and made their way to his hair where she massaged his head. The magic in the tips of her fingers drove him crazy, drove him harder into her. He didn't slow down once as her climax hit. She pulled his hair so hard he actually bit her lip from the pain. He stroked his tongue where his teeth claimed her mouth, soothing her ache as he held her tightly as she continued to float on clouds.

Not close to his release when she came down from her bliss, her hands slowly dropped from his hair to his back as he continued to love her with his entire body and soul. He broke the kiss to lean up a little and grab her legs that were still tightly around his waist. He raised them to his shoulders, getting even deeper inside her.

Not long after, she cried out again in glorious bliss, grabbing the sheets in a tight fist. He let go finally, sinking his body into her as the pleasure flowed through him.

"That was...wow, Ben. What was that?" Rina asked in a whisper.

"That was me loving the woman I love. You do things to me, Rina. You have since the moment I met you."

He lifted, bracing his forearm on the bed, while swiping a lock of hair from her face. "I hope that wasn't too rough. I guess I went a little crazy."

"No, it was beautiful. You definitely made us late. I have to find a new outfit. This shirt is completely wrinkled now."

He laughed with her as he looked down at her nice white blouse that did indeed have a bunch of new wrinkles. "I'd say I'm sorry, but I'm really not. I would love you again if I knew it wouldn't make us horribly late. It's already bad enough I'll be a little late."

Shit. Why the hell had he said that? He retreated to the bathroom before she could ask why. Words still failed him when he came out. She entered the bathroom without a word as well. He stood for a moment, shaking his head at the idiocy of his words, and started to yank his pants back on when a soft hand hit his shoulder.

"What aren't you telling me? You said it went fine last night when you spoke to Anthony."

He turned around. "It did, I guess. Except for the part where I called him a jackass a few times. Because he is one. I couldn't help myself."

"Oh, Ben. I can't have you losing your job because of me."

He brushed a hand over her cheek. "I'm not losing my job because of you. If anything, it'll be because of me. Because I can't control my emotions. I should've known better than to say that to him. He just brings my anger out really easily. I can't stand the man."

"I can't believe I went out on a date with him. Do you really think he did it? Killed all those women?"

"Honestly, he's an asshole. There's no question about that. I don't think he's a killer. He's smarter than that, to kill his own secretary. I still have to follow all leads and clear him, though. I don't want you near him."

She shivered. "I don't want him near me."

"Call me right away if he calls you or comes to your work. Call me for anything. Okay?" He grabbed her by the shoulders and pulled her into his embrace. "I'm going to worry about you all day."

"I'll be fine at work. Trust me. One word to Dee and I'll be safe."

He chuckled and let her go so he could finish buttoning his pants. "For once, I don't mind Dee's in-your-face attitude. She's pretty great. She's a great friend."

"She is. Zoe promised her a sexy detective of her own. Can you think of someone good for her?"

He stopped buckling his belt, a smile beaming from cheek to cheek. "A sexy detective of her own? Like you have?"

"Yes. Like I have."

"I'll have to think about it."

"Zoe liked Newman for her, but he's dating someone now. Sauer seems like a nice guy."

Ben grinned and shook his head slowly. "Sauer is, but

he's also really shy when it comes to women. She needs someone who can dish right back. It's not going to be easy for the man who decides to date her. I don't mean that in a mean way either."

Rina lightly laughed. "I know what you're saying."

She walked to the closet in her underwear, flipping through her clothes to find another outfit.

"You better dress fast before I throw you back onto the bed."

Strapping on his holster, he caught her sultry glance as she said, "Or you could leave the room while I change."

"I like watching you get dressed."

"Yes, but it leads to trouble." She eyed the bed, then looked at him. "Remember, we don't want to be even more late."

"Very true. It's going to be a long day without seeing you."

"Are you sure you'll be finished by the time I get off work?"

"Yes." His voice was firm. "Do not leave without me. We'll come home together. And maybe pack some of your things. I'd like it better if you came home with me."

She almost dropped the shirt she grabbed from the closet. "You don't want to stay here?"

"I have a security system. I'd feel better in my house."

She slid an arm into a sleeve, shaking her head in agreement. "That makes sense. How long do you think it'll take to find this killer? How long do you want me to stay?"

"I'm not sure how long it'll take. But I want you to stay forever."

She slowly looked at him, her hands stalling on a button. "Are you asking me to move in with you?"

"Yes."

"Ben, I...we haven't been dating that long. We...I don't know if we should do that. I think..."

He grabbed her hands. "You think what?"

"Last time you didn't let me finish telling you what I think," she said with a coy smile.

"I will this time."

"Okay." She tried to pull her hands away, but he refused to budge with his grip. "I think we should focus on this case. I can stay with you while that happens. After that...I can't say."

He squeezed her hands tighter, then wove his fingers through hers. "You know how I hate it when you say *can't*. You said we haven't been dating long. That's true. But we've known each other for a year. If I would've asked you out right away in the beginning instead of acting like an idiot, we'd already be in a relationship for months."

"Provided I didn't say no."

"Or can't." He pulled her closer, kissing her lips. "I think if I would've asked you out earlier, you would've resisted like you originally did. I also think we still would've ended up together because you love me. I love you. It's that simple. Considering we technically would've been in a relationship for months, the next logical step in any relationship is moving in together. So, let's pretend I asked you out forever ago and take that next logical step."

"You make it sound simple."

"It is simple, Rina. Really, really simple. All you have to do is say yes."

"I ca—"

He cut her words off with a searing kiss. "Don't say that word. You can say whatever you want. But don't you dare say can't."

"I'm sorry. Don't be mad at me."

"I'm not mad. I just hate hearing that word from you."
He let her hands go and turned her around to the closet.
"Finish getting dressed. I didn't mean to bring that up right
now. I don't know why I did. Don't worry about it."

"Ben?"

Halfway across the room, he took his time to look at her.
Hiding his anger was easy, but the pain. That was impossible. "Yeah."

"I'll think about it. I won't dismiss the idea. You just
threw me for a loop when you said that. I like when you
spend the night. I'm sure I would also enjoy living with you.
It's just a lot so soon. And we still haven't spoken to my
father together."

"I like that answer better than can't. I'm ready to talk to
your father whenever you are. Hell, tonight after work
sounds great."

"It didn't sound great coming out of your mouth."

"I hate to say it, Rina, but I will. I just want to get it over
with. I want to work things out with him. I don't have high
hopes I can. I imagine, neither do you. Wouldn't it be better
if we try sooner rather than later?"

She frowned, her eyes dripping with sadness. "No, I
don't have high hopes. But you're right. I'll call him. I'll see if
we can have dinner together."

"Good. I'll wait for you in the living room."

---

THE TAPPING of the pen grated on his nerves. Ben took the
pencil he was using and whipped it across the desk.

Zeke chuckled, picking up the pencil. "Yeah, you're in a
mood all right. You were late today. You have a glow about
you. Late plus glow equals sex. Yet, there's this underlying

moodiness. That's what I can't figure out. What happened?"

"Shut up, Zeke." Ben picked up a piece of paper, crumbled it, and threw it at him. "Stop tapping your damn pen."

"Definite moodiness. I think if the captain was going to suspend you, he already would've. He hasn't called you into his office yet. Is that what has you so uptight? Morning sex before work, which also makes you late, should lift your spirits. Not bring you down."

Despite himself, Ben laughed. "It did lift my spirits. Shut up about the sex already." He sighed, rubbing his chin. "We're having dinner with Rina's father tonight. We didn't exactly argue, but it sort of felt like we argued. If there's one person I don't want to argue with, it's Rina."

"Okay, that explains things better. Rina did seem distracted this morning. She's probably nervous as hell. You need to be the strong one. Don't lose your cool with him."

"I won't. Trust me." Ben shrugged when Zeke gave him an incredulous look like he didn't believe him. "Okay, I'll try really, really hard not to lose my cool. For Rina's sake. Trust me."

"That sounds a little more believable. So this…" Zeke said, pointing to the papers strewn across their desks. "This is a lot of shit to sort through. We also need to dig into Carol's life some more. Like, visit her office and interview some of her co-workers. Did you ask Rina about any medical issues? And, if the answer is yes, she has issues, are you going to tell me what they are?"

"I asked. No issues, so we have nothing to investigate with her on that angle. Thank goodness. I'm not sure I could've handled it if she had medical problems. I have enough to worry about already." Ben shifted in his chair and ran a hand through his hair. "So you're right. We have a ton to do today. Maybe we should split up. These credit card records from the boutique could take forever. I'll sift through that and you can visit her office."

"I think—"

"Stoyer, my office. Now!" Captain Ganderson said, stopping the rest of Zeke's words. He didn't look happy.

"I think I'll wait for you to come back before I leave. Good luck," Zeke whispered as Ben stood up from his desk.

"Chance, you too," Captain Ganderson added before walking back inside his office.

"Well, shit, I didn't expect that," Zeke said, following Ben to the captain's office.

"I hope my bad luck isn't rubbing off on you, man."

Zeke laid a hand on his shoulder. "Don't worry about me. I can handle it."

They walked into the captain's office with Zeke shutting the door. He obviously didn't need to be told the captain normally liked the door closed. They both took a seat in front of the desk and waited patiently while the captain folded his hands on his stomach and leaned back in his chair.

"I thought I told you to solve this little predicament you landed yourself into. Try to make peace, I believe that is what I said, Stoyer," Captain Ganderson finally said, sitting up a little.

"I'm trying, captain. I'm also trying to do my job. Catch a killer." Fidgeting would be bad. Fidgeting would show how everything was affecting him. But the look of disappointment on the captain's face made him want to fidget like a hive of bees were chasing him.

"I received another call from the chief. He wasn't happy." Captain Ganderson stopped speaking when Ben stood up, placing his hand on his weapon. "What are you doing, Stoyer?"

"You're about to suspend me, or hell, maybe even fire me. I'm saving you time by getting it over with quickly. But, please, captain, please don't do anything to Zeke. He hasn't done anything wrong."

"I told you I could handle myself, Ben. If the captain's suspending you, then he might as well suspend me. This is bullshit! Ben hasn't done anything wrong, and you damn well know it, cap," Zeke said, standing up as well.

"Both of you. Take your hands off your weapons and have a seat. Now." Captain Ganderson sighed heavily and waited patiently while they sat back down with hesitation.

"As I was saying, the chief wasn't happy. He did not appreciate, as he put it, harassment towards Anthony Tollhorn, or the rude behavior displayed."

"I'll admit I called him a jackass, sir. He is one. But I won't apologize for doing my job," Ben said, clenching his fists. Keep the cool. That's all he needed to do. It wasn't working very well.

"Stoyer, stop interrupting me."

"Sorry, cap."

"I kindly explained to the chief that when a third victim pops up and she happens to work for the same man, that I don't consider that harassment. I consider that my detectives doing their job. Did you get in his face to crack some information? Well, that's what my two best detectives do sometimes. They get into a suspect's face and demand the truth. And yes, I called Anthony Tollhorn a suspect to the chief."

Captain Ganderson rested his elbows on the desk as he leaned closer. "I also told the chief that if he felt it was absolutely pertinent that I suspend one of my best detectives for doing his job, then he could suspend me as well because I am doing no such thing."

Ben let out the breath he hadn't realized he was holding. "Thank you, captain."

"No, thank you, Stoyer. If you hadn't called me last night with an update on the case and these possible ramifications to occur, well, then I wouldn't have had the proper information to fight back with. He backed off. He didn't realize all of that when he called me. I was even so bold enough to say that maybe he should stop calling me with nonsense if he doesn't have all the facts. I did point out he is the chief of police. He should know better. That probably put me in the hot seat, but frankly, I'm done with this bullshit. You're right, Chance. It's bullshit."

Zeke smiled. Ben wished he could summon up a smile. Hell, even a small grin would do.

"Do you two know what I want now? I want you to solve these murders. I really want this problem of yours to go away as well, Stoyer. Do I need to do something to help you out with this?"

Ben shook his head. "No, cap. I'm having dinner tonight with Rina's father. I hope to solve this problem tonight."

"You don't sound very positive about it." Captain Ganderson leaned back in his chair. "Let's move these cases along, please. Do you two need help?"

"Help? As in FBI help, cap," Zeke asked a little shocked, sitting straighter in his chair.

"Calm down, Chance. No, not that kind. But if the number of murdered women keeps rising, we might not have a choice in the matter. I meant, here, like Newman and Sauer. They obviously have a caseload like you two, but nothing like this."

"Yeah, we could probably use their help today. Those

credit card records are long. With a new victim, we need the help. What do you think, partner?" Zeke looked at Ben.

"I think I get Sauer, you get Newman."

Captain Ganderson laughed. "Go back to work. Solve these murders. Quit making me holler at the chief of police. Tell Newman and Sauer what they're doing today. If they have a problem, send them my way."

Zeke nodded and stood up, walking to the door. Ben stood up more slowly, waiting to speak until Zeke left. "Thank you, captain. I wouldn't want Zeke, or even you, to lose your job because of me. I appreciate the support."

"You're a damn fine detective. Why wouldn't I support you? I have no trouble talking to this Chastain guy myself."

"Thanks, cap, but I got it. Dinner tonight, remember?"

"Yeah, I also remember you didn't sound so positive about it. Just like now."

"True. But for love, you do crazy things. Like be nice to a man who doesn't deserve it."

Ben excused himself and met Zeke by their desks. They decided Ben would stay back with Sauer while Zeke and Newman headed to Carol's office. Ben didn't mind staying back either. He didn't need another opportunity to call Anthony a jackass. Because he probably would've.

He and Sauer grabbed all the reports and papers scattered on their desks to a conference room and set up shop for the day. They took their time scrolling through the names on the list to try and match any names involved with Beth, Ashley, Carol, and unfortunately, Rina. He hated that he had to include her in the list.

The list was long. A lot of people liked to shop at Little Red's Boutique. They had gotten a list of every credit card receipt. It was impossible to know which receipts held scarves purchased without going through each receipt itself.

By the end of the day, Ben's eyes were hurting from scanning paper after paper. Relief finally came when Zeke and Newman walked into the room. Until he realized what he had to look forward to when he left work.

Dinner.

With Rina's father.

"You two looked wiped. You didn't even leave the office." Newman laughed.

"You try looking at receipts all day, name after name after name. Pretty soon they all start to blend together," Sauer said, stretching his arms in the air.

"Did you find anything?" Zeke asked with a hopeful smile.

"Negative. We got pretty far, though. You went six months back. Thank you, by the way," Ben said sarcastically, as Zeke shrugged with a big smile. "With two people, we made great progress. On the downside, we didn't find any names that popped out at us. Carol shopped there. She never purchased a scarf based on the receipts. Beth and Ashley never shopped there before. None of their friends and family purchased any scarves from there, as far as we can tell. Same goes for Carol's family and friends, besides herself, like I said. Although, we do need a complete list of Carol's friends besides what we have."

Ben rubbed a hand over his face. "I called Rina. She's never shopped there before. Maybe we missed something. How about you two? Better luck, I hope."

"I think so." Zeke looked at Newman, who shook his head in agreement and grinned.

"Share it with the class, teacher," Ben said.

Zeke chuckled. "Is it because you've been confined to a room all day, or is it the looming dinner that has you cranky? Has he been cranky all day, Sauer? I'm sorry for leaving him in your care. I thought he'd behave better."

Newman and Sauer laughed while Ben glared. "Are you done? I've been absolutely wonderful to work with. Haven't I, Sauer?"

"Yeah, he's been fine," Sauer agreed.

"Must be the looming dinner then." Zeke decided to stop messing around when Ben's hard stare didn't waver. "So, we interviewed her co-workers. They all had nice things to say about her. Sweet girl, friendly, always had nice things to say about people. Yadda, yadda, yadda. Same as our other two victims. Apparently, Anthony and her were really good at hiding their affair. No one had any idea about it until we spilled the beans. Needless to say, Anthony wasn't too happy about that."

"Wasn't happy is an understatement," Newman said. "He made quite a few threats about having our badges for the lack of proper decorum while doing our jobs. His words, not mine."

"The captain has our back," Ben said.

"I already told Newman that. Her medical bills, which I scanned before we left, were her mother's. She had stage four breast cancer. She also didn't have the best of insurance. Carol did what she could to help her mother. She brought her to appointments, helped pay the medical bills her mother couldn't. It was rough, according to her one co-worker, who said she helped Carol on occasion when she needed time off from work."

"When did she die?" Ben asked.

"About two weeks ago," Newman answered.

"Why wouldn't Anthony tell us this?" Ben wondered.

"Because he's a jackass. And when I asked, he said her mother wasn't any of our business." Zeke tilted his head at

Ben as he grinned. "I called him a jackass for you. Once. I felt better."

Ben laughed. "That's why you're the best partner a guy could ask for."

"Did you two hear that? I'm the best." Zeke winked at Newman and Sauer, who shook their heads but laughed with him. "We did find something really interesting. Guess where Carol took her mother for her doctor appointments?"

"Where Ashley worked," Ben said excitedly. Could it be? A great connection for once.

"No. But she did take her to the doctor's office across the hall. And guess who was delivering packages when we walked in?" Zeke said.

"Jones Maverick." Ben almost wanted to rub his hands with satisfaction.

"The one and only. He was surprised to see us. We showed him a picture of Carol, but he claims that he never saw her before in his life," Zeke replied.

"That's too strange of a coincidence if you ask me. We didn't come across his name yet with the credit card records, but he could've paid in cash," Ben said.

"Zeke and I thought the same thing. We got a list of the appointment times for Carol's mother. The doctor confirmed Carol always came with her each time her mother had an appointment. We also stopped by Jones's workplace and looked at his schedule and what days he delivered to the office. Three of those deliveries coincided with Carol's mother's appointments," Newman said, pulling out a chair and propping a leg on top while he rested his arm on his knee.

"Yet he claims he never saw her?" Ben asked skeptically.

"If he's our killer, chances are he did see her and is lying. If he's not our killer, it's just a coincidence and Carol probably was already back in the room with the doctor when he arrived," Zeke said.

"You don't believe in coincidences and neither do I," Ben said firmly.

"I know. That's why we questioned his supervisor a bit. Any complaints, anything strange about Jones, you know, those sorts of things. He said he's quiet, does his job well. Really, keeps to himself. Nothing odd stuck out about him. We also stopped at Little Red's Boutique and asked the employees if they recognized Jones when we showed them his picture. Nobody did," Zeke said.

"Maybe he had someone else buy 'em. I find it strange he kept to himself at work. That strikes me as odd. I don't like the quiet ones," Ben said, rubbing his chin.

"So you don't like Sauer. That's not nice, Ben," Newman said, shaking his head with a smile at Sauer.

"He's probably quiet because you talk too much," Ben countered with a laugh.

"It's called reflecting. I like to think before I speak," Sauer said, looking at Newman. "And he does talk a lot."

Zeke laughed, slapping a hand on Newman's shoulder. "We appreciate the help today. We got a lead. Ben and I thought Jones was fishy the day we interviewed him at his apartment. He deserves a closer look. But I think that's it for the day."

"You're welcome. We know you two would return the favor. You guys wanna grab a beer?" Newman asked.

"Dinner party, remember?" Ben said, wishing he didn't have to go.

"Forgot. Good luck." Newman glanced at Sauer. "Zeke's probably heading home to the wifey as well. Beer, Sauer? I can tell you all about this cute nurse we talked to today. She'd be good for you."

"Oh, she was cute," Zeke said with a grin, as Sauer's face grew red from his neck to his cheeks. "We're just talking about a pretty woman. No need to get shy already, Sauer."

"Stop, guys. You know me and women. I...I just don't say the right things. They...you know, women, they're scary," Sauer stammered.

"No, Sauer. They're beautiful creatures that need your lovin'. Let's grab that beer and I'll tell you all about her," Newman said, putting his leg down on the floor and gesturing his head toward the door.

"Okay, fine. You can tell me all about her, but you know I'm never gonna talk to her." Sauer stood up.

"We'll crack open that shell of yours one of these days," Zeke said with a laugh.

"It's my life's mission." Newman chuckled.

Sauer's face grew a deeper red, if that was even possible, as he averted eye contact with all of them.

"Just looking out for you, buddy." Ben tried to imagine him and Dee like Rina suggested and he still couldn't see them as a couple, so he said nothing about her.

"Yeah, I know." Sauer shrugged.

"Come on. I'm gonna find you a gorgeous woman tonight. It's been decided." Newman tossed an arm around Sauer's shoulder. "See you guys tomorrow."

Newman and Sauer left. Zeke helped Ben organize the papers before they left, needing to make everything clutter free.

Zeke started the car. "Call me if you need me. Don't let him get to you. Keep your cool and try your damndest to work it out. Be the calm one, the cool one, the one in control. For Rina. She'll need you to be the strong one."

"I will. I promise."

Ben glanced out the window, watching as everything

blurred by. What a bunch of lies. He promised he'd keep his cool. Keeping that promise would take a miracle. Because the minute he faced Reginald Chastain, he wanted to punch him in the face for treating Rina the way he did, and for messing with his family. Nobody messed with the people he loved.

## 15

Ben's hand tightened on the doorknob as Rina approached him in a conservative black dress that revealed nothing of her beautiful assets. It didn't matter he couldn't see her cleavage or the creamy skin on her back or a hint of her thighs that would lead him to his prize just a little further up. She still looked sexy as hell. He just imagined what was underneath her dress, creating an uncomfortable bulge in his pants.

"You should change. We might not leave if you wear that," he said as she met him by the door, keys in hand.

Rina looked down at the dress, her eyebrows dipping into confusion. "What's wrong with this dress? It's very conservative."

"That's the problem, sweetheart. It leaves me to my imagination. My mind runs wild picturing what's underneath. I feel this insane urge to drag you back to the bedroom."

She playfully slapped him on the shoulder. "I told my father we're coming. You can't make up excuses why we can't go. Even if I like that excuse."

"It's not an excuse. It's the truth. I hope I can keep my hands to myself. They feel like exploring." Ben reached to grab her around the waist, but she managed to avoid his grasp by jumping back.

"Out, mister. We can't be late. If you touch me, we'll be late. Trust me. My father likes punctuality."

Ben sighed, putting on a pouty face for her benefit to hide the stress in his sigh. "I would never make you late for something like this."

Twenty minutes later, they made it to her father's house. Ben pulled into the driveway and stopped in front of a gate, lifting his eyebrows in surprise. Before he could roll down his window and hit the intercom, the gates started to open. Ben drove through, following the long driveway. Trees lined the way, the sun was starting to set for the day, giving an eerie feeling as the trees swayed back and forth. Maybe it was the dread filling Ben inside that gave off the eerie feeling.

"Wow, I had no idea. How big is this property?" Ben asked, taking his time to drive up to the house.

"Twenty acres or so. It's very beautiful inside."

"I'm sure it is. Just like you." He grabbed her hand and pressed a tender kiss to show how much he meant it. "You look very beautiful tonight, if I didn't say that already."

"Oh, I think you did. You always say it with the way you look at me. I used to find it unnerving. Now I just love the way you look at me."

"You make it difficult to continue this drive when you talk like that. Now all I want to do is look at you."

She giggled, glancing away from his heated gaze. "Park the car, mister. Quit looking at me."

"If I must." He chuckled, squeezing her hand before letting it go.

He finally saw the house with a small garden centered in front. The driveway circled around the garden. He pictured following the circle back down the driveway and onto the road without stopping. As much as he yearned to do that, he knew he couldn't.

To the left of the garden, two vehicles were parked. To the right, there was a pathway decorated with flowers on the sides leading behind the house. He followed the road around the garden and parked the car in front of the door.

"Come on, we have five minutes to spare. I like being early. Even if it's a few minutes," Rina said, opening her door without waiting for his response.

That didn't sound like a request. More like she was telling him to get his butt in gear. He shut the car off and opened his door quickly. He couldn't help but take another glance at the two parked cars. One was a black Cadillac, and he automatically assumed that was Reginald's vehicle. He saw a huge three-stall garage, wondering why two cars were sitting outside. Reginald looked like the type who would have five vehicles. He also appeared like the type of man who would build additional space if he didn't have enough room for all of his vehicles. Strange. Why did he have two cars parked in the open?

He rounded his car, smiling at Rina, then took another look at the cars. The second car was a dark-blue sedan, not as fancy looking as the black car. The license plate suddenly glared like a bright ray of sunlight. He stumbled.

"Are you okay?" Rina grabbed his arm as she helped him correct his stance.

He turned to her with a smile that he instantly pulled from nowhere and covered her hand with his. "I'm fine."

"Come on." She kept a hold of his arm as they climbed

the few stairs to the door. A smile brightened her face when the door opened before she could knock.

"Welcome."

"You just couldn't let me knock, could you?" Rina said sweetly, then leaned forward to kiss a man he didn't recognize on the cheek.

"No. You know I dislike that. It's your home, Rina," the man said brightly, then turned to Ben. "I'm Thomas. Welcome to the Chastain home. If you need anything, just let me know."

Ben shook hands with Thomas. "Ben Stoyer. Nice to meet you. I do have a question."

"Of course. What is that?"

Ben turned toward the blue car, pointing, his eyes glossing to the license plate that showed the numbers one, five, six. The same description given by the witness that saw a dark car speed out of Rina's neighborhood the night of her attempted break-in. The car looked familiar to Ben, not that he made out the actual make and model of the car as it sped away. But the overall size and shape of the car was very familiar.

"Whose car is that?"

"It's mine. Why do you ask?"

Ben watched as the muscle ticked in Thomas's cheek, the way his hand trembled into a fist, then relaxed. "I think you know why I'm asking."

"Ben? What's going on?" Rina asked, pulling on his arm for him to look at her. He couldn't look at her. Not yet. She would see the rage, the fury, the absolute disgust of what was going through his mind.

"Something that you'll probably get mad at me for. We're going to have to reschedule this dinner with your father."

"But why? What's the matter?" Rina glanced between Thomas and Ben as they continued to stare at each other. "Someone tell me what's going on, please."

Thomas cleared his throat. "I do believe your boyfriend, Detective Stoyer, has some questions for me."

"I do believe you're correct. I think we'll ask them at the precinct," Ben said, his stare getting harder by the second. Things just took an unexpected turn. He had no idea how he'd explain any of it to Rina.

ZEKE LEANED against the wall as Rina paced back and forth. Staying calm as he watched her display her anger, agitation, and frustration was truly difficult. She never acted like this. He could never understand how she kept her cool all the time. How she couldn't let loose her feelings in an animated way like most people displayed. So the fact she was pacing, the anger quite visible, told him that she was upset. So upset that she couldn't control her emotions.

"Please don't make me ask again, Zeke. I want to talk to Thomas." Rina stopped, her hands on her hips in defiance. A look that reminded him of Zoe, a little of Dee as well. But Rina, an image so unlike her.

"Please don't keep making me say no. Ben is talking to him, trying to find out the facts."

"And he couldn't do that at my father's house. He didn't even give Thomas a chance to explain anything. He didn't even give me an explanation. He left me at my father's."

Zeke pushed himself off the wall and stepped closer to her. "Thomas didn't put up a fight either. He didn't demand an explanation. Why do you think that is? Ben did what he did to protect you."

She turned away. "Seems a strange way to protect me. Thomas would never hurt me, or anyone else."

"Your father must not believe that. He didn't come with you. He gave you one of his cars to come here by yourself."

She slowly turned toward him, her eyes almost as black as death. "He's probably getting him the best lawyer in town. My father would never abandon Thomas. He's like family." She stepped closer to Zeke, a breath away. "You tell Benjamin I want to speak to Thomas now or I may never forgive him."

Zeke took a step back. Damn. He never thought he'd need space from her wrath. It appeared she didn't need to yell to get her point across. "Calm down, Rina. Don't be pissed at Ben. He's doing his job and protecting you at the same time."

"I am calm."

"Sure fooled me." He walked toward the interrogation room. "Stay out here."

He opened the door and closed it quickly. Ben sat on one side of the table, his hands folded in his lap. Thomas sat on the other side, hands folded in his lap as well. Both were silent. "I hate to interrupt."

"Not really interrupting. He's not saying anything." Ben stood up and walked over to Zeke. "What's up?"

"Rina. She's not happy. She hollered at me."

---

"RINA DOESN'T HOLLER." Ben looked at him, confused, and scared for the umpteenth time that night. He knew he upset her. He hoped to make it up to her. If she was displaying her anger by actually displaying it for once, he could be in more trouble than he originally thought.

"Well, okay, not actual hollering, but it was insinuated. She got in my face, like inches from it, and...and they weren't happy words. She wants to talk to Thomas. She said she might never forgive you if you don't let her. She scared me enough that I almost believe her."

Ben ran a hand over his face, groaning. He peeked over at Thomas, who still hadn't moved an inch. Not a peep out of him. He didn't even ask for a lawyer. "Shit, maybe I should. He hasn't said a word to me. I could see the connection they had at the house."

"She may not be yelling from the top of her lungs, but she's pissed."

"If he murdered those women and tried to break into her house, I don't want her near him."

"You'll be in the room."

Ben nodded. This felt wrong on so many levels. He walked out of the room with Zeke in tow. He saw Rina pacing back and forth, only stopping her agitated steps when she saw him.

"Don't hate me, Rina," Ben said in a soft whisper as he walked up to her.

"Don't make me hate you, Ben. Let me talk to him. You're mistaken. I know you're good at your job, but you're wrong about Thomas."

"I'm not leaving the room. So don't even ask me to." He grabbed her hand, nodded at Zeke, and walked into the room. It didn't make sense to argue with her about how well he was at his job. He knew what he was doing. He knew guilt when he saw it.

Rina took a seat at the table. He stood behind her, close enough to reach out and touch her if he needed to.

"Thomas," Rina said softly, reaching her hand across the table.

Thomas finally looked up, tears instantly forming in his eyes when he saw her. He reached out, grasping her hand. "I'm sorry, Rina."

Ben flinched when he touched her. The ache, the fury to knock him back surged within him. Rina was already pissed at him. That would just send her over the edge. He certainly couldn't create a decent argument over the touch since she was the one who initiated contact first.

"Why are you sorry? You didn't do anything wrong. Please tell Ben that you didn't do anything wrong and you can go home. I'll drive you myself. I have father's car."

Thomas squeezed her hand before letting it go and leaned back in his chair. "I can't tell him that. I've done a lot of things wrong."

Ben stood a little straighter at the admission. Now they were getting somewhere. Of course, now was not the time to butt in and take over the conversation and demand every little thing he had done wrong. He'd let Rina talk first. Then he'd demand he spill everything.

"Thomas, talk to me. I want to understand what's going on here. I don't believe you would hurt anybody."

"I've never hurt anyone. Never. I would never intentionally hurt you either." Thomas dragged his hands over his face, moaning in despair. "I never meant to hurt you at all. I'm sorry, Rina."

"You're really confusing me. Just please tell me what you're talking about."

Thomas looked at Rina, then glanced at him. "Do you know how many men walked away from Rina when her father decided he didn't want them around, detective?"

Rina turned around to look at him, confusion written all over her beautiful face.

"I'm going to say every single one of them. He can be

quite persuasive." The anger in his words couldn't be hidden. Not that he cared whether he did or not. For Rina's sake, he should've. He was way past caring at the moment.

Thomas shook his head. "He can be. But you're wrong."

"How so?"

"One refused to walk away." Thomas looked at Rina with a smile, then back to him. "You."

"I could never walk away from the woman I love. No matter the trouble thrown my way. Do you think threatening my job means more to me than her? Do you think I would let that man threaten my family and not fight back? Maybe he needs to do a little more research before taking on someone like me. I will never back down from having Rina in my life," Ben said, coming closer to the table.

"I know that. I tried to tell him that. He's a man who is used to getting what he wants. I am a man who follows his orders. I have no choice." Thomas bent his head in shame.

"We all have choices, Thomas. We shouldn't let one person dictate them. I'm starting to realize that myself. I'm a grown woman and I deserve to live the way I want. So do you." Rina leaned across the table, placing a hand on his shoulder. "Look at me." He slowly lifted his head and held her gaze as she sat back down. "Now please tell me what you did. What did you have no choice about?

"All the problems Detective Stoyer had, his job, his family issues, those were because of me." Thomas held his head high as he looked at him. "I'm sorry, detective."

"Me, too. You obviously did it on Reginald's order, correct?" Ben asked, even though he knew the answer. Confirmation was always nice.

"Yes."

"Was it always you?" Rina asked. The pain in her voice

made Ben want to wrap her up in his arms and whisk her away until nothing but the two of them existed.

"I'm sorry, Rina."

"I forgive you. You work for my father and you didn't want to lose your job. I don't see how this is worth getting arrested for. Let him go, Ben," Rina said as she stood up and almost lost her balance.

Ben caught her, wrapping a strong arm around her waist. He would always help support her in any way he could. Even if he hurt her in the process. "I can't let him go. He tried to break into your house. Didn't you, Thomas?"

"That's ridiculous, Ben. Thomas would never do something like that. You said the man who tried to break in is related to the murder cases you're working on. Thomas would never murder someone. Tell him, Thomas," Rina demanded in her soft voice.

"How can you forgive me so easily? Do you really think my job is that important?" Thomas asked, the surprise lacing each word.

Rina moved out of Ben's embrace, circling the table. She grabbed Thomas's hands and pulled him to his feet. "You are family. I love you like a father. I forgive my real father every day. Why wouldn't I forgive you? Tell Ben you would never break into my house."

"I can't do that."

Ben watched as Rina let Thomas's hands go and backed away from him with slow steps. He couldn't tell if it was fear or shock pounding into each step. Triumph that Thomas basically confessed didn't hit Ben like he wanted it to. The only thing he wanted right now was to pull Rina into his arms and comfort her.

"You came over to the house that morning with a fierce determination. That made your father more determined than ever to make Ben go away. He didn't like that Ben had more sway with you than he did. He's your father. He just expects you to do as he says."

"You hurt those other women?" Rina asked in a harsh whisper.

"No!" Thomas took a step toward her, but stopped when she took a step farther away from him. "He told me to do more damage to Ben. To get the point across that he wasn't welcome in your life. He didn't tell me what to do, just to go do it. He trusts me to make it all right. I heard you talking to him. I know what Ben means to you. For once, I decided to try something different."

"Different?" Rina asked, confused, her body suddenly pressed against the wall.

Thomas looked at Ben. "I followed you, detective. I saw you meet with that woman at the coffee shop. I talked with her after. She was quite open about the conversation and her attraction to you. I thought Reginald would like another report to the chief about inappropriate behavior by you. But I couldn't. You weren't inappropriate. Not once. If anything, that woman was."

"I guess you're losing me now, Thomas. What does that have to do with trying to break into Rina's house?" Ben asked.

"I bought one of those scarves that you talked about with her. I figured they must be of some importance. I just wanted Rina to be happy for once. So I thought, instead of pushing you away, I should push you towards her. I never had any intention of coming inside the house. I left that scarf on purpose so you would think it was related to those murders. So you wouldn't leave Rina alone."

"Did you really think that was the best plan? Because right now, that scarf alone makes you a prime suspect in three murders." Dumbfounded. Confusion. And still anger. How could this man do something like this?

"I am a lot of things, detective, but I'm not a murderer," Thomas said with quiet certainty. "Give me a pen. I will write my confession to the break-in. I admit full guilt about that, but I did not harm anybody."

"Why do you do as Reginald says?" Ben asked.

"The reason why I do everything for him. The reason why I would never hurt another woman, or even look at another woman. The reason why I would hate to lose my job...I love Reginald Chastain. He's a difficult man. He's a proud man. And I love him like I've never loved another man."

For some reason, that didn't surprise Ben. He could see the love in Thomas's eyes, hear the desperation in his voice. He walked over to the table and pushed the pen and paper that sat on his side over to Thomas's side. "Write your statement on the attempted burglary. That's all I'll be charging you with for right now. I believe you."

"Thank you, detective." Thomas glimpsed at Rina, who stared at both of them, but wasn't really seeing them. He sat down. "Please take care of Rina. She'll need you. I never meant to hurt her. I love her like my own daughter. For once in my life, I had a family. I was only looking out for my family. And now I've lost them both."

"I will," Ben replied quietly.

Thomas pressed the pen to the paper. Before one word could be written, Rina grabbed the pen from his grasp. He looked up at her, the pen clutched tightly to her chest.

"I'm hurt. That may take a while to overcome, but you're still my family. What you said about my father doesn't change that fact. It's okay you feel that way about him. I don't want you writing any confession." Rina walked over to Ben and held out the pen. "Don't make him write it."

"I can't ignore what he did. Like the time you called me about what Mark did to Zoe, we didn't ignore that, and it's not happening now. I know you'll be mad at me, probably even hate me for it, but I can't look the other way." Ben brushed her cheek, wiping away a tear that fell. "I'm sorry. I won't ignore what he did, even if I understand the crazy reason behind it."

"Rina, let him do his job. I accept my punishment, whatever it may be. Go home and get some rest. I'll be fine," Thomas said, his voice cracking a bit. "And thank you. You have no idea what your words mean to me. I've always loved you as well, like you were my own daughter."

"You're all testing my emotions to the brink. Don't be surprised when I finally let loose." She threw the pen at him. He caught it with ease and watched as the love of his life walked out of the room without another word.

"I'll take the pen, detective. Take her home. I don't want her here anymore." Thomas held out his hand.

Ben handed Thomas the pen. "I'll put in a good word to the DA, for Rina's sake. Do you want to make a phone call? Maybe call Reginald."

Thomas looked up. "No. I think it's best I cut my ties clean with him. He won't want anything to do with me when he finds out the truth."

Ben smiled, for the first time that night. "And who's going to tell him? I highly doubt Rina will say a word. And my lips are sealed."

"You're a good man, Ben Stoyer."

"In your own odd way, so are you, Thomas."

## 16

Ben locked the door and gently laid the suitcase down before setting the alarm. Clueless. Scared. Terrified, even. Rina was still very angry and he had no idea how to make it all better. He took a moment to watch Rina look around his house, appreciating the fact she let him pack a bag and bring her to his home for the night. How long would it last? That was a very good question. One he couldn't seem to voice. Taking it day by day would have to do.

Thomas wasn't their killer. He believed every word that came out of the man's mouth. There was no way he faked that kind of emotion. He saw the torture in his eyes for the love he had for Reginald. For going against his wishes. Reginald wanted Thomas to ruin his life. Instead, Thomas tried to help.

Although, Ben thought he could've helped in a better way. Trying to break into Rina's house didn't seem like the best way at all. He understood the message. Thomas didn't want to see him leave Rina. The next possible victim related to his murder cases would ensure that. That's for damn sure.

Regardless, Ben didn't plan on leaving Rina ever. Unless she had something to say about it. And she might. Especially with the way she gave him the silent treatment the entire ride from the precinct to her house. After a brief conversation that she come home with him, she continued the silence as she packed. The drive to his house was painful. She still hadn't said a word as she roamed his living room.

"I can see you're still mad at me. Your father paid his bail. He won't be spending the night in jail, if that has you worried." He took a few steps in her direction.

"I told you my father would take care of it. He'll get the charges dropped."

"So now you want him using his influence. You can't have it both ways, Rina."

"Thomas didn't mean to do it. He was just looking out for me."

"Oh, I get it. Just like how he didn't mean to try and take Isabella away from Erin. Is that what you're saying? I might understand what was going through his mind, but that doesn't mean I forgive him. I'm not the law. You're not the law. Thomas sure in the hell isn't the law. He broke the law. I won't apologize for doing my job. You'd think you'd know me by now that I take my job seriously."

"Why am I here?" Rina threw her arms out wide. "You think Thomas killed those women. You think I'm not safe in my house because of him."

"No, I actually believed him when he said he didn't hurt those women. What can I say? I did ask you to move in with me." He shrugged, glancing around the room. Her things would fit right in. "You have no idea the worry, the stress I dealt with in the beginning. You look so much like those women that I just have this intense fear you could be next.

When I found that scarf outside your house, I almost went into a full-blown panic. I won't let anyone hurt you. I just need you to stay here with me until I solve this case. Please."

She walked up to him. Then shocked him completely when she placed her hand on his cheek. "I won't move in with you. Notice I said won't, not can't. I will stay with you until you solve this case. To help stop your worry. I'm not mad at you. I know what sort of man you are. You're an honest man. You have integrity. I do know what your job means to you. I'm sorry for asking you to look the other way. I know better than to think you would. I honestly don't know what I'm feeling right now. I just feel empty, Ben. I don't know how you can fix that. I don't know how I can fix it. I'm tired. Of everything."

She dropped her hand and walked around him. She grabbed her suitcase by the door and carried it down the hallway.

What just happened there? Because it didn't feel like anything good.

He turned out the lights and followed her path. She had no idea what room was his, considering she had only been to his house once. It wouldn't matter what room she decided to walk into. So would he. He knew he should give her some space, some time to deal with everything that happened, but he was afraid that he'd lose the connection he had with her. That she'd turn her heart away from the great relationship they could have. He wouldn't let her distance herself.

He popped his head into the spare room. No Rina. Taking that as a good sign, he walked to his bedroom and closed the door when he saw her suitcase by the bed. He glanced over to his bathroom, the light spilling out from underneath the door. Maybe he hadn't lost her after all. She chose to sleep in his room and not the spare room. He would've slept on the twin mattress in the spare room with her. He would've scooped her up against his body and held on tightly to her all night. He still might do that in this room.

He undressed, tossing all of his clothes into the hamper, then climbed into bed and waited for her to finish in the bathroom. As soon as she walked out, he waited patiently for her to join him. She only hesitated once. The moment she crawled into bed, he didn't give her a chance to wonder what would happen. He pulled her against his chest, spooning her body perfectly to his, and wrapped his arm tightly around her waist.

"I love you, Rina."

Silence. Nothing but silence echoed. He closed his eyes, giving up. She wasn't pulling away physically, but clearly she planned to emotionally. A little piece of his heart withered away when he didn't hear the words he wanted to. Needed to.

"I love you, Ben."

Peace settled around him. That's all he needed at the moment. He'd figure out how to fix everything else tomorrow.

---

"So, how'd it go last night with Rina?" Zeke asked, twirling his pencil with an ease that said he did it way too much.

Ben shrugged, unable to voice how it really went. "I need to make it up to her. I don't know how, though. I couldn't let him walk out scot-free."

"You did the right thing. Even Thomas said so. He knew what he did was wrong. He wants to pay for his mistakes the correct way. I talked to Sherry down in the DA's office this morning. He had an alibi for the three murders. Based on that, she's only considering him for the attempted burglary. Which isn't much, other than his statement. She's willing to give him one year probation and thirty hours community service. I'm pretty sure he's going to take the deal based on that."

"Good. That was quick. Rina will be happy to hear that." Ben glanced down at the remaining credit card receipts they had left to go through. "I think we're about to strike out everywhere in this case."

"Thomas is a no-go. He had an alibi for every murder. His third alibi, my favorite, trying to break into Rina's house at the same time Carol was brutally murdered. Jones is not looking good after the search warrant we executed at his apartment. We found nothing strange or crazy. His DNA probably won't match the hair Susan found because he has black hair, not brown. He's weird and feels really good for the murders, but it just doesn't fit, no matter how much we want it to. And Anthony, I hate that man, but he's looking to have an alibi for each murder as well. Who in the hell does that leave us with?" Ben said, scratching his head as he continued to look through the receipts.

"Holy shit. I think I might have something." Zeke held up a piece of paper and started to wave it with vigor.

"I hate it when you keep me in suspense." Ben rolled his hand in a circle for him to continue.

"Timothy Denson. You know, our first victim's best friend's brother."

"That was a mouthful. Say it again," Ben said with a laugh. "Why him? That's like out of left field, the ball just coming from nowhere."

"Yeah, I know. Maybe I'm stretching. Maybe I'm not.

Wanda Denson is on this list. Her credit card record shows she bought a white scarf two months ago."

"Who's that? His mother. That's Sauer's pile. I don't think he came across her name before, did he?"

Zeke grabbed Sauer's notes on the pile next to him. "No, it doesn't look like it. It's worth a shot. Let's go talk to Wanda, see about that scarf. I know it doesn't make sense, but we have no other suspects. He knew Beth. He was close to her. She would've opened her door no questions asked."

"Okay, I get Beth. How about Ashley and Carol? How did he know them?"

"He looked like a pretty boy. Carol is in the crowd with Anthony. He never said they had a relationship out of the office, but maybe she went to the country club to see him one time and Timothy was there."

Ben laughed. "That is stretching like you've never done before."

"Okay, dating websites. Maybe he was on there. Saw Carol's profile and picked her as his next victim."

"Why was Beth his first victim?"

Zeke rubbed his chin, then snapped his fingers. "He said he never wanted to date her. Beth was a beautiful woman. She was sweet and friendly. Why wouldn't he want to date her? He even killed spiders for her. What kind of man does that unless he likes her?"

"Any nice normal man should do that for a woman. Really, Zeke, that's all you got. Killed spiders for her." Ben shook his head while grinning. "The part about him wanting to date her sounds good. She doesn't see him like that and lets him down gently. Except he doesn't take it gently."

"God, he told Beth's parents that she died. If he really killed her then that is one sick son of a bitch."

"Agreed. Let's go talk to Wanda and go from there." Ben stood up and tossed his jacket on.

"Right behind you, buddy." Zeke grabbed his jacket as well. "Hey, I'd even kill a spider for you. That's what kind of great guy I am."

"I can kill my own spiders, thank you."

"Are you sure? Even the huge black ones with the big sack full of baby spiders? I'd do it for you, man."

Ben glanced at Zeke, laughing. "Shut up. I like killing my own spiders."

"If you're sure. But don't forget my offer."

RINA CLUTCHED the key tighter as she turned around. "Thank you, Officer Spencer, for the ride home."

"No problem, Ms. Chastain. Detective Stoyer said to make sure you made it inside the house before I left. I'll just wait for you to do that. Lock the door and set the alarm when you get inside."

Rina nodded, then inserted the key into the lock without trying to show the shaking in her hand. Anxiety all day. How would the car ride be on the way home with Ben? Would the tension still be there? How awkward would the night go with so much wrong between them? When Officer Spencer showed up instead of Ben, she felt disappointment. She wanted Ben to take her home. The anxiety vanished into thin air like a white whispering fog lifting into a bright early morning. Everything just suddenly made sense.

She turned the key and pushed open the door. Stepping inside the house, she quickly disarmed the alarm. She had no idea how she remembered the numbers Ben only gave her this morning. Nervous energy ran from the tips of her toes to the very top of her head. They should've slipped her mind instead of coming out with ease. She popped back into the doorframe with a small smile. "Do you know how long Ben will be? When he called briefly to tell me you were bringing me home, he didn't really say. He sounded busy."

Officer Spencer placed his hands around his belt and shifted his feet a little. "I'm really not sure. I do know they got a big lead in those murder cases they've been working on. Would you like me to stay for a while? If you're nervous being alone, I'd be more than happy to stay."

"Oh, no. That's fine. I was just curious. I'm okay being alone. If I was nervous, I would've went home with Zoe and her dad. If they have a big lead, that's a great thing. Do you know who the suspect is?"

Officer Spencer shifted his feet again. "No, Ms. Chastain, I don't know that information."

"Well, thank you again, Officer Spencer. Good night." Rina closed and locked the door immediately.

The alarm panel stared her down. What were the numbers again? How could she disarm the alarm with ease and now not remember the numbers if her life depended upon it? She stepped away and glanced around the living room.

A big screen TV sat against the wall atop a black TV stand. On the bookshelf next to the TV was an assortment of movies, even a few children's movies. In front of the TV was a white plush couch with a Minnesota Twins blanket folded nicely at the end. In the corner near the window was a light-brown chest. A doll's arm stuck out of the top. It wasn't hard to see that Ben loved his nieces and nephews. It also wasn't hard to picture her belongings among his.

Last night was the most stressful she'd had in a long time. The thought of Thomas behind bars sent her into a panic. She knew what he had done was wrong, cruel even. Her father wasn't always the best father, displaying cruelty to her on more than one occasion. She still loved him. She still forgave him. Thomas was like a father to her. There was no way she couldn't forgive him as well.

And his admission to loving her father. Yes, that shocked her. When she truly thought about it, it made sense. Thomas was very attentive to her father's needs. He always stuck up for her father's behavior, even when there were times he shouldn't have. You only do that when you love someone. She should've seen it sooner. None of it mattered, of course. She didn't judge Thomas for his feelings. He was her family. She would never push him away.

Her eyes glossed to the family photos lining the walls behind the couch. Photos of a happy family. Photos of a large family filled with children, wives and husbands, brothers and sisters. That's what she wanted. She wanted happiness. She wanted a family—a large family. With Ben. She could already picture him holding their little bundle of joy and loving that child with everything in his heart. Like he loved her with everything he had.

She understood his job and the reasons behind his refusal to drop the charges against Thomas. She didn't like it, but she understood it. As much as she wanted it to disappear, she should've never asked Ben to compromise who he was. That wasn't fair to him.

She stood straighter as she walked back to the alarm panel and entered the code. Joy soared around her as she clapped her hands. That was the first step to moving in with Ben. She needed to be able to handle the alarm.

Now, if only Ben would get home. He'd be ecstatic when she told him her decision. At least, she hoped so. Perhaps he wouldn't want her anymore. So indecisive. So rude last night. She knew what she wanted now. She wanted to move in. Because she loved him. Moving in was the next logical step. He was right.

She walked to his bedroom—soon to be their bedroom —and set her purse on the bed. Quickly changing into comfortable clothes, she decided to make something to eat. Regardless of when Ben got home, she would have a nice, hot meal waiting for him.

Digging through the cupboards, nothing seemed to jump out at her. Something easy would be best. She didn't need to impress him with anything, but she wanted to make up for the way she acted yesterday. She realized how unfair she truly had been.

Now, what would impress Ben? He was a simple man, not needing fancy things to make him happy.

Silly. Trying to overdo herself. A simple meal would suffice.

She pulled some chicken from the freezer and started to grab other ingredients from the pantry as the chicken defrosted in the microwave. It took a few tries to find where everything was located, but she eventually found the silverware drawer and snatched a spoon, and then a bowl from the cabinet near the stove. She took the milk from the fridge and measured a cup.

*Thump. Thump. Thump.*

Milk splashed around the bowl as the cup fell from her hand.

The pounding on the door didn't sound friendly. Not many people should know she was here. And the people who did, she trusted. She didn't trust the knock booming throughout the house.

Slow, steady steps to the front door ceased the moment she heard Anthony yell, "Rina, come on. I know you're in there. I just want to talk. Let me in, please."

Unable to help it, also reminding herself she was no coward, she peered through the peephole. Anthony stood with his usual air of confidence, still dressed in a suit and tie. He must've come straight from work.

He pressed the doorbell this time. "Rina, please. I just want to talk."

Biting her lip, indecision battled within. She jumped back from the door when Anthony pounded again, harder this time.

"Rina, I'm not leaving until you open the door. You can ignore me all you want, but I know you're in there. I tried your house. You weren't there. So, I know you're at this damn detective's house."

Backing away from the door, her hand covered her mouth to stifle the cries that wanted to escape. Anthony had never scared her before, but this behavior scared her.

"I just want to talk. Open the door before I break it down."

Rina didn't need any more confirmation. She remembered what happened to Zoe last year and refused to let that happen to her as well. Running to the bedroom, she spilled the contents of her purse onto the bed. Her hands brushed over everything but her phone. Where was her phone?

## 17

Ben leaned back in the chair and stretched his arms. "I could say we have all night, but we don't. I want to go home, and I know so does my partner. The only place you're going to is a jail cell. You could help yourself by telling us why you did it."

Timothy leaned back in his chair as well. "I'm not sure what you're talking about, detective. I can say I'm thoroughly embarrassed by the way you showed up at my work and arrested me as you did. Murder charges? You've got to be kidding me."

"Well, let's paint a picture for you since you seem a bit confused. We had a visit with your mother. She likes scarves. Actually, she likes almost anything from Little Red's Boutique. She recently bought a white scarf from there. Do you know what she told us?" Zeke said, standing near Ben with his arms crossed.

"I have no idea. But yes, you're right. My mother does like Little Red's Boutique. It makes it easy when her birthday and Mother's Day comes around. I know exactly where to go to get her something."

"She likes to update her wardrobe and accessories quite often is what she said. She also likes to donate her things when she's done with them. She asked you to drop two bags to the donation center for her about a month ago. Did you?" Zeke asked, although his smirk indicated he already knew the answer.

"Do I need a lawyer? Murder charges sound like I need a lawyer," Timothy said with a smug smile.

"Sure. We can get you a lawyer. Do you want a lawyer?" Ben asked patiently.

"I'm not sure. Are you charging me with murder?"

"Yes. We are. Since you avoided my question earlier, I'll answer it for you." Zeke opened the folder on the table near Ben. "You did drop off two bags for her, but before you did, you went through it and took out five scarves. Each scarf was a different color. One red, orange, yellow, green, and blue. Do you recognize these three scarves?"

Zeke laid the photos of the red, orange, and yellow scarves used to murder each woman. He didn't just show the scarves themselves. He showed them wrapped around the neck of each victim.

Timothy's eyes lit up with excitement. His face stayed neutral, but there was no mistaking the excitement in his eyes. "Those could be anyone's scarves. What makes you think they are my mother's? And that I took them?" Timothy said calmly, like he didn't just look at three women who were brutally murdered.

"Good question, Timothy," Ben said, pulling out another piece of paper from the folder, pushing it near him. "You know the place where your mother likes to donate her things. Well, they catalog each item. Your mother clearly remembers putting each scarf into one bag. The donation center does not have any scarves listed on the receipt when you dropped off those two bags. So, somehow, those five scarves went missing from when your mother put them in the bag to when you dropped them off at the donation center."

"Go on, Timothy. Take a look at the inventory list they made when you dropped off the donation. No scarves listed." Ben pushed the paper a little closer to him, noting the way the muscles in his cheek started to twitch.

"I don't believe my mother made a mistake. I guess the donation center miscalculated when they did their inventory."

"Yeah, I don't think so. Kerry was a very nice woman. Superb manager, if you ask me. She's very meticulous and doesn't miss things like that. You took those scarves so you could kill those women. Did you plan it? Or was it an impulse that took over?" Ben asked, tapping the inventory list with his hand. "We found two of those scarves. Green and blue. Did you have someone in mind that you were planning to use those on? Or do you randomly pick your victims?"

"So you bought some scarves and are now claiming they are mine? Is that how you make arrests around here, by framing innocent people?" Timothy asked with a crazy laugh.

"Detective Stoyer wasn't done. We found those scarves in your house after we got a search warrant to search every nook and cranny in your place. We found them tucked away in your closet. On the top shelf in the way, way back in a box. Guess what else we found in that box? No, you don't want to guess," Zeke said with a wide smile.

Ben couldn't help but enjoy the way Timothy's face started to form into fury. He knew he was screwed. That he made a huge mistake. Ben also felt the biggest relief. Rina was safe. Finally. Now if only he knew how to repair their relationship. Of course, now was not the time to think about that.

"I think it would've been better if you didn't take souvenirs. Cutting off a piece of your victim's hair just seems kind of dumb for a man who almost got away with murder. Three murders, at that." Ben took another photo out of the folder. "See. You cut a lock of their hair after you raped then murdered them and tied it with a ribbon. And because they all had the same color of hair, you tied a ribbon around the lock of hair using the same color of ribbon as the scarf you used to kill them with."

"You know when the lab confirms the DNA with all of that hair it'll come back to all three women. Plus, we found a hair fiber at Beth's house. You were sloppy. Now, you have blonde hair, and the hair fiber we found is brown. But you know what? It looks like you need another hair appointment. You dye your hair, don't you? You normally have brown hair. Don't worry. The lab will confirm that as well. Why don't you tell us now why you wanted to kill these women? Why would you kill your sister's best friend and then tell her own parents she died? What kind of sick son of a bitch does that?" Zeke asked, leaning closer to him with the rage displayed on every corner of his face.

"I have no idea. If I ever meet someone like that, I'll ask them for you. I loved Beth. She was a beautiful woman." Timothy grinned at Zeke, then glanced at Ben. "These other women were just as beautiful."

"Which says you knew them, saying shit like that," Ben said with disgust.

"Of course not. You showed me a picture of them. That doesn't mean I knew them," Timothy said, pointing to the pictures on the table.

"Only a sick bastard would think a picture of a strangled woman is beautiful." Zeke swiped the papers and photos on the table into a pile, shoving them back into the folder.

"What was the meaning of the notes you left under their bodies?" Ben shuffled through the folder, trying to find what he needed after Zeke made a mess of everything. "Here we go. Red for the heat, I love so deep. Orange for the glow, that hangs so low. Yellow for the sun, I only have one. What does this mean? Or does it just confirm you're a sick bastard?"

"I'm no poet, but they are beautiful messages. What do you think they mean?" Thomas countered.

Just then, the door swung open. Captain Ganderson nodded at him. "Stoyer, out in the hallway."

Ben barely glanced at Zeke as he walked out of the room. "What's up, cap?"

"There's a situation at your house." Captain Ganderson laid a hand on his shoulder when he started to walk away. "Rina's fine. She called nine-one-one because you didn't answer your phone. Officer Spencer is the closest. He's heading back there."

"He's not there yet? How do you know she's fine?" Ben asked, feeling his belt for his phone. Shit! He left his phone on his desk.

"She told the operator the alarm is set and the doors are locked."

"What's the problem?"

"She said some man was trying to get in. Anthony Tollhorn." Captain Ganderson shook his head as Ben rushed past him. "Keep your cool, Stoyer!"

---

BEN SLAMMED his door shut and ran up the driveway to the

porch where Rina stood by Officer Spencer. He didn't wait for any explanations. He grabbed her by the shoulders and slammed her fiercely into his embrace. She was okay. Thank God, she was okay.

"I'm fine, Ben," she whispered, holding him tightly.

"Nothing's fine when you have to call the police. I'm so sorry I didn't have my phone on me. Shit, Rina. I'm so sorry."

"Really, I'm okay. Officer Spencer wasn't far away. It took him less than five minutes to get back here. I promise I'm okay."

Ben loosened his hold, but still held her to his side as he turned to Officer Spencer. "What happened?"

"I dropped her off. I made sure she closed the door and locked it before I walked away. Just like you told me. Less than ten minutes later, a call came in for a disturbance from this location. I arrived to see Mr. Tollhorn pounding on the door. I even saw him kick it once." Officer Spencer pointed to the right where Anthony sat in the front yard, hands cuffed behind his back. Another officer stood by him. "He wouldn't tell me his business for being here. Ms. Chastain said he kept saying he just wanted to talk and to let him in. He also threatened to break down the door if she didn't open it."

Ben kissed the side of her head, inhaling the sweet scent of vanilla. "Did you talk to him, sweetheart?"

"No. I was too scared to say a word. I just ran to the bedroom to get my phone. I couldn't find it at first. When I finally found it, easily enough on top of everything, I called you. You didn't answer, so I just called nine-one-one. He really scared me, Ben. I didn't know what else to do."

He kissed her again. "You did the right thing."

"Is he...did he...kill those women?" she asked in a small voice.

He turned her slightly, grasping her face and rubbing a soft thumb to soothe the fear away. "No. He didn't kill those women. We arrested our killer earlier this evening. We have enough evidence to put him away for all three murders. You're safe. I'm going to have a word with Anthony." Ben dropped his hands and kissed her lightly on the lips. "You're not going to ask me to forget about what he just did, are you?"

She lifted her lips with what could be considered a small smile. "No. Throw the book at him."

"Good. I plan to." Ben looked at Officer Spencer. "Thanks, Spencer."

"You're welcome, Stoyer."

Ben walked over to Anthony, gesturing for the officer to make him stand up. Anthony struggled at first, but dropped his eyes when he met Ben's glare.

"Care to tell me why you're banging on my front door threatening to break it down? Why are you scaring the life out of Rina?"

"I just wanted a word with her," Anthony said through clenched teeth.

"Pounding on my door and making threats isn't the way to do that. What did you want to say to her?"

"None of your damn business. Let me talk to her."

"You made it my business when you came to my house. You're not getting within a hundred feet of her. You're going to stay the hell away from her or I will make your life a living hell." Ben got closer to his face. "Do you understand me, Mr. Tollhorn?"

"I'm sorry for my behavior. I just wanted to tell her I'm

sorry. That's all. I didn't mean to hurt her in any way. I'm sorry for everything."

"So because you're changing your tactics, trying to sound nice, I'm just going to say, 'Okay, Anthony. We're good.' Not gonna happen. Officer Dorscher is going to bring you down to the precinct and charge you with harassment and trespassing. I might even tell him to throw in attempted breaking and entering. You did threaten to break down the door." Ben looked at Officer Dorscher with a smile. "That sounds about right, doesn't it?"

"Sure does, detective," Officer Dorscher responded, grabbing a hold of Anthony's arm a little tighter when he started to move.

"Oh, yeah, Anthony. You better call your dad. I hear he's the best defense lawyer in town. You're going to need him."

"Screw you, detective," Anthony screamed as Ben walked back toward the house.

Ben held up his middle finger, then swooped Rina into his side and opened the door. "Thanks for your help, Spencer. Make sure Anthony gets the best treatment down at the precinct." Ben winked at him and closed the door.

"What are you charging him with?" Rina asked, leaning her head against his chest.

"Harassment, trespassing, attempted breaking and entering. I could think of more if I really wanted to. Are you sure you're okay?"

"I am. I remembered Officer Spencer saying you had a big lead on the murder cases. When I heard Anthony pounding on the door to get in, I thought maybe he was the killer. It scared me."

"It's definitely not him. It's a guy who knew the first victim. Apparently, he had issues as a child. He was on a lot of meds to help regulate his behavior. His mother and sister thought he was on his meds. Zeke and I don't think so. We didn't find any in his house, but we did find lots of evidence to tie him to all three murders."

Rina grabbed his hand, weaving her fingers through his. "Why did he do it?"

He squeezed her hand. "I have no idea. Maybe Zeke got him to talk after I left, but he wasn't saying anything when I was there. He wouldn't admit to anything. I wouldn't be surprised if he claims his innocence through the entire trial. Hell, his lawyer could probably even go for insanity. He didn't seem right in his mind. But enough of that. Are you sure you're okay?"

"I'm fine. Are you okay? Do you have to go back to work?"

"I should."

"Then go. I'll be okay. I was just making dinner. I'll have it ready for you when you get back."

He kissed her as he lifted her around his waist, wishing he could take her to the bedroom instead of going back to the precinct and finishing up with a lunatic. "I could get used to this. Don't spoil me too much." He kissed her again before releasing her. Too much temptation if he kept holding her.

"You should get used to this. I was acting silly last night. I'm sorry for the way I acted. I love you."

"What are you saying?"

She placed a hand over his heart with a sweet smile. "I want to move in with you. We should take this relationship to the next level. I'm ready. Does the offer still stand?"

He picked her up and twirled her, his lips connecting with hers, the passion loud and clear. "That offer never left the table."

She wrapped her legs tightly around his waist when he

stopped spinning. No hesitation. No decision-making. He knew exactly what he wanted.

She giggled into his mouth when he started walking down the hallway. "What are you doing, Ben? You said you had to go back to work."

He kicked the bedroom door shut. "Screw work. This, right here, is more important. You're more important. Loving you in *our* bed is way more important right now."

He gently laid her onto the bed, moving slowly over her body. "I'm going to love you all night long. I'm going to mark every spot in this house with your presence. I'm going to make it impossible for you to ever leave me."

"I can't wait," she said softly.

He laughed. "That's the only time I want to hear you say the word can't." He claimed her lips with a searing kiss, drowning out everything else around them.

## 18

He took a right, trying to concentrate on the road. It was difficult when he dreaded the destination. A smile touched his lips when a small, soft hand curled around his.

"Are you okay, Ben? You haven't said much. Did you have a bad day at work?" Rina asked quietly.

He lifted her hand, lightly kissing it. "Work was fine. The DNA results came back today. Confirms everything we suspected. He's going to prison for a very long time."

"Did you doubt it? You sound surprised."

"No, I didn't doubt it, but it's always nice to have the confirmation. I'm surprised it came back so soon."

"Did he confess to why he killed those women?"

"No. I don't think he ever will. He's still maintaining his innocence. He says he loved Beth. He never says he would never hurt her. He just says he loved her. Most people would also add in, they would never hurt the person they love. Beth's ex-boyfriend, Steven, brought us a box of her things that she never grabbed after they broke up. There was a journal. I'm surprised she would leave that at his house for so long. Maybe they didn't break up as amicably as he said, or maybe she just didn't care, but I thought that was strange."

"That is strange. I'm sure most women would keep that close to them. Maybe she just had a lot going on in her life that she forgot."

"Have you ever kept a journal?" Ben glanced at her. Beth had written some pretty private, powerful stuff. He didn't think Rina would keep a journal.

"No. You know me. I keep my emotions hidden inside fairly well. Writing them down would feel like I wasn't hiding them well enough."

"Don't be afraid to share with me."

She shyly smiled. "I won't be afraid anymore. What did she write?"

"Plenty. The most important parts that concerned us was about Timothy. Before she started dating Steven, about eight months ago, Timothy asked her out for the first time. She always suspected he liked her, but he never did anything about it. She turned him down gently and told him it was because she was best friends with his sister and it didn't feel right. What she didn't tell him was that she didn't trust him. She knew the sort of problems he had. On the outside, he could pretend he was fine. On the inside, there was just too much turmoil waiting to escape."

"He obviously took that badly. What compels someone to take another life?"

"Actually, he took her rejection fine. She said everything was still normal after that. She met Steven and life went on. She still saw Timothy now and again. She wrote her suspicions that he went off his meds, but she didn't tell his sister.

She didn't think it was her place to tell. Maybe she should've." Ben took a deep breath, letting it out slowly. "He had multiple issues going on since childhood. He was prescribed so many different medications to stabilize his moods and behavior that I'm not surprised he stopped taking them. He doesn't think anything is wrong with him. He's refusing to take his meds right now in jail. I honestly can't tell you what possesses someone to kill another person."

"That must be frustrating not knowing why he killed them."

"A little, but we have our suspicions. He's not on his meds. He's not thinking clearly. Beth breaks up with Steven and he thinks he has another chance. She rejects him again and he kills her. That's our thought. When it comes to Carol and Ashley, the other two victims, we're not exactly sure. He worked at a sports store. We spoke to his manager who remembered Ashley coming in to purchase golf clubs for her husband. Timothy helped her. His manager said he was always good with the ladies. He zoomed in right away to always help the women. His manager never complained because he made sales like crazy. Ashley purchased several items, some having to be ordered. That's where he was able to get her address. We don't know why he attached to her like he did. Maybe because she looked so much like Beth, the one he truly loved."

"And Carol?"

"That's still a mystery. Anthony—" Ben paused, glancing at Rina, whose smile never wavered at his name. "He said he recognized Timothy when we showed him a picture. He saw him at the country club a few times. He never suspected that Timothy had the issues he did. He always acted normal. He also said that Carol did stop by the country club a few times to drop off paperwork that needed to be signed. Timothy probably saw her there. But until he talks, we won't ever really know."

"And Anthony? Did anything else happen between you two? I didn't realize you talked to him again."

"No. We were cordial. He seemed more amicable to talk. He reiterated that he only came by the house that day to apologize. Of course, he was drinking that day. I was so upset when I got there, I really didn't process the alcohol on his breath. He's taking Carol's death hard. He said that day he was thinking about Carol, then thinking about you and the date you two had, and he felt guilty. He wanted to apologize for the way the date went, and for letting it happen in the first place. He always wanted Carol but was too afraid to go for what he really wanted. So he says."

"You don't believe anything he says? Why didn't you tell me this?"

"I can't stand the man, so it's hard to believe him. What he said sounded real. I thought I even smelled alcohol on his breath this last time we talked to him, and we talked to him at work. Like I said, he's taking her death hard. I don't know why I didn't tell you. I guess I was putting it off. I don't like talking about him."

"I understand. Let's not keep secrets, though."

"Never. I'm sorry." He lifted her hand and kissed it.

"Well, I'm glad you two arrested Timothy and got him off the streets. He can't hurt anybody anymore." She smiled as Ben pulled into her father's driveway and drove through the gates that opened automatically.

"You distracted me. Making me talk about the case so I wouldn't think about this dinner." He kissed her hand again. "Keep the details about the case to yourself."

"I won't say anything to anybody. You seemed nervous driving. Everything will go great. I promise. My father seemed eager to have this dinner."

"Yeah, eager, huh? That surprises me."

"He's trying. Thank you for trying as well."

"Anything for you." He parked the car, then leaned across the seat and kissed her sweetly on the lips before backing away with a small sigh. "Ready?"

"I am. Come on, you'll love the inside of the house. It's gorgeous. Remember I told you that the last time we were here. You never saw it."

"I promise not to arrest Thomas this time."

"That's not funny, Ben," she said, looking at him as he rounded the car and grabbed her hand.

"You're right. Forgive me?"

"Yes. For a kiss." She displayed her cheek, waiting for a peck.

"Please...for a kiss means on the lips, sweetheart." He cupped her chin, making her turn her face. He kissed her deeply, but not for too long. He had no idea if cameras were positioned outside the front door like they were near the gate. Not the greatest way to impress her father. "So he was eager. Does that mean he doesn't hate me anymore?"

"I don't think he hates you. He's coming around. He wasn't too happy about the thought of us moving in together. He needs some time to process that."

Ben grabbed her hand as they walked to the front door. "Would he feel better if we were engaged?"

Rina stopped in her tracks as her jaw dropped. "Are you asking me to marry you, Ben?"

"Well, think about it. Technically, we should've been dating for almost a year, which means we would've moved in a couple months ago instead of just a week ago. So technically nearing the time when I would ask you to marry me. I respect your father enough to ask him for his permission. What do you think my odds are?"

Her hand trembled. "I have no idea. Like you said, it's been only a week since we moved in together. Are you sure about marriage?"

"I haven't asked yet. Don't worry about it. But I'm always sure when it comes to you." He grinned wide, kissing her hand. "Let's have dinner."

"You are a devious man, Benjamin."

"Does that mean I'm in trouble now? I always feel like I'm in trouble when you call me Benjamin."

"Yes, you might be in some trouble. I will think of your punishment before we get home."

"Does it involve handcuffs? I might be up for that." He laughed when she blushed and playfully slapped his shoulder. "I should've said that quieter, huh?"

They walked up the remaining steps. Rina held her hand up to knock when the door swung open. There had to be cameras out here. Ben glanced around, yet didn't see anything remotely close to a camera.

"Still wanting to knock. Will that ever change, Rina?" Thomas asked with a warm smile.

"I don't think so, Thomas." She kissed him on the cheek and pulled Ben inside when Thomas stepped back.

Thomas closed the door, holding his hand out to Ben. "Good to see you again, detective."

Ben shook hands with him. "You, too, Thomas. Call me Ben, though. We're past the formalities."

"Agreed. Welcome to the Chastain home. I hope your stay is longer than last time. No ideas to arrest me again, I hope."

"Not yet," Ben said with a chuckle. "I never had the idea the last time until I saw your car. You should've parked it somewhere else until I left."

"Well, I know to be on my toes next time. You are a smart man. I will never underestimate you again."

"Please tell me there won't be a next time, Thomas. For Rina's sake." His smile dipped a fraction. Just what he didn't need. More tension between him and Rina. Because he would arrest Thomas without hesitation again.

"Of course not. Welcome to the family."

"Thank you, I think." Ben leaned closer. "So, between me and you, if I ask Reginald to marry his daughter, will he say yes?"

"Are you asking me, Detective Stoyer?" Reginald said, suddenly appearing out of nowhere. He walked over to Rina, kissing her cheek lightly. "Well, then, detective, are you?"

"You're like a cat. Stealth-like. I didn't even hear or see you coming," Ben said, backing away from Thomas, who shrugged in answer. Whether to his previous question, or to Reginald appearing out of nowhere.

"I always like to keep my opponents on their toes," Reginald said, stone-faced.

"And I'm an opponent? So the answer is no." Ben tried to keep a smile on his face, but found it difficult to do.

"You didn't ask me a question." Reginald looked at Rina. "How are you? You're early. Dinner isn't quite ready."

"We worried about traffic and didn't want to be late. I'm good, Father. I finally have everything moved into Ben's house," Rina said confidently.

"Ah, yes, moving in already. A little fast, I must say." Reginald held Ben's gaze as he spoke to Rina.

"I love your daughter. I will until the day I die. May I have your permission to marry her?" Desperation swirled around his gut, wanting the man to say yes. Praying he would. If only to make Rina happy.

"And if I say no?" Reginald's uneasy stare never wavered from Ben.

"I guess you'll find out if you say no. Is that your answer?"

"Father, I love Ben. He loves me. Can't you be happy for me for once?" Rina said quietly, yet her sweet voice echoed around the house as if she bellowed in despair. Couldn't he hear the love in her voice? The fear as well. She thought her father was going to say no, just like he did.

"Perhaps you don't see it, but all I ever want is for you to be happy. Is this the right man to make you happy? I'm not so sure," Reginald replied, looking at her as he did.

"What makes you so unsure? What did I ever do to make you dislike me?" Ben asked. He really wanted to know. If he did something wrong, truly something wrong, he'd do everything in his power to make it right.

"You don't have to do anything. I don't have to like you. Rina's my daughter. It's my responsibility to protect her, even when she doesn't think she needs it." Reginald tilted his head as he eyed Ben carefully. "You had Anthony arrested."

"Forgive me if I don't appreciate someone coming to my house and threatening Rina to open the door. I think you have your signals crossed a little. You practically pushed that man into her arms while trying to shove me out of the way. All I want to do is love Rina and protect her. Protecting her is also my responsibility."

"Thomas said you're a good man, an honorable one. He said I should give you a chance." Reginald glimpsed at Thomas, a smile emerging slowly. "I respect and value his opinion. I will also expect him to help me get rid of you if you ever hurt my daughter in any way."

Ben raised his brows. He had a feeling Reginald didn't just mean making his life a living hell. "So that was a yes?"

"You have audacity, I'll give you that, detective. That is a yes," Reginald said, gesturing his hand toward the right. "Dinner will be ready soon. Shall we?"

"Of course. Just one thing first." Ben cleared his throat, pulled a box from his pocket, and got down on one knee in front of Rina. Opening the box revealed a small diamond encircled by several tiny diamonds. Her eyes went wide with shock as Ben grabbed her hand. Good shock, he hoped.

"Rina, I love you. I have since the moment I met you. Maybe that seems impossible. When it comes to you, I find everything possible. Will you marry me?"

She bit her lip as tears touched the corner of her eyes. "Yes."

Ben slipped the ring on her finger and stood up. Wrapping her tightly in his arms, he kissed her deeply, although made it quick, even though he wanted to take his time treasuring the beauty in his arms. "I love you," he whispered against her lips.

"I love you."

Reginald cleared his throat. "You couldn't wait?"

Ben pulled Rina into his side and turned toward Reginald. "Honestly? No. I didn't want to give you a chance to take back your permission. And why wait when I know what I want. I want Rina as my wife. I knew that a long time ago."

"Congratulations! I'll pull a bottle of champagne from the cellar," Thomas said, shaking hands with Ben and kissing Rina on the cheek.

"Set it up in the library, Thomas. We'll have a celebratory drink before dinner. Also grab a bottle of wine for when we eat," Reginald said before Thomas walked away.

"Well, you'll be a beautiful bride. Just like your mother." Reginald smiled brightly, grabbing a hug from Rina. "I do miss her every day. I see her every time I look at you."

Ben stepped back in complete awe for the first time. The happiness in Reginald's face when he spoke about Rina's mother. If he could love a person with such emotion, why did he act the way he did with Rina?

"I think a summer wedding would be wonderful. The gardens in the backyard would be absolutely perfect," Reginald said.

Rina smiled politely. "Of course."

"Or, you could let Rina act like a bride and make the decisions herself, Reggie," Ben said, clasping hands with Rina, squeezing lightly.

"Do not call me Reggie," Reginald said with thin lips.

"Don't try to control Rina and I won't call you Reggie. Deal?" Ben said brightly.

"I can already see interesting family dynamics."

"Are you welcoming me into the family already? That's so nice of you. I'm glad to be joining your family, Reginald." Laughing would be bad, but oh, how he wanted to. The enjoyment of messing with Reginald. Like the times he wanted to see Rina lose her control, he now ached to see Reginald lose a little bit of control.

"Let's join Thomas. I'm sure he'll be back soon with the champagne." Reginald turned, then glanced at Rina. "I would love to hear what would make you happy for your wedding."

"Thank you, Father. I have no idea what I want. This was a surprise," Rina said, leaning into Ben as she rested her head on his shoulder.

"Well, then, you won't mind some suggestions," Reginald said with a tiny smirk as he glanced toward Ben.

"We'd love to hear your suggestions," Ben replied.

Reginald continued forward. They slowly followed him. Ben stopped her before walking into the library.

"I can't help myself when it comes to your father. I don't like it when he treats you that way. I'll try harder to be nice the rest of the evening," he said quietly.

"I think that went very well, actually."

"Are you kidding me? We weren't exactly cordial to each other."

"For my father, that was cordial. He surprised me. I guess I have Thomas to thank for that."

Ben thought about it before saying anything. "Or maybe he just saw how happy you are and realized he needed to back off a little. He really loved your mother."

"He did. He does. He was a softer man when she was alive. It broke his heart when she died." She lifted her finger, tracing the diamond. "I can't believe you asked me to marry you already."

"I wasn't lying. I really didn't want to give him a chance to change his mind. I would've hated to get married without his permission. But I would have. Because I love you. Remember, it's the next logical step," he said, raising his eyebrows playfully.

"You and your way of thinking. I like it. And I love you."

He leaned closer, whispering in her ear, "I can't wait to love you at home."

"You'll always love me?"

"Always."

DON'T MISS the rest of the books in this exciting romantic suspense series!

One Taste of You
One Taste of Crazy
One Taste of Sin
One Taste of Redemption

FOR ZEKE AND ZOE'S STORY
ONE TASTE OF YOU

*One night will never be enough...but a killer has other plans.*

One night of glorious bliss.
One night turned into utter humiliation.
Zoe Sullivan doesn't want to see the man who took her for a prostitute ever again. But when her boss is murdered, she can't believe who the lead detective on the case is.

One idiotic mistake.
One more chance to make it right.
Detective Zeke Chance vows to make it up to Zoe for the way he treated her. Nothing will stop him—except maybe the killer.

*It all started with a dance. Then it turned into a sexy, dirty night of fun.*

Everything, from the moment he met her, scared the shit out of him. He left after one night. Now, thrust back in her life, Stitch can't help but pull her into his arms knowing it can never last. He's a good guy, most days. He has a record. She works for the police department. Definitely doesn't mix well with his tough and tattooed image.

Life is complicated, especially at work. Stitch walking back into her life adds another level of difficulty she didn't expect, but Susan wants Stitch as badly as he wants her. She knows she's setting herself up for heartbreak. Focusing on work helps to keep her mind off the one man who can turn her upside down with one heated look. The latest string of murders needs her complete attention. She has no evidence, no leads, and no idea how close the killer is to making her his next victim.

*He lied. He cheated. He lost everything.*
*One missing boy could be his redemption...*

Detective Newman—well, not a detective anymore—wants to be left alone to lick his wounds after his life fell apart. He can't blame anyone but himself. When a gorgeous woman with vibrant pink hair and a sassy attitude knocks on his door, he doesn't want anything to do with her. Except Amelia Benedict doesn't understand the word no. Her brother is missing. The police refuse to help because they believe he ran away. But she knows her brother is in trouble and insists he's her only hope. He's definitely not the right guy for the case. He's nothing but bad news, and if Amelia sticks around, he'll destroy her as he destroyed himself.

# ABOUT THE AUTHOR

I'm a *USA Today* Bestselling Author that loves to write sweet contemporary romance and romantic suspense novels, although I am partial to romantic suspense. Honestly, I love anything that has to do with romance. As long as there's a happy ending, I'm a happy camper. And insta-love...yes, please! I love baseball (Go Twins!) and creating awesome crafts. I graduated with a Bachelor's Degree in Criminal Justice, working in that field for several years before I became a stay-at-home mom. I have a few more amazing stories in the works. If you would like to connect with me or see important news, head to my website at http://www.a-mandasiegrist.com. Thanks for reading!

Made in the USA
Middletown, DE
12 September 2021